Lost Identity

By

Karl Braungart

Book 1

The Remmich/Miller Series

ISBN 13: 9780985219376

Dedication

This novel is dedicated to the US Army for teaching me to identify and use personal values, especially the desire to become better educated, to plan, and for helping me to develop those values and skills to accomplish my goals.

In the US Armed Forces, I learned that with a group effort, we are and will remain a nation that exemplifies a thriving democracy.

Acknowledgments

A book takes many hands touching it before it's ready for publication. Two people especially deserve acknowledgment. David Aretha at daretha@live.com did an excellent job of editing and my wife, Sandy, was not only my biggest cheerleader but also spent many hours reading and editing.

I also want to thank Micah at 100 Covers for her, and her team's patience, skill, and experience in helping me to craft a cover that I feel represents my genre as well as my book itself.

(Legal) Disclaimer

Principal Characters & Locations

Paul Stanley Remmich – American citizen, grew up in England. West Point graduate. Stationed at 32nd Security Intelligence (S-2), Hindenburg Kaserne, Würzburg, Germany.

Eric Miller – West Point graduate. Works in US Army military intelligence. Stationed at 32nd Security Intelligence (S-2), Hindenburg Kaserne, Würzburg, Germany.

Lilly van Horn – Paul Remmich's girlfriend. Manages Schiller Hotel in Amsterdam, which is owned by her parents.

Candice Harper – Graduated from USAF Academy '97. Employed by DELTA Airlines. Eric Miller's girlfriend.

Lieutenant General Ed Sutherland – Graduated from Citadel Academy. Commander, V Corps at USAREUR (United States European Command), Patch Barracks, Stuttgart.

Major General Gerald Elliott – West Point graduate. Stationed at Patch Barracks, Stuttgart, Germany (G-2).

Colonel Joseph Collins – Commanding officer at 32nd Security Intelligence, Hindenburg Kaserne, Würzburg, Germany.

First Sergeant Ed Randolph – Head of non-commissioned force at 32nd Security Intelligence (S-2), Hindenburg Kaserne.

Master Sergeant Terry McClain – Security office assistant at 32nd Security Intelligence (S-2), Hindenburg Kaserne.

Diane Elliott – General Elliott's wife. Lives in Stuttgart.

Julia S. Mitchell – Secretary of State, Washington, DC.

Andrew Black – CIA director, Washington, DC.

Oskars Linkov – Russian ambassador in Washington, DC.

Yury Nikulin – Russian spy.

Arif Yildiz – Major, Iraqi Tariq'Allah and chargé d'affaires in city of Istanbul, Turkey.

Adnaw Alzuhari – Captain, Iraqi secret service. Works for Major Yildiz.

Tara Yako – Iraqi secret service. Works with Alzuhari.

Faisal Mustafa – Iraqi chief of dental surgery at Leighton Barracks.

Iyad Aboona – Iraqi secret service. Works for Major Yildiz.

Leighton Barracks – CIC (Army Counterintelligence Corps) offices, Würzburg, Germany (S-2).

Patch Barracks – V Corps, USAREUR, Stuttgart, Germany (G-2).

INSCOM – (US Army Intelligence Security Command), Ft. Belvoir, VA.

Hindenburg Kaserne – 32nd Security Intelligence offices (S-2), Würzburg, Germany.

Table of Contents

1
The Meeting

The two men placed their semiautomatic pistols under the car seat and got out. They entered the living quarters for the United Nations International Military Institute (UNIMI) in Stockholm, Sweden, with confidence. Because false ID cards hung from lanyards around their necks, a security guard passed them through without question. After the guard station, they got on an empty elevator. When the door opened on the second floor, they stepped out into the flow of soldiers; some dressed in civilian clothes, some in uniform. The intruders were dressed as civilians, and both had olive skin. The tall one had a black mustache, and both had dark, coarse eyebrows. They turned to the left, the busy corridor helping them blend in with the crowd. Because they also modeled a clean-cut military appearance, other soldiers would assume they were army officers from the Middle East. Luckily for them, socializing in the corridors rarely occurred, so no one questioned them. When they got to room 207, the taller one stood alongside his partner, blocking others' views. The shorter, stocky one deftly jimmied the lock and opened the door. They entered, locked the door, and waited.

This week, ten military officers were participating in a program designed to teach them to minimize the threat of war through negotiation with foreign rebels. The idea was to reduce killings and destruction. Captain Eric Miller, a tall, clean-cut Black man, stood behind the lectern, presenting his thoughts, followed by various solutions. When he finished, the group exchanged theories. This type of self-teaching was routine at UNIMI. Unfortunately, and to Miller's displeasure, four disagreed with Miller, while three agreed and two abstained. The four Middle East soldiers didn't like the solutions, believing they were harsh ways to negotiate. They appeared to feel as if the harshness was directed toward them. Miller didn't back down from his assessment. He knew his West Point background gave him insights some of the other soldiers lacked.

The class ended at 4 p.m. Miller headed to his small, one-bedroom apartment, which was not much bigger than a good-sized hotel room. It had amenities but wasn't somewhere he'd want to live indefinitely. Graduating was the goal.

He entered the apartment, flicked the wall switch, and let the door close. He stopped in his tracks, seeing two men sitting in the side chairs. The taller one with a heavy mustache appeared older, while the other was clean-shaven but shorter. He instinctively looked for weapon bulges inside their clothing but saw none. "Who are you?"

Rather than answer him, the older one said, "We came to offer you a proposition, Captain Eric Miller. Are you interested?" Surprisingly, he even recited Miller's military serial number.

Maintaining his composure, Miller aggressively answered the man's question with a question. "What do you want?"

The younger man said, "We want to make you a proposition, but we can't explain here. You have to come with us for a little while."

They stood up, and Miller could see that the older man was a few inches taller than his partner, but both were significantly shorter than him. He said, "I'm not going anywhere until you tell me more. What is this about?"

The shorter man smiled and said, "You are in no danger. We only need one hour of your time, and then you can come back. You can even follow us in your car." He described their vehicle, a Volvo. "I will flash my headlights for you."

Miller chuckled quietly, thinking that if they [illegible] harm, they were nuts to let him drive his own car. "C [illegible] He was starting to believe it was all a trick set up b[illegible] UNIMI managers. He knew they planned test scenarios to test a student's response. Besides, these men had official-looking lanyards and IDs hanging from their necks. They couldn't be villains, he thought, but he'd be ready if they were.

They went downstairs, and the two men went to their car. Miller went to his dark blue Saab a short distance away and unlocked the trunk. Out of sight of the men, he casually lifted the spare tire cover to get one of his 9mm Beretta pistols. Sitting in the car, he checked the magazine to be sure it was fully loaded. The weapon disappeared into the inner breast pocket of his winter jacket. When he drove out onto the street, the lights of the other car flashed. He followed them until they parked in the back of a large building. There were two vehicles parked next to each other. *Nothing unusual.* It looked like an embassy building, but its nationality couldn't be identified.

The men were now wearing heavy overcoats, which they didn't have on before. Miller wondered if they had armed themselves as well.

They entered a separate building from the central section. The shorter man opened the door to a room furnished like a living room, with a sofa in the middle facing them and several chairs and tables around it. Miller noticed Iraq's national flag hanging flat on the wall above a photo of Prime Minister Jalal Masum.

"Okay, I did my part by following you. Now, tell me what this is all about. Why am I here?"

"Captain Miller, we know that you are connected with military intelligence, and can obtain classified documents," said the shorter man. "My associate and I work for a government committee based in Baghdad." He walked past the sofa to stand near the wall with the flag, his hands folded behind his back. He ooked at Miller and said, "We have been informed the US Army headquarters in Stuttgart is going to receive some vital information about a scientific discovery. The United States has not shared this knowledge with any other country. Our country knows about it, wants it, and we want you to get it for us."

The taller man walked behind the couch and lifted a large, heavy duffle bag. He opened it and struggled to turn it upside down. Tens of thousands of dollars dropped onto the cushions and the floor. His partner rifled a wad of $50 bills and said, "We are offering this money to you." He let it drop to the floor, adding, "We will pay half now, and the remaining half when we receive the information. The information we seek is a scientific research project developed in the United States. It deals with the production of energy by combining certain natural resources."

Miller, still thinking it was a joke or test of some sort on the part of the UNIMI managers, dutifully played along. "How am I going to obtain this discovery?"

"When you leave UNIMI for good, any duty station they assign you to will have access to the information. We know that you are a military intelligence officer, so you will not have any problems. You have access to all documents, correct?" Miller was silent. "I must tell you, however, that if you refuse us, you face death. We cannot have our plan discovered." As he said this, the younger, shorter man removed a pistol with a silencer from the side of his waistband.

Miller quickly rejected his assumption of a UNIMI setup. Still wearing his winter coat, he gripped both zipper sides of the jacket. He looked thoughtful, as if considering their offer. The taller, older man motioned toward the pile of money with his left hand, and his partner's eyes followed. As the two looked down at the bundles of cash, Miller stepped to the side and quickly pulled the 9mm out of his coat's inner breast pocket. The short thug with the silencer looked up and turned as Miller fired two rounds in quick succession. As the bullets penetrated his body, he fell back against his partner. They both dropped to the floor. Miller could tell by the pulsing blood that he had hit the carotid artery. The second wound, in the man's abdomen, also bled profusely, his shirt growing redder by the second.

The taller man grabbed the pistol and tried to get up but slipped in the pool of blood. His gun went off accidentally, one shot went into the ceiling, the other hit the door frame.

Miller pulled the trigger again but missed as the man kept slipping in his partner's blood. The bullet only grazed the man's free arm. The guy groaned from pain as Miller turned around and raced out of the open door before the killer could get off another shot.

Once out of the building, he got into the car and quickly drove off the premises. While heading back to UNIMI, he checked the rearview mirror often. No one appeared to be following. At a red light, he rested his head against the steering wheel and breathed deeply, trying to understand what had just happened.

Damn. Damn. Damn. As his heartrate slowed he became pissed off at himself. How stupid was he to go along with these guys?

A car horn interrupted his brooding, and he quickly drove ahead to return to the apartment. He needed to alert his superiors.

2

Planning

Yury Nikulin is a ruthless spy. He manages and works with a crew that cleans offices at night. The team walked out of the rear entrance of the Dirksen Senate Office Building at 4:00 a.m. Two of his men pushed a large, square canvas cart that was too heavy and bulky for one man to maneuver. Another cleaner pushed a lighter cart. The trash bags were spread wide open at the top, concealing anything under them. The fourth man handed a clipboard to the night guard with a page indicating the offices cleaned. The man skimmed the contents of each cart and signed the paperwork for their release; all he saw were the contents of the opened bags revealing paper debris. The group moved to the dock and secured the bags with ties.

Hours before, an argument arose between Nikulin and a coworker who, like him, was a secret agent. The two were vying for an espionage position that would release them as janitors. Both were qualified and their ambassador had briefed them on the new assignment in DC. Although Nikulin had tenure, his competitor had worked in the nation's capital and knew the territory well. During work, they argued. At break time Nikulin casually offered to buy drinks and snacks from the machines. Callous and ambitious, he had a plan to ensure his own success. Stopping briefly in the hallway along his way back to the team, he twisted off the cap and poured the powder from a capsule into one of the juice bottles, shook it, and replaced the cap. The capsule contained a deadly substance he kept in his wallet in case of enemy capture, but it would serve this purpose equally well. Returning, he put the bottles and snack bags on a windowsill, except his and the other man's drink. He pretended to twist off the caps of both bottles. Minutes later the coworker was dead. Fortunately, the other men hadn't liked the agent either, so they had no qualms in helping the manager dispose of the body. They lowered him into a cart and covered his body with plastic bags filled with paper debris.

Their van backed into the loading dock and stopped at the hydraulic lift used for heavy objects. When the carts were on, one of the men pushed the button to lower it. They wheeled the carts to the van and put them inside. The heavy one needed four men to lift it into the vehicle.

During the ride back to the office warehouse the vehicle stopped in a secluded and dark section of North Capitol Street in DC. After emptying his pockets, they leaned the coworker's body against a tree. Nikulin kept the wallet to dispose of elsewhere. He also wanted to get the dead agent's cyanide from his wallet to replace the one he'd used. Twenty minutes later, a right turn onto I-295 south got the remaining crew to their headquarters.

***

Nikulin made a right-hand turn out of the embassy of the Russian Federation onto southbound Wisconsin Avenue NW. He had already changed his clothes at the embassy.

It was 6:55 a.m. This was the assignment he wanted. After all, he had been trained by the Russian Foreign Intelligence Service, better known as the SVR. Its name in Russian is *Служба Внешней Разведки Sushma Vintner Rusedski*. It is also the successor to the KGB. The loss of his cohort was of no consequence to the embassy. Many immigrant workers were found dead in the nation's capital. It was survival of the fittest.

Before being assigned to the Russian embassy in the United States, he was a scout who followed other counterintelligence spies throughout Europe for information for the SVR. Several years had passed since then. In between Europe and now, he supervised the cleaning of congressional offices. He used this time to also snoop around for essential government documents. Now the ambassador didn't have to choose who he believed was the one qualified to pursue a more intricate espionage campaign.

As Nikulin reached the middle of Wisconsin Avenue in Georgetown proper, he ground his teeth in frustration. Cars coming north wouldn't yield to let anyone come southbound. It reminded him of Moscow's motorway madhouse. A minibus stopped to unload passengers in the northbound lane. He raced through.

He sped through a yellow traffic light at the end of Wisconsin Avenue and turned left. The speed limit sign posted twenty-five miles an hour. He turned right onto C Street and drove until he reached the US Department of State building. Two DC cops patrolled the front grounds, and one man dressed in civilian clothing strolled by the building's sign, talking on his cell phone. Since it was early, Nikulin found a place to park at the end of the street. He got out and put coins into the meter, although paying was not required until eight o'clock.

Nikulin opened the passenger-side door and leaned in. He inserted a thin memory card into a remote radio receiver and compact recorder before putting the unit between his shirt and undershirt. Then he put a wireless, flesh-toned plastic bud into his right ear. He turned on the remote and adjusted the volume. A listening device had been planted in one of the building's conference rooms behind the chair railing. Walking away from the car, he flung his right hand backward toward his shoulder and pressed the car's remote-control button. There was a slight beep from the horn. He liked these American rental cars.

It was now 7:30. Workers were entering buildings all up and down the street. He looked around and relaxed, now he wasn't the only civilian near the building. Walking onto E Street was an uphill exercise. He fiddled with the dial, but still only heard scratching noises. *Was the unit working? Was he close enough?*

He reached the midpoint of the back of the State Department building, and the scratching sounds diminished. Walking across a grassy area, he reached inside his shirt and fine-tuned the remote. He heard voices talking about the eight o'clock meeting. He leaned on a concrete retaining wall just high enough to be comfortable while he watched the traffic below.

***

The Russian embassy was already busy at 8:00. Ambassador Oskars Linkov accompanied his emissary, Galina Trofimoff. They walked the outside grounds to discuss her standing in for him today at an important meeting. Linkov was a tall man with a thick salt and pepper mustache, in contrast to Trofimoff's slender, five-foot-seven height.

Later in the morning, she was going to confer with members of the Senate Economic and Security Commission regarding US oil drilling partnerships in Siberia. Since the United States and Europe were being taken advantage of by Middle Eastern oil masters, Russia was the only nation with petroleum potential for the United States.

It was a touchy international situation. The United Arab Emirates had raised and lowered oil rates over the past decades, and market uncertainty began to take a toll on the world. Although the United States had acres of its own untapped oil fields and a lot of refined reserves, Russia's vast petroleum underground needed a buyer. The United States refused to partake unless they shared drilling rights with Russia and had a written contract.

It was up to Russia to negotiate an oil price with the United States, and this was the reason for this first congressional meeting.

Linkov knew this meeting was a waste of time and would only be an exchange of words. Today, he had another concern.

As he and Galina walked, the ambassador read off questions the congressional committee would likely ask, and Galina answered. The quizzing helped her feel prepared.

Linkov looked at his watch. "Galina, it's already 9:00." They walked back toward his office building, one of the two white buildings. She shook his hand and went into the two-story office building. Linkov walked into the other building. It not only served as his office but also held the two-floor penthouse apartment.

"Excuse me, Ambassador Linkov, Minister-Counselor Mikhail Berolsky is here." He was second in command at the embassy. They took their seats.

***

Yury Nikulin walked back to his car to find a parking ticket stuck under the windshield washer blade. The time was 9:47. "Dammit!" he mumbled as he pushed it into his back pocket. As the spy sat in his car, he smiled smugly. His first day on this job and he had recorded a special meeting between State Department personnel! He drove back to the embassy to meet with the ambassador and the minister-counselor.

After closing the door, he took a seat alongside Berolsky. Linkov buzzed the receptionist and said to hold all calls, except from Moscow. "So, Yury, let's hear what you got for us today." Linkov put the memory card into the computer and another one in a second port to record. Before they could start the recording, the phone rang.

Linkov picked up the telephone and said with a smile, "Yes, President Borodin, I'm doing fine. And you, sir?" He made hand signals indicating the two men should wait outside while he took the call.

"I do not have a lot of time, Oskars."

"Yes, Mr. President. I understand. Please, continue."

Borodin said the Russian ambassador to Iraq informed him about a new political faction called Tariq'Allah. They were sending spies into Germany. He explained these people obtained jobs from the US Army, claiming they were ISIS defectors. "But they must be doing more than just cleaning offices. I don't believe they are ISIS traitors. I do think this political faction is gathering security intelligence information. They are gaining access into army offices by doing the same thing your scouts are doing in Washington, DC."

"How is this possible? How can Iraqis get these jobs, especially since the US security policies are more stringent with Middle East people?

"It's not a mystery the jobs are available. They advertise for workers and take whoever they can get because the Germans do not want to work for them anymore."

The president changed the subject. He told the ambassador the Russian spy in Iraq found out an espionage project had been approved. "It deals with obtaining information of a scientific discovery developed in the United States. So far, there isn't any more information. I want to find out more. This may require assigning another spy to watch what is going on. I just don't know who we will pick. I will keep you informed."

3

They Listen

The receptionist alerted Berolsky and Nikulin that they could return to the office. Linkov turned on the recording, and they heard Secretary of State Julia S. Mitchell say, "Welcome to our weekly meeting, everyone. Please be seated. Today, CIA Director Andrew Black will discuss foreign policy. Please proceed, Mr. Black."

Black said there were items on the agenda dealing with Russia, Syria, and Iraq. The first item was a CIA belief Russia was trading underhandedly with foreign countries. He said their information came from satellite pictures that revealed train transports from Syria into Iraq and beyond.

Mitchell chuckled and remarked, "This is interesting."

Black pointed out that the infrared satellite images revealed a train carrying military weaponry across its own country and into Iraq. It stopped at Sinjar, a town west of Mosul, Iraq, ISIS' foothold.

The secretary of state couldn't believe a train transported arms across a country at war. She asked if there was any physical identification of what was being transported, and its country of origin.

Black said his agent had done some research that could answer her question. He looked at Thomas Nolan. "Tom, it's all yours."

"Thank you, Director Black. Yes, Secretary Mitchell, we know the origin of this shipment. To begin, however, I want to show you the territory we're talking about." Thomas Nolan, Ph.D., was a Marine veteran who had been with the CIA for eight years. He walked to the side of the room. An overhead projector displayed a large map onto a screen. As the room lights dimmed, he said, "This map covers Europe and the Mideast." His laser pointer identified the geographical areas. "As we are all aware, the former Soviet Union comprised a large area within the circle I'm making with the laser pointer. The Ukraine country, down here, is included. It's in this region where tanks, missiles, and war-related materials are stored in mountain caves. The precise number is unknown, but we believe they number in the hundreds. When the Soviet Union disbanded in 1989, Moscow's underground mafia confiscated many files. They contained information about the quantity, types, and storage locations of the weapons. The Russian mafia sells the military equipment to Middle Eastern countries like Syria, Iraq, and others.

"The Ukrainian government will not return any of the tanks and other materials to Russia. They argue Russia refuses to share the costs. Anyway, military equipment is being shipped from the port of Odessa on the Black Sea. Then, it goes from the Odessa port down here to the Syrian docks of Al Ladhigiyah, which is here." He held the pointer to that map location and focused on Mitchell. She had a fleeting thought about Russia's involvement. *Why would they bomb Syria and take credit for offensive fighting against ISIS when they are sending weaponry to ISIS?* Nolan saw her stern look and realized his comments didn't make enough of an impression. He focused on Black. "I'll let you take over from here, sir." The room lights were turned back up.

Black opened a large brown envelope and pulled out photographs, which he distributed.

"These are from the satellite imaging I spoke about a few minutes ago. They show large canvas covers strapped to these train cars. The infrared satellite photos reveal there are metallic rectangular objects under the tarps. There are seven of these hidden objects, and five of them are so big that only one object fits into a train car. The photos show a tubular object, like a cannon barrel. We assume it is a Russian-built tank with a 240-millimeter cannon. The last two tarp-covered train cars before the caboose contain electronics and tank mortar rounds," explained Black. "It's hard to accept, but the Russian mafia markets this equipment by employing Ukrainians to do the hard work."

Mitchell's eyes opened wide. *That was it,* she thought, *the Russian mafia. We're getting it from two factions; the mob and the Kremlin.*

Black admitted that it was a preliminary guess, but the CIA believed ISIS was financially supported by a more powerful source in the Middle East. He didn't say anything for another five minutes, letting the people view the photographs. The spiel ended by reminding everybody of the 9/11 incidents and assuming they knew where the funding for that mass murder came from.

Mitchell thanked Black and Nolan. "The next item to discuss is from FBI Agent Gregory Andrews."

"Good morning, Madam Secretary. We have information about an Iraqi political group called Tariq'Allah. Some members of this group are getting permanent residence in Third World countries, which is not illegal, but we're concerned because it's only happening in countries the United Nations is not funding."

Secretary Mitchell folded her hands on the table, and her expression became firm. "Yes, it's a shame the UN has reduced its focus on smaller nations. But for now, what are the Iraqis doing that has you so upset?"

"Well, the most aggravating aspect," Andrews said, "is they are using the UN's standstill to introduce and promote their mission. We found out because Somalia asked the UN if this was legal."

"I still don't get it," stated the secretary. "I see nothing wrong with a Middle East nation trying to expand its own economy, as long as it's legitimate and doesn't violate UN sanctions. This situation certainly seems different from the one Mr. Black described."

Major General Elliott leaned forward and interrupted. His height and broad torso made him easy to see. "Since I've been at Fort Meade in Maryland, I've worked with Mr. Black and Mr.

Andrews for several months. It's not all war games between them. Iraq wants to expand economically."

Mitchell said, "I have no cause to concern myself with what Iraq is doing."

The general smiled. "Yes, but let's not forget, Russia's diplomatic friendship is at best strained with Western nations because of their bombings in Syria. And it's a growing problem with their mafia aiding ISIS. They will not stop until they sell everything. Putin won't do anything. ISIS will continue their efforts at mass destructions and killings. This could broaden into other Middle East nations. We must be cognizant of these matters."

"What a soap opera," Andrews remarked. There were quiet laughs around the table.

Mitchell said, "Yes. But I wish to add to what you said, General. Many Middle Eastern countries are major elements in the foreign community but hide behind strict religious rules in order to do what they damn well please."

Everyone at the table looked grave. Finally, the secretary said, "Okay, what else do we want to talk about?"

General Frommer was stationed at INSCOM. He leaned forward, rested his arms on the table, and said, "Madam Secretary, since ISIS has assumed an international position in the Middle East, they are showing aggression unlike we've seen since World War II. We know Iran has been obtaining uranium and working to produce atomic weapons. They argue they need nuclear energy, but we don't believe their efforts are all about energy." He took a sip of coffee and added, "We must maintain some form of surveillance with all unfriendly countries. Let's continue talks with them and use satellites to scan the world. We'll not only protect ourselves but show how to deal with many international problems. We know that's what the UN is supposed to do, but sometimes it takes them longer to make a decision than our own Congress." He sat back.

"I wonder about that, but I see your point, General," said Mitchell.

The secretary thought for a moment and then said, "One other thing. Are all of you aware there is an Iraqi entourage visiting Washington, DC?"

FBI Agent Andrews stated, "Yes, Madam Secretary. They're touring some agricultural areas in Maryland, Pennsylvania, and North and South Carolina. We think a few are associated with the Tariq'Allah group and we're keeping an eye on them."

They heard her say, "Good. Okay, let's take a break and get some coffee."

Linkov pushed the "stop" button on the recorder. He remembered visiting the State Department building many times and discussing foreign affairs issues in the same room. He turned around and said, "You have done an excellent job on your first mission, Yury."

Berolsky added, "Yes. I agree. What we are hearing is important information. But, for the moment, Oskars, let's have a break as well."

Linkov walked out into the reception area. Nikulin followed Berolsky but branched off to use the bathroom. The receptionist gave Linkov a message, which said the Iraqi diplomats were going to be a half hour late and asked him to hold lunch until then. Linkov sneered and thought: *They are nervy bastards, especially since they requested this meeting.* He told the receptionist to call the kitchen for coffee service. He gave the note to his minister-counselor to make him aware of the delay.

Nikulin stood on the outside terrace smoking a cigarette. Linkov joined him, and they puffed and talked for a few minutes. "Do you feel confident enough to continue to do this work?" Nikulin raised his heavy eyebrows and said he'd been waiting for something like this ever since the transfer to DC. Pleased with that confident assurance, the ambassador said, "Let's get back to our meeting, Yury."

Before they entered, Nikulin pulled out the parking ticket from his back pocket and handed it to Linkov, who smiled and agreed to take care of it.

He started the recording. They listened to Mitchell talk about the Russian underground fueling war in Syria and Iraq. They knew the finger could not be pointed to the Russian mob or its military. They had no proof. "Also, if the suspicion of Middle East spies in Germany becomes a fact, then we will get involved diplomatically and legally. Next, I must admit the double-dealing with Third World countries is fair trading. There's nothing we can do except look into it." She put the page aside and added, "During the break, I spoke with the DIA and learned Russia denies manufacturing tank ammunition for the tanks transferred from Ukraine. However, the Russian black market might be supplying the ammunition.

"We have to adjourn because I'm sitting in on a conference with a subcommittee on Capitol Hill. They're getting together with the Russian delegation regarding the oil drilling agreement. We won't meet next week because I'll be in Berlin. We're considering broadening our diplomatic relations with Iran, believe it or not, and the president thought a midpoint location would be best. At least he's willing to try again. A few other countries also will participate." After hesitating a moment, the secretary added, "I can't wait to see the reaction from the Russian ambassador in Berlin when I mention their weapons shipments from the port of Odessa." Her smile widened. "Anyway, my office will notify all of you about the next meeting."

The recording came to a stop. Neither Nikulin nor Berolsky was worried about the Russian clique and their relationship with the Ukrainian underground. Nikulin asked, "When do you think there will be another talk?"

Linkov leaned forward and rested his arms on the desk. “You forget, Yury, your former comrades still clean the office of the Foreign Relations secretary, who is a good friend of the secretary of state.” A smile grew on his face, and he added, “Plus, we have the transmitter in the conference room. Believe me, Yury, we will find out about the next meeting.” Now I must stick to a luncheon obligation. Let’s talk the first of next week.” He told Berolsky to come back at 12:30 for the luncheon.

4

The Luncheon

The midday weather was beautiful, eighty-three degrees with little humidity and a slight breeze. The ambassador took a drag of his cigarette. Blowing out the smoke, he thought: *This wait is demeaning. I should have been more involved in the scheduling of this meeting.* He wondered whether he should have notified his supervisor, Viktor Chayka, Russia's minister of foreign affairs. *If he finds out, I'll just say I forgot to inform him.* He took another drag. *What do I care anyway? Chayka has black spots on his résumé.* He knew the Russian *Duma*, or legislature, could dismiss him for such misconduct. He massaged his nose and wondered if the Iraqis were going to mention his association with the Russian mafia. *Are they going to try blackmail? What the hell do they want?*

The sight of Yury Nikulin leaving in his car shifted the ambassador's thoughts. He thought about the future and becoming wealthy. He'd like to retire and live a less demanding lifestyle. He would have retirement income from the Russian Federation and be entitled to settle in Ukraine along the Black Sea.

His daydream was broken when he felt the heat of the cigarette on his fingers. He dropped the butt into the sand urn, reentered the office, and placed the memory card into a Moscow mail folder. He labeled an envelope and put the backup card in a file cabinet.

The telephone rang, and his secretary told him Galina was on hold. He picked up the other line, and she told him the congressional meeting was adjourned until 2:00. For the next ten minutes, they discussed the content of the conference. She said the panel director, Senator Lauer, wanted a business contract to be cowritten by the Russian government and his panel members, outlining the drilling rights of United States oil companies. Also, the senator said US oil investors wanted to receive a special discount for any crude oil Russia agreed to sell them. They wanted her to answer. "I briefly explained you had to be present. I also told them you had a more important matter to work with today. I wish you could have seen their faces."

Linkov almost burst out laughing and complimented her diplomatic authority. He believed Galina was a good choice.

The Iraqis arrived at 12:30. The officer and his assistant were dressed in summer military attire, khaki pants, and short-sleeve shirts without ties. Their rank medals were pinned onto their shoulder pads and service ribbons over their shirt pockets. Their black dress shoes were highly shined. Linkov was impressed but kept his face blank.

The ambassador and Berolsky were surprised to hear them introduce themselves in Russian. That was the purpose of Berolsky's presence; he was fluent in Arabic.

"I am Major Arif Yildiz." The man was of medium build and slightly over average height for an Iraqi, with jet-black hair and a thin, black mustache.

His younger assistant had similar physical characteristics but was a bit taller at 5'10" and had a trim goatee along with his mustache. "I am Captain Adnaw Alzuhari," he said.

Yildiz and Alzuhari had comparable backgrounds. Both were born and raised in Baghdad. They were good students in political science and foreign affairs at the university and could speak two foreign languages as well. A few years before they met, the major had diplomatic interests. He trained to work with government officials before he was invited to attend the military college in Baghdad. Alzuhari was offered a two-year degree in military intelligence. Upon graduation, the Ministry of Baghdad invited him to become a special agent. He accepted and was introduced to Arif Yildiz. Yildiz trained to become one of many underground specialists for espionage. Alzuhari was an undercover spy in training.

Linkov's receptionist politely interrupted him and told them to follow her into the dining room.

While lunch was being served, Linkov wanted to know if Major Yildiz was stationed in the United States or just visiting the Iraqi embassy.

"I am here for three weeks before returning to Baghdad. My visit is strictly diplomatic. Six other people are visiting with us from Iraq. Although the United States approved our visit, we have to wait for a day so the farms and industrial sites we want to visit can be notified again."

"Why are you visiting these particular areas of business?" asked the ambassador.

Yildiz swallowed some iced tea and then replied, "My country is interested in advancing our areas of science, like medicine and veterinary research, agriculture, and computer business."

"Where are you going to visit?" asked Berolsky.

While Yildiz took a forkful of food, he motioned for the captain to answer. Alzuhari said, "Our entourage is going to visit such places in Maryland as Johns Hopkins Hospital and the University of Maryland agricultural center. Then we go to Raleigh, North Carolina, to visit two butchering companies, one for beef and one for chicken. We will then drive into South Carolina to learn about the use of organic pesticides to protect crops."

Linkov said, "I wasn't aware Iraq was capable of agricultural expansion because of the country's arid conditions." He decided to get bolder and asked, "Has something changed in your hemisphere?"

Yildiz bristled a little, wondering if Linkov was insulting him. “No. I am merely carrying out orders.” He took his eyes off Linkov, dismissing his remarks as typical of a Russian.

“Yes, but why are you pursuing this in such a scientific way when your country doesn’t have vast agricultural territory?”

“I wanted this visit for a special reason, Mr. Ambassador.”

Linkov retorted, “Is there something I am missing? I don’t follow you.” Before Yildiz answered, Linkov added, “Anyway, it is surprising to hear your country sent you to speak with me about nonviolent pursuits rather than military materials.”

Yildiz and Alzuhari laughed out loud. Alzuhari had to cover his mouth with a napkin. “You Russians don’t give up, do you?” said Yildiz with a grin. “Yes, you are correct. Iraq has arid conditions.” He sipped and added, “And we are not pursuing military information on this trip. At least not about the Russian mafia exchanging Russian-Ukrainian tanks and electronics for their benefit in Syria.”

Linkov swallowed hard, “Where did you learn this? And where did you learn to speak Russian so well?”

“Many of us, including Captain Alzuhari, were transfer military students to Moscow. We were also taught to think like Russians, Mr. Ambassador, which is to be bold.” No one spoke for a few seconds. He looked carefully at Linkov. “I’m sure you wondered why we asked for this meeting. It’s simple. Iraq wants to expand into the world market without restrictions. However, the United States objected on the grounds we are really going to pursue political takeover through military means, like in Syria and Iran. No. We are not doing this. As a result, Iraq began a technological spy campaign a few years ago.” He wet their whistle a little more by adding, “It incorporates what we’re doing now in the United States.

“The information we receive will help to advance my country. What ISIS does is their business. They are sure to be overrun. But to be honest with you, if we want something related to military materials it's easier to get it from Europe's black market than from the American military." He looked up, smiled, and added, "Our interest in American military weaponry is of great importance to us, but only to use against ISIS, not for overall destructive purposes."

"I see," Linkov said with a smirk. "Well, if Iraq is not interested in obtaining military information, why did you want this meeting? Does my country know this?"

Yildiz broke off a piece of Russian black bread, spread butter on it, took a bite, and started to chew. *They were impatient to hear the answer.* He swallowed and said with a smile, "We are aware of your association with the Russian mafia, Mr. Linkov. Of course, you do not want this publicized. It would mean the end of your diplomatic career, perhaps imprisonment. We certainly will not tell your superiors." Yildiz leaned over, squinted his eyes, and continued, "And this information must be held a secret from the United States."

Linkov swallowed nervously. He glanced at Berolsky, who was equally stunned. "Yes, I understand, but what do you want from us, Major?"

"My second mission is this, gentlemen. Iraq wants an advocate, such as you, here in Washington, DC. We know about Russia's contribution to the Third World country campaign years ago. Putting that aside for the moment, your country has an excellent reputation in international politics. Fortunately for us, the UN and the United States have reduced their contributions to help Third World nations. These countries are frustrated and angry." He leaned against the backrest. "We want to use you, personally, as a sponsor. When a Third World country requests information as to how Iraq can help them, you are to say we are qualified."

"I am not familiar with Iraq's abilities. What am I supposed to say?"

While reaching into his briefcase, Yildiz replied, "My superiors thought ahead and prepared a short outline for you to use. You can change it as you see fit, but only to promote our goals. Don't talk about Russia being able to do the same thing."

Linkov took the single page and read the contents out loud. "You will briefly tell the Third World country Iraq is a contributor to world needs in business, education, and science, and their country can be greatly assisted in these areas." He mumbled another sentence. "Iraq has the financial means to help countries forgotten by the US and the United Nations." Linkov looked at his partner.

Yildiz spoke up and said, "There is another paragraph, Mr. Ambassador."

Linkov read the last sentence. "Tell the representative of the Third World country having a talk with an Iraqi diplomat is necessary for them to expand economically and to build a future relationship."

Linkov placed his copy of the page on the table. "It seems simple enough. I'm sure we can assist your country, but is this going to be enough?"

"We are entering an international negotiation and trade environment. We are beginning with small countries lacking the means to get on their feet." He took a sip of tea. "Iraq wants a better future, and Third World people can help us get there. I realize we are working in an under-the-table sort of way by talking to you like this, but we actually want to advance these countries. It is a win-win."

Linkov readjusted himself in the chair and asked, "What exactly can Iraq do?"

Yildiz looked at him gravely and said, "First, Iraq is going to carry out a five-year plan, much like the Soviets did in agriculture. We fully intend to exploit Third World nations' resources, but we want to promote each country for what it can best produce. Many have resources they are unaware of. We will supply machinery and teach them how to farm their lands and improve cattle and poultry breeding. We can invest in building food processing plants. They need an immediate boost from their deprived conditions. Our oil money is going to help us to do this. Naturally, Iraq plans to get a percentage return on these investments. We are going to propose a fair-trade pact with each country. What we're doing is legal in the world market."

Linkov sat silently for a few seconds. Then he leaned on the table and said, "Sir, what you are saying is too simple. There has to be another motive in all this. Iraq certainly doesn't need financial support, even though trade limitations are in effect. So, tell me, what else is brewing?"

"You are a determined man, Ambassador Linkov," Yildiz said. "Iraq will not use aggressive tactics. Do not compare us to ISIS. And just because we are Iraqis, don't associate our motives with what Middle Eastern terrorists did to the United States on September 11, 2001." His statement only deepened Linkov's confusion.

Berolsky butted in. "I don't entirely understand your motives either, other than creating a diplomatic relationship and providing food for Third World nations." His patience was growing thin. "What is the real reason?"

Yildiz avoided the question: "We have already sent people to assess the atmosphere in Third World countries. The first step has been going on for some time. It is just the start of our five-year goals." He sipped iced tea and said in a sly way, "Ambassador Linkov, you and Mr. Berolsky are people who, if you accept, can work with us."

Linkov and Berolsky thought his answer sounded like it was leading up to what they were waiting for.

Berolsky said. "What are the remaining steps in the five-year plans?"

Yildiz's face grew more serious. "I am not allowed to divulge anything more, gentlemen."

"But how is Iraq going to benefit by creating diplomatic relations with Third World nations, Major? Let's face it. Time is not on your side, and you are going to need a large quantity of agricultural assistance from—" An idea popped into his mind. He asked, "Does this plan include a secret project to harness solar power? I have recently heard about this through our sources." There was no answer from his guests, but their expressions told him he was on the right track.

Yildiz was prepared to combat this question. He answered, "I have already given you information about the areas of support Iraq will give to Third World countries. Whatever information the last years of the plan include will have to come from Iraq."

Linkov glanced at his assistant, then at Yildiz. "Okay, you just want us to talk about the good things your country can do. If we do that, you promise not to reveal our association with the Russian fraternity. What else? What is in it for us?"

Yildiz smiled slyly as he looked from the ambassador to Mr. Berolsky, knowing he was about to seal the deal. He cleared his throat and answered, "We will deposit twenty-five thousand American dollars into Swiss bank accounts for each of you every time we are granted diplomatic relations with a Third World country. We must have a signed agreement, Mr. Ambassador. You and Mr. Berolsky can do with the money as you wish."

Ambassador Linkov smiled, held out his hand, and said, "As the American salesmen say, can we call it a deal?"

The four of them stood up, shook hands, and sat again.

Yildiz said, "The United States is aware of the trade the Russian mafia is carrying on with ISIS in Syria and Iraq. Why does ISIS get the military equipment?"

Linkov spread his hands wide, indicating it wasn't worth an argument. "They are the only ones open for business at this time.

For now, the mafia does not care where the old military equipment goes. It's just mathematics."

They stared at each other for a few moments before the major added, "I know you are wondering why we are doing this. We want to succeed. I know the ISIS war gives Russia the opportunity to bomb Syria. And I am aware of the support given to opposing ISIS by the United States. But a big problem exists. Middle Eastern cultural history has taught many not to trust any Judeo-Christian country. Hopefully, Iraq will be able to open economic trade with all religious sects."

"Major Yildiz, I'm sorry to harp on the subject," said Linkov, "but I have one final question. How are you going to fulfill all your desires? Certainly, Iraq's actions will become known. Other countries will also want to do this for economic reasons."

Yildiz and Alzuhari chuckled. Yildiz said, "Yes, Mr. Ambassador, you do know how to stick to the subject. First, I already mentioned we want to be considered as friendly. Second, my country is restricted in trading with a few larger nations but not with the countries in question. I already told you we are limited in some of our own areas because of ISIS." He stared at Linkov, who had a suspicious look on his face.

"It sounds like you are double-dealing."

Yildiz, irritated, trained his grey eyes on the ambassador to respond, but was interrupted by the arrival of the desserts.

"Ambassador Linkov, are you or are you not interested in obtaining the Swiss deposits?" asked Alzuhari impatiently.

The question went unanswered again as they ate dessert. The tension eased enough for them to cordially discussed other matters, Linkov had a feeling he was going to have to watch these guys.

5

Days Later

On Saturday, Eric Miller searched the Internet for a possible clue to a geographical mystery. He liked dabbling in areas not part of his schooling, and the search took his mind off what might happen to him. Since the killing of the Iraqi thug, officially a member of the embassy in Stockholm, he was ordered to keep a low profile and not to volunteer for anything. His attention returned to the screen, and he wondered why Sweden formed as a solid body of land and then separated over thousands of years, especially around Stockholm. He couldn't quite wrap his head around the process.

He was transferred to the UNIMI because the US Army needed both a graduate military professional and a savvy person. Miller majored in social engineering and achieved top grades at West Point, which helped him to excel at UNIMI. He minored in international affairs, carrying the same number of credits as his primary. Overall, his schooling enabled him to become adept in global issues; he represented the United States of America.

UNIMI's daily class schedule included discussing global, political, and military problems, with espionage being one of the topics. Another focus was on how to minimize the threat of war through negotiation with foreign rebels.

His mind wandered to the issue of international terrorism as a global problem. The old-time surveillance tactic, one country sending a person into another country, was still used but was being challenged by Internet communications, reducing the need for a human presence.

He understood international fraternalism protected terrorists from exposure; fundamentalist chiefs defended themselves and convinced their supporters to fight for their very survival. Using spies and murderers only satisfied their aggression. Present-day fundamentalists combined spy tactics with a tainted version of an Islamic way of life. The combination produced a rebellion against other religious groups, including rival Islamic countries.

Miller focused back on his computer. He examined the shorelines of the continents of Europe and Africa, and then compared the geographical outlines to North and South America, thinking they were connected billions of years ago. After clicking the mouse to pull up the map for the Pacific land areas, his cell phone buzzed.

"Eric Miller."

"Good afternoon, Eric. This is Lieutenant Bernie Bliss in the personnel department."

"Yeah, hi, Bernie. How are you doing?"

"We haven't spoken in a while, but as you know, I handle all the Western allies' paperwork here, from getting new recruits settled at UNIMI to discharging the graduated officers. Anyway, I was told to call you. A crucial matter involving you was discussed among some of the ranking staff today. They want you to attend a meeting at 1500 hours."

Miller asked, "They're working today?"

"Yes, and the meeting is mandatory." Before they hung up, Bliss said, "Hope to get together sometime, Eric." He said goodbye and hung up.

Miller wondered if this was going to be a meeting to discredit him or return him to the States to be court-martialed for the Iraqi killing. It was only 1220 hours. After making a sandwich and grabbing a soft drink, he tried to keep his nerves steady. At 2:15 he dressed in class As and left.

He drove his blue Saab to the UN Intelligence office building at 176 Dag Hammarskjölds väg. The garage entrance gate slid backward after the camera scanned a barely perceptible decal on the front windshield. He drove to the underground parking. After an electronic fingerprint scan, he rode the elevator up to the meeting room floor. An attractive receptionist verified his information on the computer and said, "Good afternoon, Captain Miller."

"Good afternoon," he said, admiring her. He wondered if she was available and casually checked out her left ring finger. He believed good food, good beer, good wine, and just one loving woman was the ticket to real life. Seeing nothing, he made a mental note to follow up if possible.

"Please go to room eight. They are waiting for you." She pointed down the corridor to her left. When he reached the wall plaque identifying the room, he straightened his tie and jacket and walked in.

"Good afternoon, Captain Miller. We've been expecting you. Please, come in and sit down," Belgian General Jacques Dubère said. He walked around the table and noted five people, only one wearing a US military uniform.

"Since you're not entirely familiar with the UNIMI officers, I will let them introduce themselves in a few minutes. I alerted these people because they expressed concern for your remaining time here. Yesterday, my office received a transfer for you."

Thank God, he thought. He said, "Oh, I didn't think I'd finish early."

General Dubère let other officers speak, including their opinions of Miller's effective communication techniques with other attendees at the course. Dubère looked at the woman to his right and said, "Please, Vice-Admiral James, you also asked to speak to Captain Miller."

Mary-Lyle James was a robust, five-foot-seven-inch, graying redhead with over twenty-five years in the US Navy. An Academy education and years with the Pentagon and NATO resulted in promotions to her current level. She began, "Although we have never met, Captain Miller, I have studied and graded your submittals over the past two years. First, thank you for your work." She pushed aside her notes and focused on him. "You are being transferred because we believe your life is in danger. The Iraqi embassy officials here in Stockholm are outraged about the man you killed, which we all know was in self-defense. We are transferring you for your protection. You are being assigned to the US Army in Europe, or USAREUR. Your duty station assignment is the 32nd Security Intelligence in Würzburg, Germany. Your central headquarters will be the V Corps' G-2 in Stuttgart. You are to be there no later than Wednesday of next week."

Dubère handed the packet to the captain and said, "Driving directions are in here. I also signed your graduation document."

The group disbanded.

***

It was close to dinnertime when Miller returned to his apartment. He was hungry and called the sandwich shop on the first floor to place an order. Twenty minutes later he picked up the order and decided to sit at the bar to eat. After taking a sip of his Swedish Pilsner and a bite of his sub, he began to read his transfer info.

Lieutenant Bliss sat in the restaurant, eating with acquaintances. He recognized Miller, and curiosity got the better of him. Excusing himself and carrying his beer with him, he sat down on a stool at the bar.

Miller swallowed the food and looked up. His visitor smiled and said in his British manner, "How are you doing, Eric?"

Miller wiped his mouth and hand with his napkin and said, "Bernie, it's good to see you." They shook hands.

"What happened in the conference?"

Miller pushed his fries closer to him and motioned for him to take some, then continued. "As you probably know, I'm being transferred to Germany."

"Yeah, with all that's happened with you, I kind of figured you were going to be relocated." The lower-ranked officer, chewing a fry, asked, "And where in Germany?"

"My duty station is Würzburg, but my job wasn't explained."

"I'm curious, Eric. How do you feel about this?

"I honestly can't wait to leave, both for my own safety and because I'm ready to move on. I've been here for close to three years. Although I enjoy meeting people from other countries, there are a few foreigners here now that are hard to take."

"I know what you mean."

The English lieutenant noticed Miller looking into space and lost in thought. He wasn't touching his food, so Bliss said, "Please, continue eating, Eric. I'm sorry I interrupted you but it was quite boring listening to the woes of those other UNIMI members. I also appreciate you sharing your fries."

***

Sunday arrived without the need for an alarm clock to rouse him. Miller decided to leave one day early. After a shower and breakfast, he made a call to the rental management agency to verify cancelation of his lease and inform them about leaving early.

The next item on the agenda was to email his family in Ann Arbor to let them know about the transfer. He placed personals in the front and back seats and filled the trunk.

During the 270-mile trip south from Stockholm to the Swedish port of Helsingborg, Miller discharged built-up stress. His stint at UNIMI was over. Stockholm didn't get too warm in the spring, and it felt good to go south; he mentally compared the Nordic weather conditions to his home in Michigan. Traffic slowed and then came to a complete stop at the bridge that crossed into Denmark. Minutes passed, and then a flagman waved them onward.

Two car lengths behind Miller's car sat the tall thug from the Iraqi Embassy in a rented dark gray Audi. The bandaged arm itched. He rubbed it, thinking about revenge. His assignment ignored the Geneva Convention's protocol to negotiate, not kill. The Iraqi ambassador wanted retribution, despite the disapproval of his government. *No one knew about this, except the ambassador and the thug.* Being inconspicuous and waiting to make the right move at the right time was the plan.

Vehicles moved slowly onto the high arch of the bridge, where traffic once again became stalled. This time Miller turned off the engine, got out, and looked at the body of water below. It joined two international waterways, called the Sound. The North Sea was to his right and the Baltic to his left. While on the bridge, seagull cries echoed in the soft breezes. Finally, traffic began to move again, and he started the engine.

A few miles down the road multiple hotel signs appeared. He decided to stop driving for the night.

The next day he arrived in Copenhagen and found it was close in size to his hometown. This city's attractions included the architecture of the romantic Romanesque period, the Middle Ages, and the clean lines of contemporary designs. The people were fair skinned, but unlike Swedes, many of them had dark hair. He walked around the central city area near the hotel. The famous bronze statue called the Little Mermaid sat on a rock overlooking the harbor. He visited the cathedral of the Church of Our Lady, which had a brochure in English detailing its history back to the twelfth century. By then it was late afternoon. *Damn, where did all the time go?*

Being a tourist town, the Tivoli Gardens area had many restaurants. The bartender understood English and brought him a beer. He was a friendly guy. He asked Miller if it was his first time in Copenhagen. The cordial discussion led to news of a multi-vehicle accident just south of the city, which closed the highway. Miller decided to delay his trip into Germany and stay at a hotel for the night. A restaurant waiter brought him a menu.

On Tuesday morning, he crossed over into Germany. It was his first time in the country and he was impressed by the straight, well-engineered highway, the Autobahn. Without speed limits, except when entering the town limits of a big city, people cruised at speeds of approximately 160 kilometers, or 100 miles per hour. There were idiot drivers as well as good ones.

Farther south, the late afternoon traffic increased and slowed north of Cologne, or Köln, as the Germans pronounce and spell it. Traffic jammed because of another accident. Exhausted from driving, he decided to find a hotel.

The Rhine River separated the east and west sides of the city of one million inhabitants. On one side of the town, he saw an impressive bronze profile of President Kennedy attached to the masonry of the bridge that crossed the river. It was Kennedy who had inspired all of Germany, especially the then-Democratic half of Berlin. His famous words, "*Ich bin ein Berliner*," are not forgotten.

From a distance, Eric saw the second unmistakable landmark, the Cologne Cathedral, the most beautiful Gothic structure he had ever seen. Sweden and Denmark had their own beautiful architecture, but nothing like this eight hundred-plus-foot structure. The two spires were more than a hundred feet above the frame.

***

Linkov's secretary's voice came over the wireless intercom. "Excuse me, Ambassador Linkov, but you have a call from Moscow, Minister of Foreign Affairs Viktor Chayka."

Linkov frowned but thanked her and disconnected. "Now what does he want?" It was 2:45 p.m. in DC. "Good evening, Viktor. This is a late call for you."

"Hello, Oskars. Yes, it is late. I just finished with a conference, and I want to bring you up to date. First, Germany is deporting our representative, Vladimir Usmanov, for spying. He was able to obtain plans regarding our oil drilling agreements with foreign countries from a Berlin government office. He also got a list of foreign countries, including the United States, that were going to try to force negotiations to lower petroleum costs. He's leaving tomorrow and will be escorted to the airport by German detectives," said Chayka. Second, we agreed to have one of your SVR undercover agents working out of your embassy replace Usmanov."

Linkov said defensively, "Why my embassy, Viktor?"

"The agent selected to work in Berlin is Aleksei Bruy. This man has worked there before and speaks German. We will secretly fly him to Moscow. After he is briefed, he will be sent to our Berlin embassy. Word has gotten out about him, and the entire continent is suspicious and insulted."

"I am sorry to lose him, but I think it is a good transfer."

"You're not going to like my next statement. Yury Nikulin is going to be assigned to a new duty station also." The ambassador closed his eyes and suppressed a harsh retort. "You are familiar with our contact in Baghdad?" Linkov quietly answered yes. "He told us Iraq is gearing up to carry out a special mission in Amsterdam. We don't know what it is just yet."

"Viktor, he is my best man. I don't want to lose him."

"You will receive replacements, Oskars."

Chayka understood losing a good spy was a morale killer. "You know he is qualified to be in Europe. I do, also. He's worked there. And if it's any satisfaction to you, he can remain under your authority." Linkov let out a sigh, his stomach muscles releasing tension. He thanked Chayka.

Before they hung up, the minister asked Linkov if there was anything else he wanted to say. The ambassador thought it was kind of strange for him to ask since the minister called him. "Yes, Viktor, I do have a question. How soon do you want Yury to go?"

"There isn't a time set for Nikulin's transfer. All we know for now is two Iraqi agents are going to Amsterdam—at least we think it's that city. And we don't know when this will occur. I will call you when we find out."

Linkov's shoulders sagged with relief when he understood he would maintain contact with Nikulin. "I hope the transfer is not soon, because Nikulin has one more assignment."

The minister didn't ask what it was about. Instead, he commented, "And thank you, Oskars, for the State Department recordings. All of us especially liked the discussion about our espionage tactic regarding the tank transfers out of Georgia into Syria. It was amusing, to say the least."

6

The Transfer

Nikulin turned left onto Wisconsin Avenue and followed traffic. A few miles and numerous traffic lights later he reached the entrance to the Russian embassy. The security scanner accepted his ID code, and the black gate opened. He parked the car and went into the embassy.

Ambassador Linkov and Minister-Counselor Berolsky were discussing the upcoming State Department meeting and Nikulin's relocation plans when the secretary interrupted and said Minister Chayka is on the line.

The conversation took ten minutes. The ambassador hung up and told Berolsky that the agent in Baghdad sent names and photographs of two people being transferred to Amsterdam. "This is getting more interesting," said the minister-counselor.

Nikulin arrived and was told to go into the office. He didn't know why he had been summoned. Everyone exchanged greetings, and he sat down. A server placed a cup of coffee on the side table for him.

Linkov told him about the assignment back to Europe, which Nikulin received with relief. *It wasn't a reprimand.* He realized a relocation to another duty station was inevitable. For the next few moments, he listened to them explain the Iraqi expansion situation.

Berolsky told him the relocation was Amsterdam. When asked how they knew, the minister-counselor grinned and said, "There are two answers to your question, Yury. First, our SVR contact in Baghdad told the command center in Moscow the day before yesterday about an Iraqi underground organization. Our minister of foreign affairs told this to Ambassador Linkov in a telephone conversation."

They were interrupted when the secretary walked in and handed the ambassador several faxed papers.

Linkov read the information and studied two other pages. He handed them to Berolsky. "We learned a few minutes ago," said the ambassador, "about two Iraqi spies who are going to be transferred to Amsterdam."

"When will this happen?" asked Nikulin.

"We're not sure," said the ambassador. He sipped coffee and explained the length of time in Holland was unknown. "You will continue to report to me." Nikulin smiled with relief, knowing he'd return to Washington, DC, when it was over.

"I have heard on the radio this morning the German government is deporting Usmanov from the Berlin embassy."

"Yes," said the ambassador. "We have to make changes." Nikulin wanted to know why. "Because an incident with the SVR representative getting caught listening to a government conference. It opened the case to an investigation to find the transmitter in their conference room. Two others are being deported with him." He knew the story paralleled what they were doing, but he said nothing.

Berolsky said, "We can talk about this at another time." He handed two photographs to Nikulin. "You will follow these two people."

There was a moment of quiet while Nikulin studied the photos and the assistant gathered the coffee dishes. When the office door closed, Linkov said, "And one other thing," Nikulin looked up. "You have another mission at the State Department on Monday at 8:00."

***

Nikulin walked out of his apartment on a rainy Monday morning at 7:15. He drove through heavy traffic at M Street. The rain changed to a light drizzle, and he adjusted the windshield wipers to intermittent. He turned onto Twenty-Third Street and continued straight until he turned left at the Department of State building. He parked in the same place, and this time he put enough quarters into the parking meter for three hours.

Once again, he geared up. Sitting in the car, he placed the listening and recording system inside his shirt and the hearing device in his right ear. He opened his umbrella as he got out and angled it to hide his face while he fiddled with the tuning. Static persisted.

He walked up on the sidewalk at E Street and continued to fine-tune the station. He heard a woman's familiar voice, welcoming people. They, in turn, greeted her as "Madam Secretary."

Mitchell greeted the attendees by name, including Professors Rebecca Haines from Georgia Tech, Ronald Smith from Johns Hopkins University, and Henry Morris, MIT. She then introduced the other government officials to them.

Nikulin walked across E Street to the lawn and stopped at the concrete retaining wall. He moved the receiver unit around his back far enough until the reception improved. He lit a cigarette and moved the umbrella to block the drizzle. He watched traffic below and listened.

At the same time, a security patrolman walked under the canopy on the upper end of the building at Twenty-Third Street. Another patrolman approached him and said, "Did you notice the guy over there?"

"Where?" asked his buddy.

"The one holding the umbrella at the wall."

His eyes focused better, and he said, "Yeah, I see him now."

"Why would someone stand there in the drizzling rain?" asked the first patrolman. Feeling sadistic, he said, "What the hell's he going to do, jump over the wall into the morning traffic?" They chuckled.

"I don't know, but maybe we should talk to him. No one stands in the rain for the hell of it. He's up to something."

7

The Longest Ride

Turkish Airlines flight TK1587 from Baghdad landed at the Frankfurt/Main airport at 10:50. The attendant warned everyone to remain in their seats and explained the exit procedures. No one paid attention. People unlocked their seatbelts, stood up, and got carry-on baggage from the overhead compartments. The jet came to an abrupt stop at the ramp, throwing the standing passengers off balance. Yako and Alzuhari remained seated and whispered about the people who were standing and their disregard for order.

The airport's signage for arriving passengers directed them to the baggage claim. After they retrieved their suitcases from the rotating carousel, they got in line at a customs station. Minutes later they walked into the terminal lobby.

Yako, a dark-haired, olive-skinned beauty, was familiar with Germany. Her father was an Iraqi government employee. Over time, he transferred to three Iraqi embassies; England, Germany, and Holland. Her English improved at Georgetown University. Her undergraduate major was political science. She'd dreamed of becoming an ambassador herself someday. Some of her friends selected psychology as a major, and she took a few classes with them. Her interest grew, and she decided to make it her minor. At the end of her first semester as a senior, Harvard University accepted her application to the renowned Kissinger graduate program for international studies.

During the second semester, she and a group of her friends signed up for a course in hypnotism. The graduate student taught that hypnotism could help people improve, as well as get sub-conscious information from people. The graduate student used them as guinea pigs for his research work, both hypnotizing them and teaching several of them how to hypnotize. The hypnosis evaluations included charting the individual's suggestibility level from one to ten. Ten was the level at which an individual would do silly body movements while sticking out their tongue or cackling like a chicken. The lower numbers meant the person's state of mind wasn't as susceptible to orders. The more dangerous part of the work involved exploring the subject's conscious state—their feelings and thoughts about their lives and current events. When the students finished this exercise, they'd go barhopping in Georgetown.

The airport terminal's billboards displayed the bus and subway transportation schedules. They stood side-by-side. She said, "Which takes longer?" They wheeled their luggage carts to the bus billboard. She raised her voice over the noise and said to her partner, "If we take the subway, we have to walk a few blocks to get to the train station. The bus takes a little longer but will drop us off right at the *Bahnhof*." He recalled that meant "train station" in German.

They stood at the sales window to buy bus tickets. A half-hour later they boarded the bus. It took thirty-five minutes to get to the *Bahnhof*. Alzuhari had never been there before, but Yako had visited years before. She found the maniac pedestrian situation the same; many just pushed their way through, ignoring others. When they got inside, the station billboards showed the different times for the trains. She decided to take the one having a direct route to Amsterdam without having to change trains. It didn't depart until 7:00, but they bought tickets anyway.

"Let's get something to eat," suggested a hungry Alzuhari.

They wheeled their luggage through the restaurant's doorway. The head waiter greeted them, and a server moved their baggage into a closet. They sat at a table, and a waiter brought the menus. They each ordered a beer and something to eat. As they discussed their business plans for Amsterdam, Alzuhari pulled out some papers and read about the person they were to recruit. After being served, he opened the remaining envelope and found two photographs. “This man is our target.” He handed one to Yako. The waiter removed their plates, and they used the next hour discussing the potential of this new associate.

“Finding this man is going to be interesting.”

“How do we get him? What bait do we set?” she asked.

“Major Yildiz has a contact in Stuttgart who is a high-ranking officer of the US V Corps. He is going to help us.”

He continued reading and added, “Our target’s name is Captain Eric Miller, and he works with their intelligence branch.” He looked up at her and added, “He is qualified for what we want, but will he be willing?” They spent another hour there determining alternative tactics. The discussion became unproductive when they realized face-to-face contact was more likely to succeed.

***

The station’s loudspeaker announced departure times. The train to Amsterdam was leaving in fifteen minutes.

Passengers placed their tagged baggage onto the luggage racks and then got into another line to go through electronic security. Yako and Alzuhari got aboard. Inside, they walked along the train car’s corridor to their section. The compartment accommodations were plush: high-back adjustable seats with dark blue upholstery and a large window. They felt a slight jolt as their train moved out of the station.

Alzuhari frowned as he looked at his ticket. “I didn’t pay much attention to our travel time, Tara. This train takes six hours to get to Amsterdam?”

Yako removed the ticket from her purse and examined it. She looked at him and said,. "Unfortunately, it was the fastest train out of three choices."

Her reasoning didn't reduce his annoyance. He mumbled to himself while reading the list of twenty stops along the way. "We can almost ride a camel from Baghdad to Baqubah in the time it will take this damn train to reach Amsterdam. Why didn't they allow us to fly or rent a car?"

They heard a knock on the door, and a man wearing a white shirt, tie, and a black vested suit slid the door back and entered the compartment. He asked for their tickets, examined them, punched them, and left.

Tara explained, "The airline security check is too sophisticated. They electronically examine all luggage and carry-ons since the Syrian war has escalated. The security check for the train is minimal. We got through the gate without a problem. Since neither of us has driven to Amsterdam before, I didn't consider a car rental."

The train ride was quiet, the only sound being a mesmerizing *click-clacking* of steel wheels over iron track joints. They returned to reading the newspapers. Suddenly, Yako was distracted by a man looking at them through the door's glass window. He slowly walked on, so she disregarded it. Moments later, the guy stopped again and looked at them.

Strange, she thought. *Is he just looking for a specific compartment? Was he going to join them?* She started to alert Alzuhari, but then the man looked down at some papers in his hands and briskly walked away.

"What's the matter, Tara?" asked Alzuhari.

"A man just walked past our compartment twice. He stared at us and then looked down at some papers in his hand. They looked too big to be tickets. When I stared back at him, he walked off quickly."

"Maybe they were photographs." Alzuhari got up quickly and pushed the sliding door open. He looked both ways in the corridor, but only saw a woman and children leaving a compartment further down the car. He closed the door and pulled down the shade. "Whoever it was, he is not in sight now."

Some time passed while he finished looking at the newspaper. Yako said, "I want to read some more about this officer."

She took the packet. It was the last thing her partner remembered before falling asleep. Yako read through it for a while, then fell asleep too.

They woke when the train's brakes screeched as it pulled into Central Station. Through their window, they were surprised to see many people walking and scurrying along the station's inner walkway at 2:30 in the morning. Just as they were leaving their compartment, Tara advised, "We have to speak either Dutch or English now, Adnaw."

"Yes, I remember."

They hailed separate taxicabs. The drivers loaded their bags, and each gave their driver their respective apartment address.

***

Nikulin was confused because they took separate taxis. He also got into a cab and told the driver to follow the taxi just ahead of them, the woman's taxi. He leaned forward anxiously and looked out of the windshield to make sure Yako's cab was in sight. As they entered a residential apartment building section of Amsterdam, Nikulin told the cabby to slow down. He again leaned forward to look out the window. "Pull over to the curb and stop the cab," he said.

The two taxis, one driving the man and the other taking the woman, stopped at neighboring buildings. *Good,* he thought. He watched them enter different apartment buildings next to each other. A minute later the Russian ambassador's voicemail in DC said the embassy was closed. He left a message: "I followed Yako and Alzuhari to where I believe they are living. I will be in touch."

8

Midweek Arrival

Cologne was busy at daybreak. Miller turned over in bed and pulled the comforter over his shoulder. The noise from car horns, diesel trucks, and a siren came through the window he'd opened a tad. He pressed the night-light button on his watch: Wednesday, 5:09 a.m. He got up, shaved, showered, and repacked. Downstairs a continental breakfast awaited guests. He finished eating and checked out.

Traffic on the Autobahn outside Frankfurt was heavy. He toyed with the radio until he found the armed forces station. An American voice announced in English, "This is Sergeant Teresa Borders at your military forces radio, Frankfurt. Stay tuned for the eight o'clock news and weather."

Traffic moved faster now. Up the road, overhead signs came into view. The radio commercials finished, and the news resumed.

The newscaster reported over the past two years, German labor working for the army had reduced to almost nothing. She identified the bases at the US Armed Forces under the V Corps in Stuttgart and the Air Force at Frankfurt and Ramstein airbases. They were being flooded with the only labor available, immigrant workers from the Mideast. The reason given was the upsurge in the industry in what used to be Eastern Germany. They only hired Germans. The Criminal Investigative Division (CID) increased its number of security investigations from espionage crimes. Soldiers who worked in the security intelligence offices insisted they turned off their computers before leaving for the day. Higher-grade NCOs working in these places backed up the soldiers' statements. But one morning a workstation in Frankfurt was discovered with engineering formulas for the Ferret communication satellite displayed on its monitor. The cyber tampering was being done by experienced people. CID contacted the FBI in Frankfurt for help.

Miller never believed CID would contact the FBI. He assumed all investigations remained in-house. *Someone had to have turned on the computer to get this information,* he thought.

It was 10:15 when he drove onto a hilly road in Würzburg. Unsure which way to go, he stopped at a red light and asked a pedestrian how to get to Hindenburg Kaserne. The woman understood English. She directed him to take a left at the light and go straight. "You will see it," she said.

After a few miles, he slowed the vehicle as he approached the army post's fenced side and read the name, Hindenburg Kaserne. Old Glory waved high above the post's grounds. He made a right turn and stopped at the Military Police gate entrance. The Iraqi thug in the dark gray Audi slowly passed Miller's Saab seconds later. He made a U-turn and parked at the curb down the road.

Miller noticed the soldier's name on the shirt. "Morning, Sergeant Phillips; I am reporting to the 32nd Intelligence Headquarters." She noticed his civilian clothes and the jumble of belongings in the back seat. He handed the orders packet and his ID to her. She verified the ID name and photo and compared them to the transfer document. "Yes, sir, Captain Miller." She gave him directions to the post's headquarters. He took the envelope and drove off. There was an open parking space across from the building.

Nearby soldiers watched him get out of the car and walk into the building. He appeared military, with his clean-cut look and the way he walked; straight, proud. Without a uniform no one knew his rank, so they didn't salute. They also noted the license plates were European, not the typical army olive green with ivory numerals.

He walked inside and admired the spacious design. He sensed another person behind him and turned around. A black man in starched fatigues held out his hand. "It's good to meet you, Captain Miller. I'm First Sergeant Ed Randolph. Welcome to the 32nd, sir."

Smiling, Miller said, "I'm pleased to meet you too, but how did you know my name?"

"It's official protocol for the MP to telephone my office about any new arrival. We've been expecting you."

"I'm to see Colonel Collins."

"Right this way, sir,"

The old Nazi billet with its high ceilings, decorative hanging lights, huge windows, and tall office doors resembled a well-maintained museum.

He knocked on the door before walking into the room. Stepping aside, Randolph said, "Presenting Captain Eric Miller as directed, sir."

Miller walked in, came to attention, and saluted. "Reporting for duty, sir."

A full bird colonel stood up and returned the salute. They shook hands, and he said, "Captain Miller, how do you do. You're early!"

Randolph left, and Collins began to look over Miller's paperwork. "I see that you graduated from West Point the same year as your new working associate." Collins looked up. "He's second in command to me here at the 32nd."

"Who is that, sir?"

"Oh, an American with an English accent, Captain Paul Remmich."

Miller grinned broadly. "So this is where Paul is stationed!"

Collins uttered, "You know him?"

"Yes, sir, we're good friends. After graduating from West Point, we went to Fort Huachuca for advanced intelligence training. We transferred to different bases and lost contact."

He sat patiently while the higher-ranked officer reviewed the file. Miller reminisced, chuckling about their friendship. "Yeah, that accent!" he said smiling.

Collins focused on Miller. "I want to finish with this first, but if you want coffee or a soft drink, the snack room is down the hall."

"I'll wait, sir," he said good-naturedly, remembering adventures with his buddy.

"Better yet, give me another minute, and I'll show you the way to the base snack bar. We can brief you on your security position later." The colonel finished, and they made their way across the compound. Miller chatted about his friendship with Remmich. They also compared notes on where they had been stationed.

"*Guten* afternoon, Colonel," Sophie Litz said in her German way. She sold the *Stars and Stripes* newspaper, *The Wall Street Journal*, *The New York Times*, Frankfurt edition, and magazines and paperbacks. She nodded to Miller.

Collins returned the greeting while looking around the snack bar until he spotted Remmich.

"You are looking *für* somebody?"

"Yes. Captain Remmich. I just spotted him."

"*Ja.* He is sitting over there by the center post," she said, pointing.

"Thank you, Sophie." He told Miller, "Come on, let's get in line for lunch."

It was already past noon, and the place was noisy and crowded. They grabbed trays and utensils wrapped in napkins. Collins said, "I forgot to mention, but we will be having a short in-house meeting at 1:00 to prepare for General Sutherland. Your briefing can be later."

They moved up three spaces to the stainless-steel tray slide. Miller asked, "What's it about?"

He repeated what Miller heard on the morning news about the potential spies at the US Army posts.

Collins hesitated while he grabbed a plastic-wrapped half-sub. Miller said, "I didn't understand the whole gist of the radio news, but why don't the Germans work in these areas?"

"The German middle- to lower-class individual refuses to work for us anymore. When the Russians left East Germany, more profitable work became accessible to them." They moved forward in the line and Miller grabbed his lunch. "For example, they have had work for new construction in East Germany for the past decade. It has provided thousands of jobs. German manufacturing increased because businesses in West Germany expanded. These opportunities created a domino effect. Berlin, once again, became the capital. Working for us? They feel it's beneath them." Miller nodded, showing he understood.

They moved ahead again, and Collins changed the subject. "I won't be sitting with you and Paul, but please try to talk some sense into him."

"About what?"

"He's mentioned resigning."

Surprised, Miller said, "What? Why?"

They moved a few feet more. Collins grimly explained Remmich's dissatisfaction with the US supporting the UN's policies toward Third World countries. He hesitated for a few seconds and said, "It could also be because his girlfriend in Amsterdam wants him to resign." He looked in his captain's direction, and remarked, "But we need guys like him. He should be thinking about getting promoted, not resigning, dammit."

Collins paid for both lunches as a welcome gesture. They each grabbed an empty soda cup and went to the fountain station. Splitting up, Miller walked to Remmich's table. He was reading *The New York Times*. "Mind if I sit here, sir?" He waited for the man's reaction despite his excitement.

Paul Remmich grew up in London. His father, Peter, represented the United States at the embassy there after he got his doctorate. Twenty-Four Grosvenor Square was his permanent residence before he met his future wife, Sally. As a result, Paul and his siblings absorbed a lot of the culture.

Out of the side of his eye Paul noticed a man in civilian clothing and said without looking, "No, no, go right ahead." His British mannerisms made Miller laugh quietly. Remmich realized that laugh and the man's voice were familiar. He looked up and focused on the person next to him.

"Eric, I'll be damned! It's really you!" Paul was a bit taller, with short, sandy blond hair brushed to one side. He got up and grabbed his buddy by the shoulders, almost knocking over the soda.

"I wanted to let you know I've been transferred here." Miller placed his tray on the table. They laughed and shook hands heartily, drawing attention from everyone nearby. After they sat down, the cafeteria returned to its normal cacophony.

Collins finished his lunch and excused himself from the other officers at their table. He saw the two captains engrossed in conversation and decided, *Hell, the 1:00 meeting can wait. It's only about Sutherland's visit, anyway.*

When his buddy got quiet, Miller asked, "What are you thinking about?"

Remmich's eyes were somber and he looked away. He leaned over the table and fiddled with a paper matchbook. He remembered the goals they had planned together and felt terrible, but said, “I know this will be a shock as you’ve just arrived, but I have decided to resign. It seems our timing is off.”

Miller tried to hide his emotions. He swallowed hard to ease his thickening throat. “It’s hard for me to accept you’re resigning. I told the colonel about our friendship, and he told me the bad news. Paul, why are you doing this?”

“I just don’t have the enthusiasm for this life anymore. My loyalty to our country hasn’t diminished. It just bugs the hell out of me the way the US followed the UN’s decisions and greatly reduced assistance to Third World countries. Politicians and diplomats pay more attention to the ISIS crisis, North Korea, and Vladimir Putin.”

Miller nodded while sipping some soda. “I’m not up to date on the UN’s role in Third World nations.”

Remmich explained how six years ago the UN promised to cultivate relations with Third World nations. Plans to get them into the world market included sending qualified people to help them. Then and now, they needed education facilities and modern hospitals. A hard fact to accept was the situation with natives from Third World countries who were fortunate enough to get teaching degrees as foreign-exchange students. They wouldn’t return to their own country. Remmich stopped for a moment and asked, “Are you telling me you never heard about this?”

“The last thing I heard in any detail was, gosh, maybe three years ago. I didn’t have the time to care for anything else, except my training at UNIMI. They wanted the international group to center on improving relationships. Until now, I never knew about it.”

Remmich lit a cigarette and offered one to Eric. “I quit after my transfer to Stockholm. I see you’ve destroyed that matchbook. Why don’t you use a lighter?”

“I lose them.” He held it up and said, “These are cheaper.”

They were silent. Miller watched his friend fiddle with the cardboard cover. Remmich's mind wandered while he wrapped the loose section around the striker section with both hands. He bent the whole thing in half, then back and forth with a forefinger while the thumb and middle finger of his right hand held the bottom part of the bend. He knew his buddy would ask questions, but the silence and digital manipulation provided a distraction.

"Have you considered any alternatives?"

"I've contemplated talking to the counterintelligence group. Their office is always working on projects.

Miller didn't want to dig into Remmich's plans and start an argument. Instead, he asked, "The colonel mentioned a meeting we are to attend today. Who is General Sutherland?"

"A lieutenant general. He is our CO at V Corps Military Intelligence within USAREUR. The main office is in Stuttgart, better known as our S-2. The organization now covers Europe, Northern Africa, and parts in the Mideast."

"Who are we getting together with?"

"A few officials from NATO, but mostly our people."

A tall, broad-shouldered NCO interrupted Remmich. "Excuse me, sir, but the CO asked me to give this note to you."

Remmich introduced him as the office manager. Miller stood up and shook Master Sergeant Terry McClain's hand. "Terry, this is Captain Eric Miller. He'll be working with us."

McClain said, "I look forward to working with you, sir."

Remmich read the note out loud, telling Miller, "The one o'clock meeting is postponed. McClain left.

"He is also my aide when we attend meetings in Stuttgart, and my attaché and vehicle driver. I guess I should say he's now *our* attaché."

Miller wanted to know more and leaned back in the chair. "So, is there another reason for your plan to resign?"

"My Dutch girlfriend, Lilly, wants me to move to Amsterdam." He lit another cigarette and hesitated for a few seconds. After exhaling, he stated, "And by the way, my plan is not changing, Eric, but I won't bail out until I get the resignation approved."

"Have you written one yet?" he asked.

"No." Remmich sipped his soda and opened a new cigarette pack. He again offered one to Miller, who accepted this time.

"I forgot to ask. Why do you want to leave your position when you're going to get a promotion from captain to major next year?"

Remmich ignored the question. "Have you been in the security office yet?"

Miller felt his stomach clench with Remmich's disregard to his question. "Not yet."

"We'll have enough time to get you oriented since the conference has been postponed."

Remmich's cell phone vibrated. He said, "It's from Klaus Schneider. He wants me to call him later."

"Who's he?"

"Klaus is my German buddy. He's also the city's chief mechanical engineer for water and sewage. We met at the Kiliani beer festival, which takes place each July. It was the week when I arrived here."

They left the snack bar. Before entering the S-2 office, Remmich swiped his ID card through a reader mounted on the door frame. Collins was already there. He spoke to Remmich, while McClain told Miller about his security intelligence responsibilities. First Sergeant Randolph walked in.

"Excuse me, gentlemen. I have important information," reported Randolph "The jet arrived at Leighton Barracks with NATO military personnel. They'll be staying at the base hotel. Second, General Sutherland's aide telephoned. They are in a traffic jam on the Autobahn. The general postponed the security get-together until tomorrow morning at 0900 hours."

Collins slapped his hands together. "Well, I guess that means we don't have to rush." Everyone laughed at his gestures. Looking at the new officer and smiling, he said, "You can have the rest of the day off and get settled."

Randolph explained, "I'll have Sergeant McClain ride with you to direct you to the Leighton Barracks post. One of my men can follow you and bring him back."

They walked outside, and Remmich asked, "Have any plans for tonight, Eric?"

"Like I really know where to go. What's on your mind?"

"Wait a minute while I return the call to Klaus."

"*Hallo?*"

"Good afternoon, my friend."

"*Ja*, thanks for calling back. How are you doing?"

"Good. Hey, listen, I have a friend I want you to meet, and I thought we could all get together for dinner and beer."

Klaus said, "Ja, I called you to suggest we go to my uncle's restaurant. And, yes, bring your friend."

"Yes. Excellent suggestion. The chef prepares a delicious, breaded schnitzel. How about 6:00?"

"*Ja*, 6:00 it is."

They hung up, and Remmich told Miller to meet him at the Leighton Barracks PX at 5:30. "We'll leave from there to rendezvous with Klaus."

9

The General Upstairs

Collins glanced at his watch. "Damn, it's 8:15 already." He wondered if the conference room was set up as he had directed. He walked into the security office and said, "Captain Remmich, go upstairs and make sure the overhead projectors are working, the seating is in order, and coffee tables are ready."

Recognizing the colonel's tense mood, Remmich stood up and motioned for Miller to join him.

While they walked upstairs, Miller asked, "Why's he so uptight this morning?"

"He's always on edge before one of these meetings, especially when Sutherland is on his way. They get along, but he gets uneasy."

They walked into the briefing room and looked to see that everything was in order. The projector worked, and the kitchen workers had the pastry trays on each table, as well as hot coffee and hot water for tea. Miller and Remmich decided to stay in the room to avoid Collins. They each got a coffee and a pastry.

By 8:40, NATO army participants from Russia, France, Germany, and the US walked in groups into the room. Invited military from the Middle East arrived and were told to go upstairs. Everyone crowded around the tables.

A *Stars and Stripes* army reporter sat in the back.

Sutherland entered the room with his entourage. There was a loud call from Major Dunlop, and everyone stopped talking. Dunlop immediately yelled, "At ease." Colonel Collins told everyone they had one minute to finish their conversations. The general positioned himself behind the dais and reviewed his notes.

The group sat down. "Good morning, everyone." He was fifty-five years old, six-foot-one, and physically fit. Some graying hair brushed his temples. His complexion was somewhat rosy because his father came from Dublin and his mother was second-generation, born in the Irish sector of East Baltimore in Maryland. He attended Mount Saint Joseph High School before being accepted to the Citadel.

His sergeant first class brought a cup of coffee for him. He took a sip, looked above his reading glasses, and said, "The purpose of this meeting is multifold. First, to discuss espionage problems in V Corps. Second, the transport of illegal weaponry into Syria. Third, Iraq's determination to negotiate and work with Third World countries.

"There has been an influx of Mideastern workers into Germany. They apply for work from ads posted by the army, because the German workers won't do it anymore. The V Corps MPs found out classified security intelligence information had been confiscated. A few have been caught. This is an act of espionage." He looked at the Middle East guests while he spoke about occurrences at Frankfurt and Stuttgart posts.

Sutherland began his second agenda item by telling them how weapons and supplies were being transported into Syria. Knowing who the benefactors were, he decided to mention the Russian mafia. He also said they didn't know who the backers were, but he acknowledged underground money paid for the weaponry. The Middle Easterners in the audience began to murmur but he ignored them.

For the next fifteen minutes he talked about how some Third World countries were diplomatically approached by Iraq. "This is not illegal, but we consider a Middle Eastern country being involved with the ISIS crisis as threatening," commented Sutherland.

The general had to raise his voice to quiet the audience. He told them how the United States Congress questioned whether Iraq pursued the Third World nations for economic reasons. No one said anything. "The United States discovered Cuba, Nicaragua, and Somalia negotiating with Iraqi diplomats." He looked at the Middle East attendees and dropped a bombshell. "We want to know if Iraq is aiding the smaller country in good faith, and plans to provide educational, medical, industrial, and agricultural assistance. Can these smaller countries provide equal trade? If not, then we have an international problem."

An olive-skinned man from Saudi Arabia, General Rashid al Rudin, stood up. *Oh, boy,* thought Sutherland. "I resent your accusations, sir. Neither my country nor any nation in the Middle East is helping ISIS."

Sutherland looked around the room and told everyone, "Someone is funding ISIS. This is fact, not hearsay."

General al Rudin said, "I think much of this morning's presentation lacks a basis in truth. The one fact I can state is the United States does not do enough to counter ISIS. Russia certainly does more." He sat down. Every Mideastern officer looked toward Sutherland with a firm stare.

The Russian generals smiled.

Sutherland was aggravated. *That son-of-a-bitch!* He had to repress the urge to counter al Rudin's remarks because it would just invite more argument. Instead, he ignored him.

Collins noticed the irritation in the general's face. He looked at General Elliott, but his demeanor gave nothing away. The colonel motioned to his watch, signaling Sutherland to take a break. He got a yes nod. "I think we're ready for a fifteen-minute break. Please be back by 10:30."

Everyone stood up. Most of the guests went to the restrooms. Some got more refreshments. Sutherland joined them. Elliott glanced at Miller, sizing him up for a particular future assignment. Miller was in a group with NATO officers. He noticed Remmich looking at him, so he excused himself and walked over. "What's up?"

"I'm going to take my coffee and go out to smoke. Care to join me?"

"Sounds good to me."

They walked outside and talked about the gist of the meeting. While sipping and puffing, Remmich asked sarcastically, "Hey, man, I thought you quit?"

"I did, but you're a bad influence on me." The comment caused laughter among others.

"So, how come you didn't show up at the PX to go to the restaurant last night? I called your number, but there wasn't any answer."

"I was held up waiting for my lease agreement for over an hour. It was frustrating as hell. What a bunch of dumb foreigners we hired. When I got back to my apartment, I didn't notice the time and thought I'd rest for a few minutes. When I woke up, it was a little past 2:00. I didn't bother to call you then and fell back to sleep."

"No problem. I'm sure you were exhausted. It happens to the best of us."

They heard a call to return. They drowned cigarettes in their remaining coffee and dropped the cups into the trashcan.

Dunlop called for quiet, and everyone stopped talking. Sutherland returned to the dais and politely ordered everyone to sit down.

Collins wrote a note and handed the message to the general, inviting him to stay overnight. Sutherland wrote on the back for the colonel to get him and his men, along with General Elliot, rooms at the post's hotel. He had planned to stay anyway to discuss Paul Remmich's future.

The general smiled at the group, enjoying the fact that he was going to prove a point. "Are we ready?"

"Yes, sir," Master Sergeant McClain said.

McClain turned on the overhead projectors while First Sergeant Randolph brought up the presentations on the laptop computers. Sutherland walked toward the screens holding a laser pointer. The aerial photos were the same ones presented by the CIA during Defense Secretary Mitchell's meeting at the State Department. He talked about how an Echelon satellite could detect anything from the transporting of military equipment to troop movement at night. They clearly saw the massive size of the covered items on the individual train cars.

Sutherland turned and said, "Quite remarkable that the satellite can x-ray the tarps and provide a clear picture of what the train cars are hiding." When he asked if anyone had a question, he was bombarded. He quietly chuckled to himself. This time he called upon Elliott to assist him.

Many questions were asked and answered in the remaining thirty minutes. Collins interrupted. "I'm sorry to break up this meeting, but it's all the time we have this morning. The second half of this session is for NATO military personnel only." Middle East officers didn't like it, but there was nothing they could do. "We will resume at 1330 hours." The room got noisy, and Collins yelled, "Hold it, everyone. Quiet down, please." The room noise stopped. "Before we adjourn, I want to invite all of you to a luncheon."

Sutherland knew he needed to be diplomatic and soften the dispositions of the Middle Eastern military, so he accompanied them in the bus to the officers' club.

As the group walked off the bus, the aroma of roast beef became more intoxicating the closer they got to the building. Inside, the line slowed while a full sliced beef platter replaced an empty one. Roast lamb was for the Middle East attendees.

Waiting in line, Remmich suggested to Miller, "Since our plans were changed for today, let's visit the castle tomorrow? Then, if you still have the energy, we can plan something else on Sunday."

"Great," said Miller. "I wish they'd hurry the hell up. I'm hungry."

10

They Looked West

It was peaceful on the tenth floor in Iraqi Major Yildiz's condominium in Istanbul. It was May. The opened windows and the balcony door let the breezes ruffle the sheer curtains. Only faint sounds from vehicle horns elevated to this level.

The furnished villa included a large open floor plan with a living room and a dining area. The kitchenette had all the necessary amenities. On the opposite end of the suite were three bedrooms. He chose the largest one for himself, using the other two for offices. This was the first time his government bought living quarters for someone like him. His staff lived less luxuriously in rented flats. From the balcony, he saw the historic Sea of Marmara.

There was a sound from the outside. It got louder. It came from the magnificent Blue Mosque. It was the 3:00 call to prayer.

The staff communed in prayer to Allah. They knelt and bent forward on the prayer rugs in silence. The singer's voice ended minutes later with, "I respond to you, oh Allah. I respond to you." The music continued.

With his two Iraqi assistants, the major rose to an upright position on his knees and bent forward again, saying the *Shahadah* out loud to end their prayers: "I testify there is none worthy of worship except Allah, and I testify Muhammad is the messenger of Allah." They got to their feet after rolling up the prayer rugs. All of them put their shoes back on and handed the carpets to the woman. She prayed in a different room as required by Islamic religion.

Yildiz prayed only in the mid-afternoon when his group attended a meeting. Otherwise, like many other Muslims, he didn't think it was necessary to pray several times a day.

Istanbul is a city built on two continents. The Muslim tradition is prevalent on the east side of the Bosphorus Canal, and the Christian tradition west of the river. This group found the Turkish Islamic traditions similar to their Iraqi customs, but they maintained their Iraqi foundations.

Yildiz had moved here three months earlier. He was on active military duty. What he hadn't told the Russian ambassador was that he was a specialist in security intelligence; the Tariq'Allah underground division. A re-attempt of the failed mission in Stockholm was now assigned to him; find the officer and make him a mole and courier for espionage.

When the major returned to Iraq from Washington, DC, he handpicked a group of specialists to work with him. Being stationed in this Turkish city separated them from the UN's repeated investigations in their country.

"Let's get on with business," he said. They sat down at the hand-carved mahogany dining room table. Turkish rugs covered parquet floors.

Like he said to the Russian ambassador, Iraq had a multifaceted goal; keep the military away, establish internal financial stability, and build a trade of goods and services. Over the decades, geological satellite expeditions revealed Iraq, the neighboring country of Kuwait, and parts of Iran possessed the second-highest volume of crude oil after Saudi Arabia. It literally floated on pools of deep oil fields and natural gas. As a result, this Istanbul team and the two in Amsterdam had all the financial backing they needed.

Reducing the need for oil for energy; conversion of solar energy to electric energy was the idea Linkov mentioned. No one would need nuclear power any longer.

"There is a long-distance telephone call for you, sir," said Luma Samir, the office manager. "It's the Russian ambassador in Washington."

What timing!

He called to tell Yildiz that the Swaziland ambassador had contacted his office about Iraq's international proposal. "I told him Iraq has a good relationship with Russia, and your country's reputation in foreign business development is worthy. I explained Swaziland can benefit from contemporary agriculture development and advances to their education system. Did you know most of the people live on only two dollars a day? But, as always, Major, I tried not to say too much."

Not surprisingly, Linkov wanted to know about his commission so Yildiz assured him: If Iraq secured a contract agreement, money would be deposited in the Swiss accounts.

Before ending the conversation, he added, "You are becoming a rich man, Mr. Ambassador. I hope to visit your palace someday." They laughed together before saying goodbye. He walked out of his office and joined the others.

One of his men, Iyad Aboona, graduated from MIT. Electronic engineering taught him how to design and construct computer chips, working on both communications and robot assembly. He contracted with Tariq'Allah to build a special microchip. He wanted to know how much information was going to be discussed.

The major brushed his fingers over his mustache and leaned forward. "I will elaborate in a few minutes." He leaned over to get the outline for the talk. "As you know, we have already selected someone to obtain the scientific document that will guide our work. Tara Yako and Adnaw Alzuhari will recruit this man."

The last person in the group was Faisal Mustafa. He'd arrived one hour before this meeting. He got a pre-med degree from the University of Maryland, and his dental degree from the

University of Maryland in Baltimore. During the residency, he learned how to hypnotize nervous patients, instead of giving them a numbing injection or sedating them before surgery. It was a specialty he and Tara Yako shared.

His first job after dental school was at Fort Dix, New Jersey. One year later he and his wife vacationed in Baghdad, their hometown. He learned the Tariq'Allah's development was in its infancy. During the next two years, he earned a higher status at the dental hospital. He asked to be transferred to Germany. An interview followed one week later after the review of his résumé. Others talked with him and decided he was qualified as a dental surgeon. They also liked the fact he was fluent in English. He got the job at central headquarters for the five-thousand-man infantry division at Leighton Barracks, a subdivision of USAREUR. Officers and NCOs liked him because of his ability to discuss politics and US sports. After five years, he earned a promotion to second in command to the chief surgeon, a colonel.

Yildiz contacted an operator on the conference phone, wanting to connect with the spies in Amsterdam. The operator tried two times but couldn't get through. She said a return call would come when the lines were not busy. He hung up and looked at his watch. Everyone heard him say, "Let's take a break for dinner."

They ordered chicken kebabs and salads from a carryout menu. Samir wrote down everyone's choices for food and soft drink items and called in the order. The delivery was fast, and Yildiz paid for everything. As the boxes were opened, wonderful smells filled the room and made everyone salivate. The major didn't think prayer was needed and for the moment, work also took a back seat.

The meal ended, and everyone helped to clear the table. The group reseated, and Samir handed out a folder to each of them. Yildiz said, "Tariq'Allah's instructions are in this plan."

The telephone rang, and Luma looked at the caller ID. She pressed the speakerphone button. The operator said the two people were on the line.

Yildiz greeted them, saying, “Yes, hello, Adnaw and Tara. We have been waiting to talk to you.” He let the others exchange greetings with them. “I have a new update. My undercover US Army officer contact at V Corps in Stuttgart called me. He said our target is going to visit Amsterdam with a friend, whose girlfriend lives there. My contact approved a three-day pass. The other man’s name is Paul Remmich. You have two photographs of the man we want and his name. You two will be able to meet up with him over the American Memorial Day weekend.”

“Do we have a location?” asked Alzuhari.

“Yes. Go to the Blues Alley nightclub together. Go every night, starting tomorrow. Socialize with people speaking American English. And, of course, their military haircuts will also identify them. Since both of you lived in the United States, you shouldn’t have any trouble communicating. You know what to do from there.”

This was Mustafa’s first day in Istanbul and he hadn’t been fully briefed beforehand. He asked, “Who is this man we’re seeking?”

“He is a West Point Military Academy graduate, Faisal,” said Yildiz.

“Why are we meeting this person in a bar?” asked Yako.

“It’s a jazz bar and restaurant. US bands tour in this city to entertain and make money. US soldiers frequent Amsterdam and this establishment,” Yildiz explained. “My contact knows where they are going to go because they’re required to report their plans in detail before they go into another country. They wrote down one establishment. You and Tara will be notified by this office when Captain Eric Miller will be at the Blues Alley nightclub. When you talk to him, ask for his line of work. Make sure he is the right person."

Tara Yako said, "I'm confused, Major. How can I acquaint myself with a strange man in a bar? He'll think I'm a prostitute trying to pick him up."

She couldn't see the grins on the men's faces.

"What this man might think of you isn't important. Just get him to talk with you. Be friendly."

Yildiz told everyone to open their binders. He talked to Yako and explained how she would gain the target's trust. She said she understood. At the lower section of the page, section C's instructions included the final act.

"Adnaw, Section D is when you get to be involved in helping Tara."

He asked if they understood. He got yes answers.

Yildiz focused on Dr. Mustafa. "You already have his dental records, Faisal. You will prepare a series of appointments, one for a standard dental examination. As soon as you determine this person's molar size, Iyad will build a robotic-engineered computer chip for you."

Dr. Mustafa said, "Everyone, go to the dental chart page and look at the picture of a lower jaw showing the larger molars." He described in more detail the dental procedures.

Yildiz said, "Miller will have a dual role. The first is to find a military intelligence document. He will also be used for diplomatic purposes.

"In the beginning, we will limit his travels, but we want him to eventually resign from the army. We now know he is a security intelligence officer. Let's understand, Tariq'Allah wants the secret information. Their army employs civilians in his line of work. Since he is trained and experienced, they may want to keep him. Let's not forget—we already have a highly ranked officer secretly working for us at Patch Barracks, V Corps headquarters. Let me discuss the matter with him."

Alzuhari smiled and said, "He will become one of us."

The meeting ended.

11

The Invitation

Early morning radio babble woke Remmich. He got up and stretched. Twenty minutes after his bathroom rituals, he got coffee and made a telephone call.

Miller reached for the vibrating cell phone on the night table. Caller ID showed it was Paul. He leaned on his elbow and pressed the talk switch, yawning

"It's Saturday. Get out of bed. We're going up to the castle, remember?" He stopped speaking when he heard the 7:00 armed forces radio station mention Sutherland's name.

"Turn on your radio and tune it to our army station at 92.5."

The newscaster stated that shipments of military armor, munitions, and computer equipment were transported into Syria. She quoted the general saying, "To the best of my knowledge, this has been going on for more than a couple years."

"Yeah," said Miller. "The general's dig at the Saudi general kind of pointed the finger at him. I liked it when he declared Mideastern countries say they are our friends but jump on the opportunity to draw attention about sanctions against their neighbors."

The newscaster continued to talk, but they ignored her.

"I am glad he was direct with that guy," said Remmich. It showed the other Middle Easterners present he wasn't backing down."

"How did the radio station get the information?" asked Miller.

He listened to the explanation about Sergeant Maribeth Higgins being a reporter from the *Stars and Stripes* newspaper.

"Well, let's get on with today's business. I have things to do. Until then, I'll see you at 1100 hours in front of the PX."

"Sounds good," said Remmich.

***

At 7:50 Collins sat outside at the officers' club puffing on his pipe. He banged out the tobacco from his pipe on the side of the bench. Sutherland's car arrived, and he stepped out with a briefcase strap hanging from his shoulder. They casually saluted, greeting each other, and entered the building. A sign read, "Seat yourselves."

The waiter came by, and both ordered coffee and breakfast.

"How are you doing this morning, Ed?"

"I am doing okay, Joe." Grinning, he said, "The meeting yesterday sure irritated the complainers when I insinuated a Russian complicity."

"Well, look where they're from."

The two went on to discuss the morning's radio report in more detail, satisfied with the news.

"I'm glad we're having this meeting, Joe." He focused on the colonel. "Captain Remmich's resignation concerns me."

Looking grave, he said, "I am troubled about it too, Ed."

Sutherland reached into the briefcase and pulled out a hanging file folder. The waiter poured coffee and took their breakfast orders.

"I think this is interesting, Joe." He had reviewed the captain's profile. It listed specific accomplishments. "His performance since he graduated from West Point has been excellent. I remember when he transferred to our headquarters as a first lieutenant. He was with us for three months before coming to you at the 32nd." He mentioned letters of commendation from two duty stations in the states. The general referred to Remmich's introduction of the new military intelligence database he learned at

Fort Huachuca. "I looked at Miller's file, also. They schooled at Huachuca together."

"I reviewed Captain Miller's portfolio the day he arrived. He told me about their schooling," said Collins.

"At Remmich's suggestion, we sent a fax to Fort Huachuca requesting the new software package. I didn't realize how antiquated ours was until we received the new one. After we reviewed it, I had it sent to you and the other security offices in my command."

"And it was a big hit when we had it installed," said Collins.

They paused while the waiter served their breakfasts. They ate and talked.

"Let's change the subject for a moment, Ed. I'm disturbed about the Middle East immigrants entering Germany. I don't like it because it puts the onus on us to hire them and some are spies. Maybe I'm paranoid, but you know how General Patton felt about ignoring a hunch."

He ate another bite of ham and sipped. "It's impossible to get factual answers about their backgrounds," said the general. "Criminal records are not available. The Iraqi government won't give us any information."

"I know." He swallowed a section of egg and put down his fork. "It reminds me of the way the Russian communists infiltrated the old Seventh Army German labor crews here in Germany after WWII. It wasn't all Germans doing the work we needed."

"Yeah, now the Middle East spies are here. I'm repeating myself, but why can't the armed forces limit hiring those immigrant workers based on these facts? Consider the influx of Hispanics into our country. They could be hired to do the same thing. It's money in their pockets."

"First, World War II laws are still active, Joe. We must follow the rules and hire immigrants under German regulations. Your Latino workers idea is something to think about."

Sutherland took another bite and then said, "You heard about the DIA uncovering a transmitter hidden behind the wood trim in a conference room at the State Department?"

"I heard a little bit about it on the radio and read it in my *New York Times*."

"Okay, then you'll appreciate this one." He talked about the State Department's grounds' police arresting a Russian spy.

Collins chuckled. "Yeah, I read about that too. That sneaky bastard. And the ambassador denied it."

"Well, anyway, the FBI followed through on the guy's deportation."

Sutherland wanted to get back on track and said, "The reason we're reviewing Remmich's folder is that he doesn't realize his own worth. I hope he stays active. If he doesn't, I want him to stay as a civilian decryption specialist and advisor."

Collins added, "Yeah, we can do that, but will he agree? It would keep him semi-active. He could continue to decode classified documents. His buddy, Captain Miller, is being introduced to all of this. He's a smart guy too. But what if Paul goes home right away? What then?"

"We won't be within our military-legal capacity to use him as an advisor." Before the general said anything else, a server poured more coffee.

***

Miller sauntered along the sidewalk and stopped to look in the window at a cigar store next to the PX. A horn honk caught his attention. He saw a black BMW with Remmich at the wheel and got in

Remmich returned a salute from an MP as they drove out through the security gate. A kilometer down the road a German policewoman directed traffic at a four-way stop. He drove onto the main drag. “This street is named after a guy named Wilhelm Rhöntgen. He invented the X-ray machine at the beginning of the nineteen hundreds.”

“Interesting” His enthusiasm picked up when they passed a streamlined streetcar.

“They are in some European cities. No exhaust fumes.”

He downshifted into third gear and sped up the hill. He turned left onto a two-lane road and shifted into fourth gear. A road sign read Marienberg Schloss.

Miller wanted to know, “I saw a diagram on the sign, but what did the words mean?”

“It’s German for “Marienberg Castle.” It’s the direction we’re headed.”

He downshifted into third again as the road continued to wind from left to right. Ahead, a clearing brought the area into view.

“Jesus, it’s enormous.” It was slow driving into the parking sector. “I never thought a medieval castle would make it through both world wars in Germany.”

“Indeed, you’re looking at it firsthand. It survived. It dates from the eight hundreds.”

“Are those cone roofs actual straw or thatch?”

“The straw-looking stuff is actually a textile, Eric. This is a historical structure preserved with modern materials.”

They strolled to the end of the parking lot where it adjoined the two-sided, massive vineyard hill. It surrounded the fortress on three sides. He pointed toward the Main River. “The cultivation of this hill goes back more than a thousand years when feudalism was practiced by the Church and the upper class. People worked these sloped fields manually, so the dense vegetation kept the enemy from getting to the top of the hill too fast."

"This area ever attacked?"

"During the religious Reformation, the fortress remained intact. One reason this part of Germany was so important to the ancient Franks was its relationship with the Catholic Church. Karl the Great, the ninth-century Germanic ruler, was part of the reason for its beginnings here. Also, this place has the oldest chapel east of the Rhine River in Europe. I think it was first constructed in the year 808."

"Isn't he the guy the French called Charlemagne?"

"Correct."

"So what Julius Caesar couldn't accomplish east of the Rhine, the church did."

"Yes, it became more involved centuries later. But until then it wasn't easy for the Romans. They didn't get past the Rhine until the fourth century. The area today is the city of Hanover; it became their military base. From there they went south."

The entrance was a massive horseshoe arch with a wooden door lifted by two steel cables. An open courtyard followed. Walking around to the far side offered a full view of the town. Remmich pointed out the All Saints Bridge crossing over the river. He explained its construction occurred at the outset of the 1500s. The statues represented both saints and aristocracy. The allies' air raids avoided destroying the cultural history of this city.

He looked at his watch and asked, "You hungry?" Miller nodded, and they went to an outside restaurant.

They seated themselves. Miller's attention focused on a building in the middle of town. Pointing, he wanted to find out, "What's the huge palace-looking building over there?"

"It's the Residenz, the palace of the Franconian Bishops. It's been there since the mid-seventeen hundreds. It took two decades to build, and the air raids spared it during the wars. Inside is an architect's work of art. There are beautiful marble floors, Rococo fresco paintings, and beautiful hand-carved furniture."

"A palace, huh?"

A waitress interrupted. They looked like Americans from their haircuts, so she spoke English. "Can I get you something to drink, gentlemen?"

"We'll have beers."

"And you're having lunch?"

He ordered meals for both of them. She finished writing and walked away

"So when are you planning to fill me in with the facts about your resignation?" He sat with crossed arms and a frustrated look. They stopped talking when the waitress returned with the Würzburger Hofbräu beers.

Remmich didn't want to talk about it. Instead he described the different sections of the castle. The waitress placed the bratwursts and potato salad along with fresh garden salads on the table. When they finished lunch, his colleague's annoyance was noticeable. Miller grabbed a cigarette from Remmich's pack and lit it.

"Eric, being irritated will not do either of us any good. I know you're disappointed with me, but it pisses me off the army allied with the UN and reduced aid to Third World countries. I can't change either of these facts."

Miller sat up from a slouched position. "It's just that I was really looking forward to working with you again." Relenting, he said, "We've had a long friendship. Let's try to keep it that way, regardless of where we work."

Remmich agreed and motioned for the waitress to bring the check.

An hour later they drove back to Leighton Barracks. He dropped Miller off but didn't mention getting together on Sunday.

He felt a break might reduce his friend's discontent and reconcile him to the resignation decision.

***

On Monday morning Master Sergeant McClain spent an hour and a half going over computer codes with the new captain. Someone's watch beeped, and the noise of chairs being pushed away from desks indicated snack bar time!

The breakfast line moved steadily along the tray rack. Remmich and Miller paid for coffee and breakfast and sat at a table by a pillar. When it came time to leave, Remmich said, "You didn't forget this coming weekend is Memorial Day, did you? You still in?"

"Of course. You have anything planned for us?"

"Yes. Lilly's parents own the hotel adjacent to their restaurants, and we don't have to pay."

"Yeah, great. Thanks."

"We'll have a good time. And of course, I want to introduce her to you. You'll meet her parents and sister too."

Miller smiled. "I look forward to it."

"I didn't tell you, but Mr. Van Horn offered me a job after I resign. He wants me to be the wine consultant for their family business. It'll include travel, tasting wines, and buying the wines. The vintners will take care of the shipping to Schiller."

When they returned to the S-2 office, Remmich realized his cell phone was dead. He telephoned Lilly on the military line, which he knew violated INSCOM's defense bylaws. He told her to make reservations for them. After they hung up, he explained to Miller, "Randolph needs to submit a request for our three-day passes. He has to contact headquarters and get their approval first, but I don't foresee a problem."

"I didn't know we had to inform any other office."

"We do. Our security clearances are at the compartmented information level, which allows us to handle encrypted-decrypted materials."

"Yeah, I realize that."

"Because we're going into another country, we have to provide its name and who we're going to be with. I wrote Lilly's name as a friend when I gave the details."

***

On Wednesday morning, the colonel marched into the S-2 room with a CID officer. "Excuse me, everyone. Someone called long-distance to Amsterdam on the secure line. Will you identify yourself?" He knew the culprit, but he needed to follow protocol.

Soldiers glanced at each other. Remmich stood up and admitted he was responsible. The colonel ordered him into his office. A loud reprimand echoed in the hallway. When it was over, he commanded Remmich to wait outside in the corridor. Collins dismissed the CID officer in an angry tone. The guy walked out with an irritated look. He told the captain to reenter. "Due to your service history, I'm overlooking courts-martial. But don't let it happen again. If you want to talk to your girlfriend, do it with your own phone and on your own time. You understand?" Before he answered, the colonel made a dismissive arm gesture and stated, "Now get the hell out of here!"

***

Friday couldn't have arrived too soon. Remmich walked into his colonel's office and requested permission to leave in the afternoon, instead of Saturday morning. Collins thought the captain had a lot of nerve after his recent blunder. Remmich appeased him by saying they completed all the security clearance and NATO paperwork, so the CO granted his request. Instead of eating lunch on base, they returned to their apartments, packed, and were on their way forty-five minutes later.

When they drove to the north side of Cologne, they made a pit stop. They bought sandwiches and a drink and ate in the car heading northward to Düsseldorf. Many kilometers later a bypass led westward toward Holland.

Traffic always slowed entering Amsterdam, where there were more cars and jaywalkers. They drove into a section of the city called Rembrandtplein, named for the painter. Remmich turned right and stopped at a parking lot gate behind the hotel. The attendant electronically verified his license plate number, allowing him to park in the lot.

Sections of the hotel were built back in Rembrandt's era, but owners added extensions over the centuries. The restaurant and bar part was a trademark of the Van Horn family, dating back to the sixteen hundreds. Before them, the owner's name was Schiller. Since then, a slow, steady growth had occurred. Never having a son, Franz and Karelle divided the property between themselves and their two girls, Lilly being the eldest. The name of the Hotel Schiller came from the original owner.

It was 4:45 and guests filtered into the Brasserie-Schiller bar-restaurant section. The two men walked inside looking for Lilly. Not seeing her, they sat at the bar. Remmich felt a tug on his shirt sleeve. When he turned around, the smiling woman said, "I'm happy to see you made it." He smiled and said, "Yes. Finally." He stared into her green eyes, loving how her brown hair enhanced her natural rosy skin tone.

She looked away from him and asked, "Is this your friend?"

"Oh, excuse me. This is Eric Miller, the fellow who attended West Point with me." She shook his hand. They spoke for a while until Lilly got a text on her cell phone to return to the front desk. She advised them to order her a beer. "I won't be long."

"Eric, do you remember eating raw oysters at the Lexington Market when we visited Baltimore?"

"Yeah. When we attended the Army INSCOM School at Fort Belvoir. Why do you ask?"

"If you're interested, they serve them here, as do many other bars and restaurants. This is a coastal area. Are you interested in sharing a dozen?"

"I'm not too sure, man. Oysters are an aphrodisiac, and I've been without a woman for a long time."

Remmich laughed while the bartender, Kerk Felders, greeted them. "I heard you talking, but we're sold out. I had three bushels delivered this morning, but we have had guests all day. There is also a stag party for a young man who is getting married tomorrow. They alone ordered a bushel. Tomorrow, gentlemen." With a shrug, Remmich introduced Eric to Kerk.

Lilly returned to the bar and sipped her beer while she explained, "I have to maître d tonight. Sorry. But I won't have anything tomorrow, so we can go anywhere you want and dine with my parents and friends later in the evening."

"Good idea. I'd like to walk around Rembrandtplein. But what's happening tomorrow evening?"

"We'll be having dinner in the smaller dining room. My relatives will be here, and my parents want you and Eric to meet everyone." Lilly's sister, Anna, walked up and exchanged greetings with them. She needed Lilly to assist her for a moment. They walked away.

"Well, what are our plans for tonight?"

"You're still a jazz fan, right?"

"Very much so."

"There are great jazz bar-restaurants in this city. I think you'll enjoy the international blend of people."

Lilly returned and gave each of them their hotel room cards. "I know you are going to the Blues Alley," she remarked with an ornery smile.

Remmich chuckled. Lilly's suspicions made her say, "I will have my detectives watching you all evening until you are safely back here." Miller laughed, and his pal put a hand over his mouth to prevent spitting out his beer. She kissed him goodbye on his cheek and told him, "Have a good time."

***

Yako and Alzuhari received an unexpected conference call from Major Yildiz. He talked about his US Army undercover connection at V Corps. They listened to him say their target would be in Amsterdam that weekend. "My contact told me the hotel where he is staying," said the major. "We know this is fact because he had to provide his plans to his superiors before he left. From what I understand, Tara, he will visit the jazz bar we spoke of earlier. I'm sure you will feel comfortable. It's also where American army soldiers go."

They hailed a taxi outside her apartment building. It was 5:30. "Go to Blues Alley restaurant in the Leidseplein district," she said in English.

***

Nikulin told the cabby to stop and park two cars behind the yellow taxi. He called the embassy in Washington.

The receptionist contacted Ambassador Linkov. "Yury Nikulin is on the phone from Amsterdam, Mr. Ambassador." She transferred the call.

"Hello, Yury, do you have more information?"

Nikulin explained, “I followed the Iraqis from their apartments to a nightclub. I’m still in the cab.” He continued. “From my flat I have watched them walk into their buildings. With my binoculars, I can also see into their apartments because my room is across the street from them. They each have flats on the second floor facing the street. I can place a hidden microphone in each apartment.”

Linkov said, “Since you know where they live, do some exploring. First, go inside this nightclub and make sure they are comfortable. Then take the cab back to where they live. I am sure you can use your tools to unlock the doors.”

12

Barhopping

Paul Remmich walked out of the hotel elevator. He looked for Eric while going into the lobby, but he wasn't there. He sat on an empty couch and faced the corridor. The reception area grandfather clock showed 6:30. Relaxing, he focused on the front-page caption of *The New York Times* on the coffee table. He picked it up and read. "US Army General Confronted." The editorial mentioned more than he had heard on the radio.

"This is absurd," he mumbled, then became aware of someone sitting at the other end of the couch.

"What's absurd?" asked Miller.

Remmich looked disgusted and folded the paper on his lap. "This article elaborates on the radio station's blurb regarding Sutherland's meeting. I wonder if this is going to limit the chances of getting the crooks. How the hell did it get into the hands of the press? I thought the meeting was only covered by *Stars and Stripes*."

"Good question, but Paul, it's just a typical news caption. I wouldn't worry about it." He leaned over toward Remmich and added in a low pitch, "Let the politicians handle it! Come on, let's go out."

When they approached the shiny, golden exit doors, a doorman swiftly pressed the wall button to open them. "Good evening, gentlemen," he said in English with a Dutch accent. They returned the greeting.

"Can I be of help?"

"Can you get a taxi for us please?"

The wave of a white glove brought a cab. "Where are you going this evening, Mr. Remmich?"

"We want a ride into the Rosse Buurt."

The doorman had a confused look. He knew these men were too sophisticated to associate in a district of prostitutes and gay bars. "And what else, sir?"

Remmich explained they wanted to go to the Rosse Buurt first, and then they were going to the Leidseplein.

The doorman opened the cab's back door and spoke in English. "I want my guests to be taken to the center of the Rosse Buurt. Drop them off at the middle of Damstraat."

"Okay," said the cabby.

"What's the Rosy Burt?" Miller wanted to know as they got into the cab.

"The red-light district of Amsterdam. We're going there because I wanted you to become better educated."

"Yeah, right! Like I'm going to want to waste my efforts on a hooker who wants me to buy her drinks, takes me to a room, drugs me, then runs off with my watch and wallet."

"They're not all that way, Eric. You can't compare these professionals with the prostitutes in the States. These women charge, of course, but it's a legitimate business here. You will have to see for yourself."

Miller had an idea and said, grinning, "Although she could be professionally gifted to handle both of us." The cabby laughed.

"And what are you suggesting?" asked Remmich, as he leisurely turned to look at Miller.

"Hey, man, we're still sharing buddies. Right?"

Remmich couldn't hold back a smile, and in his British way stated, "You're insane!"

The cab came to a stop. "Damstraat," declared the cabby. Remmich handed him a ten-euro dollar and told the cabby to keep the change.

After they had walked around for a while, Miller commented, “I don’t understand why people in this area keep their front window curtains pulled back. Any passerby can see inside their house.”

“That’s intentional. The Amsterdam city homeowner wants us to see how orderly and clean their home is, regardless of the neighborhood. It’s their way of saying their homes are worth living in. Home break-ins are rare here. When the robbers are caught, they get a much stiffer penalty than in the US. Of course, the average passer-by doesn’t look into the window.”

They walked onto another street, and Miller asked, “What’s the deal with this half-naked woman sitting sideways behind a big window?”

“This is a professional prostitute. She’s actually advertising. It’s her way of letting a man know what he’s going to get.”

“Is she knitting something?”

“She is. It’s one of the ways they pass the time. Another might be reading a novel. She’s advertising constructively, believe it or not.”

Miller chuckled. “What follows that?”

“They perform in private.”

“Constructive, huh?” Do they work in the same house they live in? I mean, this place looks like a family home.”

“Well, not exactly. It’s a brothel. This entire neighborhood is brothels. It’s why you don’t see kids.”

“Okay, I’ve seen enough.”

Remmich laughed. “We just got here, Eric. What the hell’s wrong with you, my good man?”

“You can stay!” stated Miller while he patted his back pocket to make sure the wallet was there. “I plan to look for a real woman, and I know they’re here because you got one.” He started to walk ahead and loudly asked, “You coming?”

Remmich smiled at the woman looking at him out of the window and followed Eric. They crossed a bridge arching over the river canal and headed to another street. Remmich waved for a taxi. “Take us to the Leidseplein.” It was dusk, and the streetlights came on.

Decorative signs illuminated café and restaurant entrances. Remmich said, “Follow me.”

They walked into a high-tech electronic music venue called the De Ijsbreker, which specialized in heavy rock music and smelled of pizza and beer. The music was loud, so Remmich yelled, “Hey, let’s drink a half-liter each then get the hell out of here.” He leaned toward a barmaid and said, “*Twee lagers*.” He returned his attention to Miller. “This isn’t my type of bar scene, but I did it this way in the beginning. It’s a good starting point for you. Next time, you won’t ask me about this place and that place.”

Miller shouted, “Where did you learn to speak Dutch?”

“I don’t. I only know a few words.”

Miller nodded.

Just then, an aroma other than cigarette smoke caught their attention. Marijuana joints were being passed among the multigenerational clients, who were as vibrant as the music. Both members of one couple had striped hair. The guy had green hair on one side, orange on the other, with a natural dark center, and his girlfriend had red and blue with her natural color in the middle.

Miller took another sip and motioned to leave. He couldn’t handle the noise. “C’mon, let’s look for someplace else.”

They headed for the Blues Alley bar and restaurant, where quieter music played. Soft lighting set the atmosphere. On the stage were eight male musicians, both black and white. They played string and wind instruments to accompany the singer. The vocalist played the piano and sang Nat King Cole’s version of “Unforgettable.” The group’s music and vocal harmony were soothing.

Miller commented, "Man, this singer and small orchestra are terrific."

"Indeed. The bands usually are here in Amsterdam," said Remmich.

They sat at the bar. A barmaid approached, and Remmich said, "*Twee lagers, als't u bleift.*"

"Two beers coming right up," she pronounced in perfect English. They laughed.

Paul saw a waiter carrying two orders of raw oysters and nudged Miller. "Do you see what I see?"

Miller watched the waiter as he placed trays and condiments on a table behind them.

Their beers came. The vocalist ended the song, and Remmich asked the server, "Can you bring us two plates of raw oysters?"

The lounge and table areas were neatly arranged. Miller nudged him and said to look at a classy-looking woman across the bar. She eyed him too and smiled with recognition. Her olive skin tone suggested to them she might be Spanish or Moroccan. Sitting back and sipping their beers, they heard several languages spoken around the room. Miller raised his eyebrows and said, smiling, "A few of these people come out of the good old USA."

"Yes, that's definitely American English.

Miller added, "There's a group of women sitting at a table on the left over there speaking our lingo too."

A server placed two cloth napkins with seafood forks on the bar in front of them. He set down two plates of raw oysters in their half shells on a bed of rock salt. On the side were small bowls of horseradish cocktail sauce. The men squeezed the juice out of netted lemon halves over their oysters and into their sauce containers.

Miller chewed and swallowed. "Delicious." He lifted his head and looked across the bar, noticing the olive-skinned woman looking at him again.

His attention returned to the appetizer. "Man, these oysters are fresh." He added, "They have a sort of sweet taste."

They finished quickly and Remmich asked for the check. "Are we leaving already?" questioned Miller. Remmich pulled out his wallet, but Miller grabbed the check and said, "This one's on me." He waited to sign the credit card bill.

Remmich said, "I want to take you to a couple more places, the Alto Jazz and Bourbon Street scenes. They're close by. We can come back here later if you want. But you need to see these other places too." They put out their cigarettes.

Yako recognized their target. As the men walked toward the entrance, Alzuhari commented, "I think we should follow them. We can't afford to lose Captain Miller." He placed money on the bar, and they left.

They walked farther up the street and heard Dixieland music. Miller commented, "It's interesting these establishments are named like places in New Orleans."

"Yes, it is," answered Remmich, smiling.

They walked in and ordered two half beers and a slice of pizza for each. They talked and listened to the ragtime music for a half-hour. Meanwhile, Yako and Alzuhari waited patiently on a bench a few doors away.

"I need to buy a pack of cigarettes," she said. Her partner looked at her, confused. She didn't smoke. "I'm doing it because our man smokes. I want him to be relaxed around me."

Meanwhile, in an entryway two doors away, the determined thug continued his surveillance of Miller. His arm wound had healed, but it was still sore.

Remmich spoke up. "Eric, I have something to tell you. I've decided to propose to Lilly this weekend."

Surprised, his buddy smiled and shook his hand. "Well, I think you're getting a real prize."

Remmich agreed how lucky he was to find someone as pretty and smart as her.

When they finished eating, Miller excused himself to go to the restroom while his buddy paid the check. They passed each other in the corridor, and Remmich said, "I'll see you outside."

When they met on the sidewalk, Remmich said, "I know we talked about going to the Alto Jazz café, but it's seven-thirty, and these places are filling up. Let's go back to Blues Alley. I enjoyed the combination of jazz and blues music."

"Yeah. The band was great. I hope the group of US women is still there." He smiled and cleared his throat. "This is too good of an opportunity to give up."

The Iraqis followed them back into the bar. Remmich saw two empty places on the opposite side of the horseshoe bar. He nudged his buddy's arm and said, "Follow me." They scooted around people and sat down. The Iraqis waited out of sight among people. So did the thug.

Miller looked for the olive-skinned woman. He didn't see her and assumed she'd left. Remmich looked for the group of women at the round table. He motioned for two beers. His interest in the table of women was not for himself.

The bartender placed the beers in front of them. They sipped for a while, and Remmich said, "I think I'll stroll around a bit. Why don't you stay here, and if I see something interesting, I'll come back and let you know. And save my seat." Miller nodded,

He noticed Paul's pack of Camel cigarettes and matches, which he moved next to him. He passed the time watching people. When the music stopped, a different band of musicians took over.

A woman sat in Remmich's seat. "They switch bands every couple of hours."

Miller turned around to find the soft voice belonged to the olive-skinned woman. He smiled and said, "Thank you. I didn't know." He wasn't used to being accosted by women. He wondered if prostitutes worked in this kind of establishment. *No way*, he thought. He sipped and looked at the band setting up.

The audience clapped for the pianist and vocalist. "Thank you very much. My name is Bobby McCarron. My fellow band players and I left Chicago last night and arrived in Amsterdam this morning. Jetlag has not set in yet." Those listening to him smiled. "My partner tells me some of you requested a song called 'Unforgettable' as sung by the great Nat King Cole. First, we're going to play Cole Porter's songs, but later I'll sing more Nat King Cole. Now I want to introduce Sally Thomas, who will be sharing the vocals with me." The band continued to set up.

Miller sipped his beer and awkwardly reached for the cigarettes. As he turned to look at the woman, he noticed her face glowed in the low bar lighting. She pulled a cigarette pack out of her purse. When their eyes met, she placed a cigarette between her lips. He politely struck the match to light it. As she thanked him, he blew out the match and looked at her again and smiled. She didn't inhale and turned away to blow out the smoke.

"I should introduce myself. I am Eric Miller."

His introduction delighted her. Yako switched the cigarette to her left hand and extended her right. He moved his cold hand into hers, and they squeezed momentarily. "My name is Tara Yako."

"It's nice to meet you, Tara. Do you come here often?"

"A couple times a week," she lied. "I enjoy the music, and the people are friendly. How about you, Eric? Do you come here often?"

He heard her American English pronunciation and wondered if she'd ever lived in the United States. "This is my first time. I'm here with a friend."

"Are you traveling, or do you work with the embassy?"

Her friendly manner put him at ease. "Actually, we're with the United States Army stationed in Germany. My friend Paul comes here about every two to three weeks to visit his Dutch girlfriend." He turned away to sip his beer and took a drag on his cigarette. *This woman was something else to look at; oth her face and her body.*

She knew the answer to her question, but for the sake of conversation, she asked, "Is he the man who was sitting with you, the blond-haired one who just walked away?" Before he answered, she continued, "And are you both officers, Eric?"

He hesitated, feeling that question was kind of pushy coming from someone he just met. He decided to overlook it, smiled, and said, "Yes. We're both captains."

Adnaw Alzuhari sat on the other side of the horseshoe. Yako turned to sip her drink and glanced at him. Anxious, he came half out of his seat, so she smiled and shook her head to tell him not to interfere, not yet.

As she turned back toward Eric, she saw the man who had looked into their compartment on the train. He was at the center horseshoe section looking at her. He glanced at Alzuhari, then turned back to look at her. Before either of them could react, the Russian paid for his beer and disappeared into the crowd.

Miller saw her looking across the bar and wondered what had caught her attention. The bartender came over and offered to bring another beer. Miller ordered two and asked Tara if she wanted another drink. She accepted, and the bartender nodded and walked away. She thanked Miller; hazel eyes filled with promise. Eric regretted leaving at that point but excused himself and said he'd be right back. She watched him walk out of sight.

The drinks came, and she told the bartender to take Eric's half-empty beer glass. Quickly and with precise motions, she reached into her purse and removed a small white envelope. It contained several tablets of Rohypnol. Spy agencies in many countries used the drug to sedate people. Based on the dosage, it could either knock them out or create a feeling of well-being. Either way, the drugged individual revealed information. When administered, the person would also experience short-term memory loss.

She looked in the direction of the bathrooms, then placed her right hand around the rim of one of the full beer glasses closest to her and dropped in the pills. They fizzed a little in the beer. She used a cocktail stirrer to help dissolve them. Alzuhari watched, nodding approval.

Miller returned.

"I hope the bartender didn't try to charge you." He didn't realize his half glass of beer was gone.

"No, I wasn't asked to pay. But it was kind of you to buy me another drink. Thank you." She moved the spiked beer directly in front of Eric.

He didn't want her to imagine he was drinking too much so he didn't pick it up immediately. They talked for a while, learning about each other. He asked if she ever lived in the United States.

"Yes. I attended Georgetown University."

That's where she learned to speak English so well. He remembered she was Saudi, but he never thought to ask her what she did in Amsterdam.

Remmich returned from talking to the group of American women. He casually nudged his arm between her and his buddy and reached for the cigarettes and match pack. "Sorry. I didn't mean to butt in," he said as he smiled at Yako. "Eric, can I talk to you for a moment?"

Miller excused himself and got off the stool. They moved a few feet away, and Remmich said, "You seem to be having a good time. Do you want to keep talking to her? I'm asking because there's an interesting woman at the round table over there I think might be your type, Eric."

"Sure, I want to meet her. But I like talking to this one too. She's so pretty, and her body is unreal."

Remmich chuckled. "Listen, I took the opportunity of introducing myself, and they invited me to sit. If it weren't for Lilly, I'd definitely make a play for one of them." He hesitated while lighting his cigarette and continued, "But while talking to them I found out they all work for Delta Airlines, either out of Frankfurt or Amsterdam. Why don't you mosey on over there and I'll hold your spot here at the bar?"

Miller nodded. "I ordered more beer for us, by the way, but haven't touched either glass yet"

"What do you know about the woman you were talking to?"

"From what I got out of her, she's from Saudi Arabia and went to Georgetown University. You can entertain her while I'm on scout patrol." They laughed and bumped fists.

Miller walked back to his seat and nudged Yako on the arm. He introduced Remmich, who sat down in front of the spiked beer. Miller grabbed the other beer glass and left.

Yako frowned; the drugged beer was sitting in front of the wrong man. She watched him fiddle with the empty matchbook. Hoping to distract him from drinking, she blurted out, "Oh, I didn't introduce myself. My name is Tara Yako."

He stopped bending the slaughtered thing and looked at her. "Can I offer you an American cigarette?"

She looked at him thoughtfully, calculating whether walking away would be the best thing to do. Fighting the urge to bolt, she looked down at the pack. "I've never smoked Camel Filters before. Thank you."

"I'm Paul Remmich." He shook her hand. Yako appraised him, admiring his handsome features, but distracted by the upset of her plan. He pulled out a cigarettes for both of them and repositioned the beer closer to him. "So, Tara, cheers," he said, getting ready to lift the spiked beer glass.

She wanted to prevent this disaster. *What if this person wasn't competent? Worse, he wasn't the first choice of Tariq'Allah!* He picked up the drugged glass of beer, and she asked him, "Is the beer cold enough for you, Paul?" She put her hand on his arm to discourage him from sipping. "Perhaps you can order a colder one," she suggested.

"It's fine." He took a few big sips.

She realized, given the circumstances, she might as well find out as much about him as she could. She wondered how experienced he was as a military man and what he did. How did he think? "Tell me, Paul, do you keep up with current events?"

"Yes. I am always in touch with what happens globally. As officers, Eric and I have to be aware of our country's relationship with the United Nations." He added irritably, "Personally, I really don't care for their influence and control over our interaction with foreign countries."

"What do you mean?"

He took a few more quick sips. "I feel they've been double-crossing Third World countries rather than helping raise their overall standing in the world. It seems history is repeating itself with wealthy and midsize countries ignoring the poorer ones. If the UN was doing the right thing, less prosperous countries could receive specialized help. It would have a positive effect on all of us."

"This is fascinating," she said, smiling and thinking this may not turn out so bad after all.

The conversation turned into a one-man show. He continued to criticize the United Nations for not doing more.

"Because of what is happening, I feel I can no longer serve my country. I'm going to resign." He drank more beer.

She wasn't sure how long the drug took to take effect. Unfortunately, if this man didn't work out, they'd have to get rid of him. She took a deep breath and asked, "So, Paul, you told me what you think about global events, but what exactly do you do with Eric?"

"We're stationed in Germany."

She shook her head. "Yes, he did tell me, but he never said what your functions are or where you work."

Since she seemed to agree with his views about the United Nations, he felt comfortable telling her. "We work in the city of Würzburg, which is between Frankfurt and Nürnberg." Eric and I are in military intelligence. He flicked his ash into the ashtray and asked her about herself. *She began to hope she'd avoided a disaster, and that perhaps he is the better target of the two.*

"I was born and raised in…" She paused. "Saudi Arabia."

Remmich didn't pick up on her hesitation. "Oh, yes, and Eric mentioned you graduated from Georgetown University." He took another sip. "We graduated from West Point, a military academy in New York."

"How is it you have a very British accent yet are a member of the American military? Are you a citizen of the United States?"

"Yes." He explained his background for the next ten minutes but his speech began to slow as he started feeling lethargic and woozy, almost punch-drunk. He chuckled self-consciously. "Is there something else you want to know?"

He leaned toward her and almost lost his balance but straightened up by holding onto the bar. He didn't understand why his vision was distorted. Watching from the other side, Alzuhari was concerned but stayed seated. Yako noticed Remmich's eyes slightly closing.

Miller came out of the men's room and decided to tell his buddy what a good time he was having. Walking toward him, the scene was surprising and puzzling. Why was Remmich leaning toward Yako with his hand on her leg? *Paul loved Lilly.* He decided he was probably just playfully flirting and returned to the table with the American women.

The noise in the bar got louder. Remmich's head dipped forward, and he felt less and less alert.

There were three servers behind the bar now, and their bodies blocked Yako's attempts to get Alzuhari's attention. Finally, she waved for a bartender. He approached. She pointed and said, "Will you tell the gentleman sitting across the way wearing the dark-blue shirt to come over to me, please?" The guy nodded and walked away. Remmich's awareness diminished further. Alzuhari arrived and nudged her free arm. Remmich reached out clumsily to push him away and almost fell off the stool.

The moment had arrived.

When Eric returned, Candice asked, "Where did you go? You were gone so long I didn't think you were coming back."

He put out his cigarette. "Oh, I went to the bathroom, then started to let Paul know where I was."

"You look troubled, Eric. What's wrong?"

"Paul is over there flirting with a foreign broad when he's supposed to be getting engaged tomorrow. I never thought he would get involved with another woman."

His sincerity deepened her attraction: he sounded like a one-woman man.

The music stopped, and the bandleader spoke. "By request, this next song is 'Night and Day' by the great Cole Porter." An alto saxophone began the music. Sally Thomas's voice was soft and melodic.

"Care to dance again?" He followed her to the dance floor. While they were among others, she wrapped both her arms around his waist and moved in close to him.

"I've told you a little about my background, but what about you?" Their arms loosened. They looked at each other, talking and dancing slowly.

"Paul told us you are West Pointers. I'm an academy graduate, also."

"Oh, really? Where did you go?"

"The Air Force Academy. I graduated in 2010 and got my wings a year later. When I served my five-year term of service, I decided to resign. Too many men tried to run my life. It soured my military career plans. But since I was used to co-commanding the big transports, the coaching and managing prepared me for large commercial jets. Fortunately, I landed a job with Delta Airlines. I work out of New York at Kennedy International. It's been a wonderful relationship for the past five years. The reason I'm here with these other Delta women is to celebrate my first overseas flight in a different capacity. I'm now a commercial airline captain."

Miller gently squeezed her hand and congratulated her. Candice leaned her forehead onto his chest and said, "I'm glad I accepted the new job."

Meanwhile, Alzuhari stood at Remmich's other side, helping to keep him upright. "I thought you were going to drug the black man. Where is he?"

Remmich leaned his head on the bar and started to laugh in a silly manner. The bartenders assumed he was drunk. One of them came over and asked her if they needed help leaving. Alzuhari smiled ruefully and said in English, "No, but thank you anyway. We are going to take our friend home." The bartender walked back to his other customers.

Alzuhari looked closely at Yako. "You didn't answer me, Tara."

"I never thought another man would get in the way, Adnaw. It surprised me when Captain Miller left, and this man sat next to me." She sighed and added, "I'll explain later, but I don't want to lose this one. It seems he may fit our needs just as well as Captain Miller. Help me get him outside. I don't want to cause a scene because his friend might see us." She hoped no one paid attention to a drunken man helped by his girlfriend.

She placed money on the bar and loud enough for nearby customers to hear said, "Come on, darling, we're going to go home." Carefully, they guided Remmich to sit up and made him lift his head. It didn't work, and he fell forward again. People looked at them. Alzuhari put Remmich's arm around his shoulder. He was just tall enough to be able to move him away from the bar. Yako grabbed her purse. People moved out of their way to let them go out. One man held the door open for them.

Yako opened the back door of the closest taxi and got in the spacious back seat. Alzuhari slowly turned Remmich around, bent him over a little, and eased him down to the car seat. He placed his hand behind Remmich's head to stop it hitting the side of the car roof. Yako had no physical control to position him better, but their captive had no control and started to fall sideways. She grabbed his shirt to stop him from falling to the floor. Alzuhari got in and pushed him upright.

"Take us to Thirty-Seven Raamstraat, please," she said in English.

Blues Alley was packed. Miller stood up and said, "I want to find out how Paul is doing. I'll be back soon." When he got to the bar, Remmich wasn't there. Other people were sitting in their seats. Wondering how long ago his friend left, he asked the woman in one of the bar seats. She couldn't speak English but showed him a pack of Camel Filters. Miller smiled and nodded as if they were his, and she gave them to him. He realized the bent-up matchbook on the counter belonged to Remmich.

***

The taxi parked at the curb at the Blues Alley nightclub. Nikulin's undercover scheme of waiting in a cab seemed to pay off. He saw Alzuhari holding onto Paul Remmich and getting into the taxi up ahead. He told his cabby to follow their black cab.

The tall embassy thug sat at the horseshoe bar and focused on Miller.

13

The Fix

Paul Remmich kept falling forward or to one side during the ride. The cabby announced their location and stopped at the curb. Alzuhari got out. Yako tried to balance Remmich, while Alzuhari pulled him out of the back seat. She paid the cabby.

They walked inside her building and got onto the elevator. Yako pushed the floor button.

They walked off; Alzuhari still had Remmich's arm around his neck. She moved ahead and opened the apartment door. Remmich's legs began to buckle. He lifted him again and said, "Paul, stand up straight!" Remmich concentrated, wobbling and trying to stand upright.

She closed the door, and he slurred the words, "I li…liked those el…e…vators." He swallowed and added, "What are we doing…here?"

Yako didn't answer.

They eased him onto a recliner sofa. She lowered it to forty-five degrees. His stomach flipped with the movement, nauseous.

Remmich tried to sit upright, but he couldn't. His limbs wouldn't cooperate. Alzuhari ordered, "Sit right here and don't get up!"

His mind whirling, he wondered if he was in a doctor's office. Yako approached with a small serving tray holding a syringe, an ampoule, and an opened package of alcohol wipes.

"Wha…what the hell is this? Where…where am I, goddamnit? Wha…t's that smell?" Alzuhari walked to the back of the sofa and held on to his shoulders. Yako grabbed the alcohol wipe. Remmich slurred again, "Wha…what's…smell?" He tried to move, but Alzuhari increased his hold. She lifted Remmich's shirt sleeve above the elbow and gripped his skin to find muscle. His muscles tensed as he watched her press the syringe's tip and saw liquid squirt out of the needle.

"Don't watch what I am doing, Paul," she ordered. He looked into her face and then back at the syringe. Alzuhari placed his hands on the sides of his face and made him look straight ahead.

"Ouch!" he yelled, without slurring, jerking as the needle stabbed the skin and pressed into his muscle. His arm stung and burned the whole time it took for the syringe to empty. Yako's inexperience and clumsiness with the injection made the pain worse. He tried one more time to pull away, but it only increased the pain. "Damn…it hurts," he yelled again, tears forming at the corner of his eyes. Finally, she pulled it out and rubbed the bleeding area with the alcohol pad. Jerking and screaming, he said, "Lemme go!" Awkwardly, he jerked his body to get up. Alzuhari continued to hold him in place.

She wiped away lingering blood and put on a bandage. "I will not hurt you again. Take it easy." Alzuhari removed his hands, and Remmich calmed down.

They walked out to the balcony to call Major Yildiz in Istanbul. He put the cell phone on speaker. She spoke in low tones, wondering how to tell Yildiz, while occasionally glancing at Remmich.

The conference call began in a friendly way. Yildiz asked how the hunt for their black soldier was going. Alzuhari said they found a most interesting man.

"Oh?" commented Yildiz.

He sensed something was wrong because generally Yako enjoyed talking to him and explaining what they had been doing, but not tonight. Alzuhari wondered if he should say more to help, but she shook her head.

"Is everything okay, Tara? You seem subdued."

For a few seconds, she kept quiet. "I'm feeling good, Major. It's just…" Reluctantly she continued. "We found an American soldier. He is with us right now. I performed the steps of initial drugging. Minutes ago, I gave him an injection to calm him and reverse the drowsy state of mind. He is doing better."

"It sounds as if everything is going according to the plan. Is there something wrong?" asked Yildiz.

She wavered, then answered, "Yes and no. The man we abducted is not Eric Miller. However, the beneficial points are the man is an officer, and he works in the same city as Dr. Mustafa. He can speak German, and he is displeased with the United Nations. I listened to him complain about their broken promise to assist Third World nations. According to him, the United States will not negotiate to change the UN's decision. I can't tell you anything else for now."

Yildiz commented, "Yes, our foreign ministry is familiar with this. And what are the bad points?"

Alzuhari motioned to help, but she shook her head.

"Before you say anything to object, let me add he is also not happy with the United States Army."

"So, he is not the black soldier we targeted?" No answer. "Well, who is he?" before she said anything, he wondered, "Do you think he is equal to the man you were supposed to get?"

She tried to reverse any negative attitude in him by saying, "I believe Allah gave us a gift. The man we have here is Paul Remmich. He was in the jazz restaurant with Eric Miller. They are friends. I briefly spoke to Captain Miller, but Remmich is also a captain, and he works with Miller. They both graduated from the same military academy." *Yildiz's mind raced. He realized if both men worked together, they must function similarly at military intelligence.* "Paul Remmich holds the views we were seeking. He also says he intends to resign. I want to see if we can persuade him to work with us." She explained how Remmich took the wrong beer. "I tried to get his attention away from the drugged beer, but he drank it anyway."

The major didn't speak for a few seconds. Finally, he said, "You must understand something. We are dealing with an officer who is, I'm certain, in good physical shape. Remember, Tara, you said they graduated from a military academy together. He can defend himself, and he will kill to save his own life." *The Stockholm incident entered their thoughts.* "If you find he isn't the right person and can't be hypnotized, kill him and dump his body into the lower canal district." Alzuhari and Yako were aware an order had to be obeyed but hoped killing Remmich wasn't going to be necessary.

Yildiz told her to get the instructions for the hypnotizing process. They reentered the living room. Alzuhari walked to the side of Remmich's chair and watched his breathing and blinking eyes. They returned to the balcony.

"I have the binder, Major," she said. For thirteen minutes, the three of them reviewed the steps for hypnosis. Although they were familiar with the manual's content, Yildiz wanted to discuss every bit of it.

"Tara, you will ease this man into becoming hypnotized. The discontent he expressed about the United States and the UN's treatment of Third World nations is to be repeated. Get him to agree with you. Play into his emotions, encourage him, and then let his subconscious follow your instructions. It's why I recommended marijuana. It will make him more relaxed before you begin."

"Excuse me, sir," said Alzuhari, "but in the local apothecary, the pharmacist said they didn't have the dried, leaf form of marijuana. They only had a liquid called *cannabis indica*."

"Interesting," said Yildiz. "Is this liquid injected in his arm?"

Yako said, "No. No. Paul Remmich smokes. I will insert some of it into a cigarette. This is our chance. Otherwise, we would have to give it to him in liquid form in a drink, and it will take time to digest. Instead, the lungs will quickly absorb the smoke."

"Yes. Good," said Yildiz.

Time was of the essence.

Yako said, "Major, thank you for reviewing the steps to convert our new ambassador."

"Before I say goodbye, I want both of you to know I spoke with Baghdad about your endeavor to get Mr. Miller. Okay, you didn't get him. I will handle it. They want our man to get the scientific discovery. He can only do this if he maintains contact. He is going to be a valuable asset. Sometime in the future, we will have him fulfill his wish to resign. We will have our undercover contact ensure that he stays in part-time. He is to be told we want him to get the information. Finally, tell Paul Remmich that he is not to forget anything he wanted to do before tonight. I mean, I want him to act the same as if he were not under hypnotic control. Again, I will notify Baghdad about you securing someone, but I will not go into detail. For now, our plan will continue. Good luck."

They thanked him and walked back inside.

Paul said, "I want a cigarette." He gestured to his pocket and said, "I don't have any."

Yako realized this was the perfect opportunity. "Just a minute, Paul, I will give you one of mine." She went into the kitchen and got an unused plastic syringe out of the box of medical supplies. Opening the liquid container and siphoning *cannabis indica* into the syringe, she inserted the needle into the end of a cigarette. Slowly, she pushed the needle into the paper wrapping as far as it could go, dampening the tobacco. Five minutes later, it was ready.

Alzuhari lit it for him. They waited halfway through the cigarette to see if he relaxed. "How do you feel, Paul?" he asked. Although he did not answer, he yawned and stretched sluggishly.

They waited patiently for him to finish the cigarette. She put it out for him, while Alzuhari moved the backrest again. Remmich laid his head back and stared at the ceiling, relaxed.

Yako rolled out a flat, portable stand with a movie projector and placed it in front of the sofa. She whispered to Alzuhari to close the windows and shades. The stove's light provided enough brightness for her to plug in the projector and turn it on. It beamed onto the oval ceiling. They assessed Remmich's condition and determined he was ready to become hypnotized.

She walked up to him and said, "Paul, I want you to know you can help Third World countries. We can stop the United Nations from doing nasty things to them. If you don't want to do it, you can get up and leave right now."

His countenance changed to a serious look. He thought about helping Third World nations. The pot made him less resistant. He answered in his British accent, "Yes, I want to help them." He didn't mention anything about leaving the army.

"Everything is going to be fine, Paul. Relax," said Alzuhari, and he patted him on the shoulder.

Yako moved Remmich's head to watch the ceiling. She turned on the projector and focused the lens. A moving nighttime galaxy of stars mesmerized him.

Alzuhari turned on the air conditioning because a cool, relaxed atmosphere enhanced the hypnosis process. Everything was quiet, except for the hums of the air conditioner and the projector. They waited. Remmich appeared to become more comfortable. When the projected spectacle rotated to the Milky Way, the display had completely captured his attention. The solemn expression on his face signaled he was ready.

Sitting on a chair next to him, she said, "Paul, you are watching a lot of stars pass through the galaxy. They are objects similar to you, and they have a particular path to follow. You have a path. It's filled with personal power. You are like the stars because your human energy is in control of the path in your life. The power of the stars lets them move to where they want to be. We are going to help Third World nations. They are our friends, Paul."

She whispered to Alzuhari to get a blanket. They each held a side of it and placed it on Remmich's legs and upper torso. She said, "You are worth more to yourself, and worth more to our goal, by deciding to help Third World nations. You want to become a member of Tariq'Allah by making yourself a friend to these countries, Paul. We want to help, not hurt, these countries. We do not want to follow the United Nations. Do you want to work with us to help Third World countries?" She hesitated for a few moments to let him stare and think. "You are trapped as a member of the army and not able to practice what you want to do to help advance the world by assisting these poor people."

She hesitated for a few seconds before saying, "You want to resign as a full-time military officer. You want to become a diplomat. You want to be happy and help Third World nations."

Her statements made him feel free. In a part of his mind, he wanted to believe these two people were going to help him counter the selfish acts of the United Nations. He wanted to be active in becoming a diplomat.

Yako remembered his displeasure. Her words paralleled his emotional state. "Paul, our goals include assisting people in Third World countries. We want to get them better educated. Some of these countries need hospital construction and medical help. They need to have better farms for growing vegetables and fruit. They need to breed livestock. They need to develop commerce and business. We desire to help Third World nations. Do you want to work with us?"

It was the second time she had asked. Remmich didn't answer. His hypnotized subconscious mind was now in a trance, a condition between waking and sleeping. Inducing a trance can control sublevels of consciousness. A subject is unaware of the surroundings. Paul Remmich's depth of trance wasn't extreme. He was aware of the stars and Yako talking. What he needed to do was make a decision on his own. Yako realized if she could accomplish this, he was sure to work with them. But will he do it? She let him relax more for a moment.

Shivering, he pulled the blanket closer around himself. Yako gently laid another blanket over him and stood at his side. Bending over, she whispered, "Paul, I want you to understand that you have a choice. You can get up and leave if you want to. You don't have to stay here and help Third World nations." She waited for a few seconds, observing the open expression on his face, and then repeated, "Paul, you want to become a member of Tariq'Allah, which helps poor nations. You are fed up with the way the US military operates. You want to resign. You want to work with us. Third World nations are not important to them. You care for them. The army just talks about the problems but does nothing to help. This is really your decision." She hesitated a moment and asked, "Do you understand me, Paul?"

Now Remmich's desire for freedom from the military was stronger. His conviction matched the thoughts she expressed. Again, she asked, "Do you want to leave the military?"

"Yes."

"Do you want to help the poor people of the world?"

Sluggishly he said, "Yes. I want to help them have a better economy, better schools, doctors who stay in their countries, and a political system that cares."

He stopped talking, but it was clear he had subconsciously retained what they wanted. His mind had accepted the suggestions. She said, "You want a new way to live. You can determine what you want, Paul."

"Yes, I can be a diplomat," he whispered.

Knowing his role in the army before and during the Blues Alley scene, she asked, "Paul, tell me everything about your job in the military."

He hesitated before answering. Yako wondered if he would rebel against the questions.

Alzuhari studied Remmich's profile. Their captive's eyes focused upward as he watched the slow, freely revolving star movement.

Yako said, "Paul, you understand everything I am saying. You can make your own decision. You can leave if you want to. You are making a democratic decision, Paul, to help Third World nations."

She leaned forward and studied his profile. His eyelids opened more. The state of subconsciousness helped him to relate to only the ideas suggested; a motivation occurring without intention, without awareness, and without conscious guidance.

"Tell me what you do, Paul."

He mumbled incoherent words.

"I have a new life for you, Paul. Now, tell me what you do in the army." She kept telling herself to be patient, but it was frustrating. It wasn't like the nights in Georgetown, where they didn't have to search for information. Instead, they gave simple commands that made people do ridiculous things. She sat in a slouched way and massaged the bridge of her nose.

Suddenly, he uttered, "I am associated with the V Corps, 32nd Security Intelligence in Würzburg, Germany." His German pronunciation was as decent as his standard British accent.

"Are you fluent in German, Paul?"

"Yes," he murmured. "I can speak, read, and write German."

Alzuhari noticed her eyes closing, relieved. He smiled.

It was a miracle. Allah had helped them find a messenger, a mole. She said in their native Arabic, "Maybe this is the man destined to fulfill Tariq'Allah's worldly desires and not the other one."

She observed their new secret agent and said, "Thank you, Paul. Tell me, do you have access to classified computer files?"

"Yes."

Alzuhari asked, "Which ones?"

"Confidential, secret, top-secret, and the SCI-level files. I work with SCI-level files and decode encrypted information. With SCI, I have to be cleared each time I work with a file."

"What does SCI mean?" asked Alzuhari.

"Special Compartmented Information. It is accessed on a need-to-know basis only. Each document has a classification above the lower three, and its level of confidentiality is determined by the Joint Chiefs of Staff and the Department of Defense."

Once again she knew the answer, but she wanted *him* to answer. "What department of the V Corps do you work in, Paul?"

"Military Intelligence, which is under USAREUR command headquarters in Heidelberg. My office is classified as security intelligence." He hesitated. "Our encrypted communication data is the most classified text within the army."

She bowed her head and closed her eyes. Excitement overcame her and Alzuhari. He smiled and leaned back in the chair. They now knew he was the right guy.

"When are you returning to your workstation, Paul?" asked Yako.

"On Monday, Memorial Day. It's a holiday for me."

"Paul, you are going to resign. You want to work as a part-time employee. Tell them what you want if they don't ask. Do you understand, Paul?"

"Yes. I want to work part-time. I will say I want to if my superiors don't ask."

They couldn't believe the cooperation his subliminal state of mind gave to them.

"There is one last thing I want to say. On Tuesday, I want you to telephone the chief of dental surgery at Leighton Barracks. His name is Dr. Faisal Mustafa. I believe you live there."

"Yes, I live on base."

They watched him stare at the revolving galaxy. Yako moved closer next to him and began to give him post-hypnotic suggestions. "You will be getting up in a few minutes. You will return to the Blues Alley jazz bar with us. You will act as you always do with your friends. You will not remember what we talked about tonight when you return to Blues Alley. Tomorrow evening, I will call you and give you specific instructions to contact Dr. Mustafa. Do you understand me, Paul?"

He waited a few seconds, then answered, "Yes."

"Write your telephone number for me, Paul." The projector provided just enough light for him to see. He followed her command and returned the pad and pen. She held up the paper and examined the number and read it out loud.

"Yes," he answered. Yako placed the pad on the table.

Alzuhari walked up to him, looked into his eyes, and said, "You are to remember the words, 'It…is…a...cloudy…day…outside.' Repeat those words to me, Paul."

"It…is…a...cloudy…day…outside."

"When you hear those words, you will obey the person who speaks to you. Do you understand?"

"Yes."

Yako got close to him again and said, "I want you to remember everything you've wanted to do in your personal life up to tonight. And I want you to agree to help us during your resignation. Do you understand?" He nodded.

It was almost dark in Yako's apartment after Alzuhari turned off the power to the projector. He moved the table to the side of the couch so Remmich could stand. Yako opened the shades, then opened the balcony door. A soft spring breeze refreshed the inside air.

Alzuhari touched on his right arm. "It's me, Paul. Remember, I am Adnaw." He pushed the button to return the chair to upright. Yako stood beside him. "We are going back to Blues Alley with you." She got her purse while Alzuhari put on a sports coat. He felt the left pocket; the pistol was there. They helped him get up and put on his jacket. When they got out into the corridor, the elevator arrived quickly.

Yako waved for a taxi. "Take us to the Blues Alley jazz nightclub."

The evening was still young.

***

He had been outside Yako's apartment building on the phone with Linkov for the last half hour. Nikulin told the ambassador there was an ampoule and syringe in Yako's apartment but nothing in Alzuhari's flat. He explained that the white, American man at the jazz bar was very drunk, and the Iraqi man helped him get into the taxi.

"I wonder if they drugged him."

Nikulin didn't respond. He watched them leave the apartment building and get into a cab.

"Yury, are you still there?" He heard Nikulin hail a taxi.

"I'm still here, Mr. Ambassador." He told the cabby to follow the white cab.

"Yury, what is going on?"

"Their taxi is leaving. I am following it."

"Call me back."

14

His Return

It was almost 11:00. Blues Alley was crowded. Cigarette smoke fogged the air above the hanging Tiffany table lights. Eric Miller's agitation about his friend's whereabouts kept interrupting attention to Candice. She sensed his uneasiness and excused herself to go to the lady's room with her friends. The mass of people made it difficult to look around. *Damn! I'll bet he left to go to that broad's apartment.* He turned back toward the table and saw Candice walking toward him.

"Looking for Paul once more?"

"How did you know?"

"Because you are standing up and have a troubled expression on your face."

"It's been over two hours." He pulled out her chair, and she sat down. He did likewise.

She gripped his hand, and reassuringly said, "He'll show up."

Outside, a cabby stopped just past the entrance. Alzuhari told the driver to wait there. He and Remmich got out. Yako spoke to the driver and waited.

***

Nikulin's taxi driver parked at the curb. The Russian rolled down the window to get some fresh air and started to call the ambassador. At the same time, he saw Alzuhari standing at a cab with Remmich. He changed to camera mode and took multiple shots as the two men walked into Blues Alley.

***

The band played the soft jazz of Nat King Cole's "Mona Lisa," as Alzuhari led Remmich into the crowd. "Try to find your friend, Paul." The noise and people distracted Remmich. While he looked around, Alzuhari disappeared.

***

He recognized the Iraqi walking out of the bar and getting back into the cab. The Russian was between a rock and a hard place because he couldn't follow both. "Follow the white taxi ahead," Nikulin told the cabby. He dialed the ambassador. There was a recording, and he pushed the number for Linkov's extension. It rang three times before Linkov's recording started.

"Ambassador, Nikulin. The Iraqis and the American just returned to the Blues Alley nightclub. The men walked into the building together, but the Iraqi came back to his cab alone. The American is still inside." He studied the multiple photos for a moment. "I am following the Iraqis' taxi. Also, I have some photographs of the Iraqi man and the American, but they are not close-ups. I will send them to you."

The ambassador recognized his voice and rushed to pick up the phone. "Yury, are you still there?"

"Yes."

"No. Don't go there. You already know where they live, and I have an idea what they are up to. Email the photographs. I will have my assistant study them and see if we can identify this man. For tonight, follow the American."

***

Remmich wedged his way between servers and patrons. He got to the bar section but didn't see his friend. He remembered where the women sat and thought that's where he probably was. He paid for a draft, then walked to their table.

Miller felt a hand on his shoulder. He turned around, surprised, stood up, and quietly asked, "Hey, man, where the hell have you been?" The table's conversations stopped. All eyes were on Paul Remmich.

Candice looked at the sharp stares from her friends. She understood Eric's stress, so she decided to get involved. "Glad you're back, Paul. Please, have a seat."

Remmich's brain was still a little cloudy. Although the effects of the drugs lingered, the post-hypnotic suggestions controlled him. He said hello to the women. Looking at the pack of Camel Filters on the table, he commented, "Oh, you found them. I thought I'd lost the pack." He took one and politely asked for a light. The table's atmosphere was subdued. Miller waited for him to lead a conversation. *Maybe he'd talk about where he went.* Candice didn't want to wait and said, "You never mentioned it before, but I understand you and Eric have a common background and a long friendship. Now you're working together."

Curious eyes focused on him. He took a drag, exhaled, and swallowed a sip of beer. "We've been friends since our days at West Point."

Bessie Martin, a copilot with Candice, asked, "Have you been stationed in a variety of places?"

The question made Remmich feel calmer. He thought it might be because the women were American and friendly.

Instead of blurting out a lot of information, he said, "Well, it's been half and half, so to speak. Half of my career has been overseas and half in the United States."

"Where did you get your British accent?" Alice Johnson asked.

Remmich smiled and answered, "England, of course." The group broke into laughter. As it subsided, he added, "Oh, it's a long story."

A waitress came around and asked if they wanted more drinks. Remmich declined, but the rest at the table ordered. The jazz band resumed playing. Eric and Candice got up to dance again, which left Remmich alone with the women. He conversed with them about his background and his travels throughout Germany and all over Europe. He appreciated their interest, and they enjoyed listening to him

At a little past 1:00 they called it a night. To the men's surprise, the women paid for everything. Eric and Candice stayed seated, exchanging addresses and telephone numbers, and then got up and met the others outside. After getting into their own cabs, Miller noticed his friend was unusually quiet on the ride to the hotel.

The cab stopped at the main entrance, and the attendant immediately opened the door. Miller handed the driver a euro note. Remmich tipped the doorman. They walked into the main lobby, and Miller asked, "Care to have a nightcap?"

Remmich focused on the lobby clock time and said, "Why the hell not!" Miller smiled.

The Brasserie-Schiller's bar was half-full. The barman placed cognacs in front of them. Remmich felt a gentle grasp on his left arm.

"Hi, Lilly," said Miller, smiling. "Care for one?"

"Hello, Eric. No, thank you. I'm glad you brought my one and only back to me. I was beginning to wonder about him." She took a sip of Remmich's cognac. She asked, "How was the evening for you two?"

"We had a great evening. Paul found me a fascinating woman."

Lilly turned to look into her lover's eyes. He nodded affirmatively. She sensed something was bothering him, but said, holding up the cordial, "To our future."

Miller looked at the time. He gulped the remaining cognac and said, "Lilly, Paul, I'm going to leave you two alone." He bid them both good night and walked out.

"Are you troubled about something, Paul? What is it?"

Staring at the bar, he seemed at a loss for words. He didn't know why, but he felt compelled to respond, "I'm going to resign from the military, Lilly." He took another sip of Cognac and added, "It has been a difficult decision. Eric and I have even argued a lot because of it."

"I don't care about your choice of profession, Paul."

He sighed and said, "Thank you."

She ran her hand up and down his arm inside the sleeve.

He twitched a little and said, "Ouch." He wondered what it was, so he lifted his shirt sleeve and saw the bandage. He didn't remember placing it there.

"Did you scratch yourself?"

He couldn't remember, so he took a guess. "Oh, I must have caught my arm on…the shirt hanger hook. It's nothing serious."

She took the final sip, then said, "Okay, are you ready to leave?"

***

Nikulin sat in the hotel lobby pretending to read a newspaper. He understood people speaking English. Lowering the paper just enough, he observed a man and woman walk to one of the elevators. He recognized Remmich but not the woman. They were the only ones to get onto the elevator. The Russian spy walked briskly to look at the floor indicator and saw the number where the elevator stopped.

He then walked to the other end of the lobby and sat in a secluded area. He telephoned the embassy. The ambassador answered. “Mr. Linkov, I am in the hotel where the white American is staying. He is also with a woman. What do you want me to do?”

“Stay with him. Get a room for yourself tonight. Get up early and wait in the lobby. I’m sure you’ll spot them.”

Nikulin walked up to the registration desk, asked for a room, and completed a registration form.

His accent didn’t strike the attendant as unusual, especially since so many foreigners came to Amsterdam. She ran his credit card through the register while getting a plastic card key.

“Do you have luggage, Mr. Nikulin?”

“Oh, it’s a small piece, and I have a few office materials. It’s not heavy. Don’t bother to ring for a bellhop. Thank you anyway.” He walked away.

***

Saturday morning brought the sound of traffic through the open window. Lilly woke first. She noticed the bandage had come off. There was a dark red spot with a tiny scab. *That’s not a scratch,* she reasoned. Her hand gently massaged his temple, which caused him to take a deep breath and turn on his back.

They were naked. The man-animal moaned like a dog yawning. She laughed at his antics. He turned on his side and faced her. Their noses rubbed and he moved closer, his fingers trailing over her bare skin. She turned onto her back. They made love slowly at first, then more passionately. Her arching back and soft moans urged his movement. As their excitement peaked and then gradually abated, she shivered with one last orgasm.

He kissed her soft lips, and they rolled to the side entwined, still facing one another.

He knew he should do it differently and have a ring to give her right then, but he was too anxious. "Lilly, will you marry me?"

Her eyes were coy as she smiled and said, "Yes, I will marry you. I wondered when you were going to ask me." Her cheeks glowed with joy.

She lay on her back, and he repositioned himself on the side of her to get closer. As they rested, distracting thoughts passed through Paul's mind, including his resignation, living in Amsterdam, going to the dentist, and maintaining a friendship with Eric.

It was the last idea about his friend that took the longest to consider. His silence made her ask, "What are you thinking?"

"Mostly things related to us, and one aspect in particular. I won't have to drive here anymore. We'll be together."

"And we'll live here, so we won't have to buy living quarters. You won't have to find a job."

He knew the answer about living there, and jokingly asked, "Oh, really? I understand the information about getting married and living here. But what other plans have you made for me?"

She elaborated about the wedding and beyond. He listened to her talk about a job after his resignation. Mr. Van Horn said if Remmich became a civilian, he'd offer a job to him. Remmich already knew the tasks included traveling and wine buying. It would reduce her father's travel responsibilities.

"Do you remember we have our family get-together and dinner this evening?" He nodded. "Tonight, I will have a big reason to want my family to get together." She laughed and ended with, "They're going to be surprised."

They discussed a possible nuptial date, his future job, and how much longer he would stay in the military.

"Eric is coming this evening, isn't he?"

"He agreed to get together, but he met a woman last night who is a commercial airline captain. I'm not sure what his plans are now." He hesitated for a few seconds and then said, "Maybe we should tell him to bring…" He paused, searching his memory. "Candice."

"Yes. Fine. But we should keep Eric far from my father."

"Why? Doesn't he like black men?"

"No, he's not prejudiced. I meant my father would want to talk on and on with him, and he might ask about their relationship. He's nosy and may think it's a bit hasty and quiz him about his intentions. Do you understand?" she said.

"Actually, no. I don't."

"Being a father of two girls has made him cautious and protective. Remember, Paul, we never told him about me staying at your flat in Germany. It took over a year before he agreed to let you stay here and not have to pay as a guest."

Remmich laughed in a low tone and said, "I'll bet he compares the situation of young people to himself and your mother."

Lilly leveled a stern gaze at him. "You don't think my parents slept together when they were falling in love, do you?"

Remmich nodded. She pinched him without hurting. When they stopped laughing, he said, "Well, yes, I understand. Your father does like to talk and be everyone's advisor."

Lilly told him to meet her down in the kitchen for breakfast. After she left, Remmich telephoned the front desk to leave a message for Eric, who was still asleep.

The hot shower was therapeutic for Remmich's neck and upper back. The scab washed off, which caused a stinging sensation. He turned away to stop the shower water from irritating the area. While the pain subsided, he contemplated buying an engagement ring. Most of the Dutch jewelry stores were members of the Benelux Alliance. They'd discovered diamonds centuries before in South Africa. It was also their slave-trading years. The business of buying, selling, and trading was the best in Europe.

Many European people visited Holland, Belgium, or Luxembourg to acquire diamond and gold jewelry. It was Saturday, and the stores were open.

Before meeting Lilly for breakfast, Remmich wanted to find jewelry store locations. He stopped at the front desk and asked one of the attendants, who wrote down several firms within the Rembrandtplein district. Remmich realized one was just at the end of the street. He needed to find out her finger size, so he called her sister, Anna. She agreed to meet him after eating and bring one of Lilly's rings.

During breakfast, Lilly explained she had to work all day.

They finished and went their respective ways. Remmich left a note at the front desk for Eric, inviting him to the dinner with Candice.

Anna met him at the other end of the hotel at the Brasserie-Schiller bar section. She gave him one of the rings Lilly often wore.

The Van Moppes Diamonds store was just down the street, so Remmich decided to go there. The owner, Peter Van Moppes, came from a long family line of jewelers. Remmich entered the store and walked to a glass counter. A clerk offered assistance. "I'm looking for an engagement ring."

Mr. Van Moppes overheard them. He approached and introduced himself. "Do you know her size?" Remmich handed Anna's ring to him. The assistant took it to size. Van Moppes told another assistant to bring out a large green cloth pouch. He selected one of the small sacks inside holding six diamonds: the largest weighed one carat, three were a half-carat each, and two were a quarter carat each. He handed a loupe to Remmich. While he looked at the diamonds, Mr. Van Moppes explained the cuts and the clarity quality. Then, he arranged them in place and explained the diamonds would look best if the large one and two small ones were set for an engagement ring. The three half-carat diamonds could be secured in a wedding band; they would align correctly. Remmich liked the diamonds' settings and agreed with the quoted price.

He explained the circumstances and asked if the engagement ring could be ready later in the afternoon. The jeweler told him if he bought all six, Paul could pick up the engagement ring at 5:30. He was advised the other three diamonds could remain in the vault until he needed the wedding ring. There was no charge to hold them. Remmich agreed and put nine thousand dollars on his American Express. He was satisfied dealing with an importer because a regular store would have charged him fifteen thousand or more.

Remmich returned to the Hotel Schiller around 2:00. The front desk attendant recognized him. He waved and told Remmich he had a note. Eric Miller wrote, "Candice will join me for the party. We will be strolling around the city for most of the day." Remmich asked the receptionist if he could use the lobby phone to call Lilly because his cell phone was dead. Her sister Anna came to the reception desk and told him Lilly was taking a nap. He handed the ring to her and talked about his purchase. Anna was thrilled and promised she would be discreet.

A nap sounded good to Remmich, especially since he didn't get a restful night's sleep. He instructed the front desk attendant to ring his room at 4:30.

He awoke, perspiring, though the room was cool. His body shook like a vibrating motor. *What is happening?* He grabbed a tissue and wiped his face to remove the sweat. The telephone rang. It was the front desk with his wake-up call. After he hung up, he wondered if perhaps it was the stress of the upcoming days and months. There was something else, but his conscious mind couldn't grasp what it was. "Oh well," he said to himself, then got up, took another shower, dressed in a sports coat outfit, and left for the Van Moppes jewelry store.

The Van Horns celebrated family reunions three times a year: a summer get-together, at Christmastime, and Easter. This wasn't the first one Paul had attended, but it was his first springtime event. Sometimes military leave was out of the question. Summertime NATO meetings interfered with visiting Amsterdam. Remmich returned to the hotel and walked into the dining area as the waiters placed dinner wines on the table. Remmich picked up a glass of champagne and was told the oysters were off-limits until the full family arrived. He heard Miller laughing behind him and turned around.

"I listened to the waiter say the oysters are off-limits, pal. Disappointed?"

"Very much so."

Remmich switched his attention. "Hello, Candice. I'm so glad you are here, despite the company you had to bring." She laughed.

Miller was about to counter when the Van Horns entered the room. It was now 6:45 and the other guests were still not there. Mr. Van Horn finally relented, and Karelle told the waiters to begin serving all of the appetizers, including the fresh oysters.

"How can you stand to eat those things?" Candice asked.

Miller put five oysters in the half shell on his plate, squeezed lemon juice over them, and spooned a little cocktail sauce on each. With the cocktail fork, he lifted one off the shell and offered it to her. She made a face but accepted. "Chew it a little, rather than just swallowing it, Candice. Trust me. You'll enjoy it." Her facial expression was indescribable. Eric, Paul, Lilly, and her sister laughed.

"Come on, Candice. You're a real international person. I'm sure you've eaten unusual appetizers or snacks before," said Remmich.

She ate the oyster and sauce. After a few moments, she said, "I kind of like it. Can I try another one, please?"

Miller forked another one for her. "You're gonna eat all my oysters."

Remmich motioned his buddy to follow him to the end of the table. Candice took the fork and plate. With their backs to the guests, Miller asked, "What's up?"

Remmich reached into the coat pocket and pulled out a ring box. After opening it, Miller quietly said, "Wow, this is beautiful! When did you buy this?"

"This afternoon." He explained how the jeweler suggested the design.

"Oh, man, I can't wait to watch her reaction. When are you going to give it to her?"

"As soon as I get a chance to refill her champagne."

Candice walked up to them and asked, "What were you two talking about?"

Miller guided her to the side and explained Paul's plan. She smiled, pleased about what was going to happen.

Lilly screamed. She held her glass up and saw something sparkling at the bottom. Remmich couldn't hide his smile, and he asked, "Well, aren't you going to get it out?"

She drank the full glass of the champagne and then struggled to get the ring out of the glass. Remmich got a cloth napkin and helped to dry it and her hand. She let him fit the ring onto her finger. She smiled and displayed it to her parents and sister, her fiancé beside her. Her father congratulated Paul. Her mother kissed her future son-in-law and then hugged Lilly. Anna hugged both of them, and the guests toasted.

***

On Sunday morning, Remmich mumbled in his sleep. It woke Lilly. She looked at the clock. It was 7:45. He lay on his back, sweating, and his body trembled a little. Waking up, the shakes stopped. Lilly witnessed everything. She wiped off the sweat with a tissue. It calmed him.

She listened to him describe having the same experience the day before.

"Yesterday?"

"Yes. I didn't say anything because it didn't seem important. Anyway, we were both busy, and I honestly forgot to tell you." He lifted her left hand to look at the ring.

She smiled and said, "Yes, it was an important day. I will never forget it." She hugged him and asked, "But are you feeling better now?"

"Yes, thank you."

The cell phone rang unexpectedly. Remmich answered and said, "Good morning to you too, Eric. How did you sleep after the fun and excitement last night?" Another voice asked who was on the line. Remmich chuckled and said, "Do I hear a woman's voice in the background?"

Miller laughed, and said, "Yeah. You don't miss anything, do you?"

Remmich chuckled and said to meet at 11:00 in the main restaurant for brunch. They hung up.

Lilly looked at the clock. It was 8:10. I have time to clean up, dress, and get down to the kitchen." She thought for a moment and added, "Let's have eggs Benedict."

Brunch time consumed over an hour. The waiter brought a ticket for Lilly to sign. Soon afterward she looked at her fiancé and asked, "What time are you leaving tomorrow?"

"After lunch."

"Candice, when are you leaving?" Lilly asked.

"Not until Tuesday. We're having a meeting about skyjacking. The presentation is being given by the British Secret Service. It's mandatory for my crew and me. There'll be about a dozen crews attending. Afterward, our flight departs Amsterdam at 5:30 for New York."

"Would you and Eric care to walk around with us and see some of the sights around here today?"

She smiled at her new boyfriend and declared, "Sure, "I'd love to."

The future Mrs. Remmich proudly escorted her fiancé and their friends through sections of Rembrandtplein. "It's named for one of the world's most famous artists, who lived in the 1600s. The word translates to 'Rembrandt lived here.'" They followed her into a few merchants' stores. She greeted those who weren't busy, introducing her fiancé and their friends to a few of the merchants. It wasn't by accident on the way back to the hotel the group stopped at the Van Moppes jewelry store. Candice told Eric she wanted to go inside. Remmich overheard her statement and smiled.

Candice asked why the building had such steep outside steps leading to the landing and entrance door. Lilly explained it was an architectural design dating centuries earlier to repel rising waters from storms and high tides. They walked inside, where a sign on the wall read in Dutch, "Family Business Since 1828." While Candice and Eric admired items in the jewelry cases, the owner and his wife recognized Paul Remmich. She smiled, and Peter Van Moppes walked over to shake Paul's hand and congratulate the couple.

Walking along the street to return to the hotel, Miller spotted a tall man who looked somewhat familiar. The guy had a similar build to the tall thug in Stockholm. He waved it off as a coincidence.

***

The Russian spy stood off to the side of the hotel. He watched a black man and a black woman accompanying Paul and Lilly. He used his cell phone and took some pictures before walking into the hotel. He decided to stay one more night.

***

The Iraqi Embassy thug followed the foursome as they walked around. It was not a good time to approach Miller, but the torment and anger lingered. He had a plan to get revenge, but not yet.

15

And Something More

Paul's eyes opened on Memorial Day to daylight coming in from the sides of the window curtains. It was 7:30. He felt Lilly's warm body next to him. When turning onto his back, his heart rate unexpectedly increased. Waking up more, he repositioned the pillow and leaned against the backboard. The thoughts in his mind were jumbled: Visiting the Blues Alley the night before, resigning, and the wish to help Third World countries. He knew something was different but couldn't grasp what it was or bring the matter to the forefront of his controlled mind. His bride-to-be moved more in his direction and interrupted the spell. He stood up on the side of the bed and walked into the bathroom. He decided to have a warm shower to relieve the unexplained stiffness in his neck.

Lilly woke up when she heard the shower. She dressed and walked into the steaming bathroom. Tapping on the glass door and looking closely, she saw his naked body in a hot cloud. His attention focused on her and she said, "I'm going to my quarters. I'll call you and give the time for brunch."

Later, Remmich packed his belongings. There was nothing else to do for the moment. He sat down and cleared old calls and some email messages from his cell phone. When finished, he watched a Dutch television game show. He thought it was comical, even juvenile because of the antics of the participants. Not being able to understand the language made it even more boring. But American and British game shows seemed kind of ridiculous to him also. The cell phone buzzed; it was Lilly telling him to meet at 10:00.

The four of them sat together in the main restaurant for over an hour talking and eating. Remmich looked at his watch and said, "The weekend together was fun, but we need to leave." After the men signed out, they drove to Germany. Candice took a cab back to the airport hotel.

Holland highway traffic increased the further they got out of Amsterdam. "Did you ever drive back this late on a Monday before?"

Irritably, he said, "Yes, the traffic is heavy, but there aren't any holdups."

His friend seemed uptight. *It was one of Remmich's odd moments. What's bugging him?* He was physically there driving a car, but his mind seemed far away. Again, he realized he didn't understand why Remmich's attitude to resign was so definite. They took an exit off the highway, which linked to the Autobahn south to Cologne and Frankfurt.

Almost an hour later, Miller noticed his friend's shoulders rested against the back of the seat. He gripped the steering wheel in a more relaxed way, and his face appeared tranquil.

Remmich saw an exit sign ahead and suggested, "Hey, let's make a pit stop."

"I thought you'd never ask."

He turned off the ramp and headed to a parking area. They got out, stretched, and went into the Badzimmern building that housed public restrooms, fast food, and news and trinket shops. When they got back to the car, Miller asked to drive. Remmich smiled and flung the keys to him before getting into the BMW. The rest of the ride to Würzburg was relaxing for Remmich; he napped.

He navigated strictly from memory into Würzburg. They passed the entrance to the castle. Arriving at the lower hill area, he remembered to turn right. Minutes later the MP guard at Leighton Barracks noted the car's bumper sticker and saluted as they passed.

Miller returned the salute and headed for the PX lot where he parked.

"Paul, wake up." He nudged him. "Hey, we're home!"

He squinted from the sunlight. "Oh."

"You slept so soundly, the tractor-trailers didn't even wake you up."

Remmich spoke in a low tone. "Yeah, I suppose I did."

They shook hands and Miller thanked him for sharing their weekend.

Remmich swallowed and acted as if he needed to talk more. "Take your time," advised Miller.

Paul closed his eyes and caught his breath. "I don't know what's bothering me."

Miller wondered if it was from a bad dream. Instead, he asked, "Do you think you're getting the flu?"

"No. It's something else. I can't explain it."

"Try."

He stared at the floor and added, "I can't describe it, because I don't know."

Miller wasn't sure if the odd condition was related to his long disappearance Saturday night. He wondered if Remmich felt guilty.

He rubbed his neck. "I had the same neck stiffness a couple times this weekend." He hesitated for a moment. "Something is bothering me, but I can't recall what it is or what I wanted to do about it."

"What do you mean?"

The answer didn't come right away. Miller waited, thinking. He wanted to find out if there was more to the puzzle with the other woman. His buddy began to speak in a rational way, disregarding the question. "I'm feeling better now," Remmich responded.

"Get some rest. We've had a busy weekend, and we're not used to three days of partying. Being out half the night and playing tourist during the daytime is exhausting. I'm even tired and glad we got back."

"Yeah, I guess you're right." He sat straight against the seatback and ended with, "Hey, thanks for sticking around."

"Well, that's what friends are for."

Miller wanted to know if his colleague really felt better and decided to tease him. "Since Candice's flight schedule includes Amsterdam, when are we going back? My reasons are almost as righteous as yours now."

They laughed while he stepped out of the car. Miller lifted his bag out of the back, pushed the button to close the trunk, and waited for Remmich to drive off. He went to his car and drove to his own apartment building.

Remmich rested for the rest of the day. When it was dark, he chose to stay in the apartment.

For dinner, he opened a can of chicken noodle soup. A while later he fell asleep while reading *Newsweek*. Around 9:00 he woke up when the cell phone rang. It was Tara Yako.

He picked up the phone and heard the six words. "It…is…a…cloudy…day…outside." He repeated the same words, which put him into a deep trance. She reminded him to contact the dentist for an appointment. "Copy this number and name."

***

On Tuesday morning he called Miller and explained he still wasn't feeling good and stayed home for another day.

***

Wednesday morning brought international concerns into the S-2 office. Military intelligence information from the NATO Internet service arrived. The items included the North Korean agreement to dismantle nuclear weapons. ISIS declared a caliphate rule would stretch across Syria and into Iraq. There was a concern because the Iranian government reopened their plutonium factories. Their argument was they needed electrical energy from nuclear power plants for homes and factories. Either way, ballistic missile air attacks could become a reality. Members learned that the next target for ISIS to attack was probably in Europe. Iran targeted Middle East traitors. Korea's agreement could not be trusted. They needed to show further disarmament. If either matter escalated, military war stations in Europe, the Middle East, and Asia would have to be relocated. The Western Alliance knew that reorganizing defense centers took time.

Remmich entered the room. Everyone stopped talking. He figured it meant they were upset about the resignation. *He knew they liked him.* As he sat down, McClain handed him printed emails regarding the international situation. "Sir, you need to review these and initial, so I can fax them to V Corps stating we read them."

Miller entered minutes later and sat at his desk.

Remmich leafed through several of the pages and stated, "Eric, I want you to look these over also."

Miller finished reading two of the documents and said, "I believe we need to inform Colonel Collins."

"Agreed. Especially since you'll be assuming the responsibilities."

Twenty minutes later they returned to the office. Remmich told his master sergeant to return the reviewed data.

Remmich noticed a pile of security intelligence applications on his desk. The workload never decreased. "Jesus, if it's not the escalation of international threats, there's always another problem," complained Remmich.

Miller didn't want to talk about it. "Let's get on with business."

"Sergeant, give half of these to Captain Miller."

For the next hour, they reviewed the individual pages of fourteen soldiers applying for top-secret security clearances. If approved, they could operate top-secret mechanical equipment from computers, including tanks and missiles. They signed most of the papers. A few were rejected due to lack of information.

"I believe we're finished." Remmich placed the batch of documents into a desk file. The wall clock indicated it was 8:58. "McClain, these are to be sent to the Pentagon. Put them into a return envelope, and then you can break for coffee."

"Yes, sir."

"Paul, ready for the snack bar?"

"Let me make an appointment with my dentist first. Save a seat for me. I'll be with you in ten minutes."

Most of the soldiers followed Miller out of the security office. Remmich, McClain, and an E-4 stayed behind. He started to look in the armed forces telephone directory. He was somewhat mystified; it wasn't clear why Dr. Mustafa's number was already in his head. He didn't recall ever meeting the dentist. He called and made an appointment. He wrote the date and time in his date binder and left for the snack bar.

16

Snack Bar Revelations

The snack bar was more crowded than usual. Remmich concentrated on the line of people. Sophie, the newsstand sales lady, said in her German accent, "Gut morning, Captain Remmich."

He smiled and returned the greeting. Again, he focused on people and saw Colonel Collins sitting with three other officers. His friend had involved himself in discussion with another group at the table next to his. Remmich got a cup of coffee and picked up a clear-boxed croissant sandwich.

He walked to the colonel's table. Collins beat him to the punch and commented, "With the look on your face, Captain, I assume you're going to ask if your resignation information arrived."

"That's correct, sir. Has Stuttgart sent my paperwork?"

"I expect to get something later today or tomorrow. I'll let you know." He sipped and added, "Although I wish you'd change your mind." The other soldiers of rank sitting at the table stared at Remmich.

He ignored them. "Thank you, sir."

He sat down at his buddy's table and unwrapped the breakfast.

"You finally made it here," said Miller. "How are you feeling this morning?"

"Much better." He bit into the croissant and sipped some coffee.

"I rarely see you eat breakfast. Didn't you eat dinner last night?"

"Just a can of soup."

Without any warning, Remmich started to complain about the Third World issues. His hypnotized, subconscious mind focused on this argument. Miller admitted it was an aggravating situation for all concerned, not just the Mideast.

The sympathetic remark had no effect on Remmich. He finished breakfast and took another sip of the coffee.

Miller had an urge to argue but it was tempered by rational thinking. *Why did his friend want to resign? Something wasn't right. Why was he so protective of these countries?* Maintaining eye contact with Remmich, he repeated the biggest challenge to ending terrorism: Prevent money getting to those militant fundamentalists, or murderers. There was no reaction from Remmich. He mentioned how the top funders of terrorism were wealthy sheiks in Saudi Arabia and large corporations in the Persian Gulf area. He reminded him about the report revealing constant funding laundered through banks in the United States and England. Remmich still didn't comment.

Miller wasn't giving up. He harped on Iraq's history of ignoring ISIS' pursuits. "I disagree," retorted Remmich finally. "Iraq has always objected to their quests." He tried once again to defend Iraq's efforts to abolish neglect of poor nations.

Miller's aggravation level rose again, but winning the argument was not the solution. He paused to sip coffee. Changing the subject to an off-the-wall question, he asked, "I don't remember you telling me when the wedding date is scheduled. Have you and Lilly made plans yet?"

Remmich responded as if they had never argued. He sat forward. Smiling. "She had already made them."

"Well, it's beginning to show who controls whom between the sheets." They both laughed.

Sidetracking the subject again he asked, "Did you make your dental appointment?"

"Yes. It's tomorrow morning."

"That soon?"

"I guess it was the right time of day. I'm lucky."

You've been there before, haven't you?"

"Numerous times. But this is an appointment with the main guy."

"Who is he?"

Remmich thought for a moment. "Damn, I had his name in my head just a little while ago. Oh… Dr. Mustafa."

Saying the dentist's name triggered a subconscious response in Remmich and he mentioned poor nations again.

Miller changed the approach and decided to discern his friend's tolerance level. He offered an off-the-wall comment. "It's not only mind-boggling that terrorist money can be wired so quickly to anywhere, but it's also frightening. You don't know when a Middle East country will strike." He swallowed some coffee and watched.

Remmich's manipulated mind reacted to the statement in an aggressive way. He objected. "It seems you are assuming Iraq has a partnership with ISIS. It's totally false. Instead, the extremists are comrades with Syria."

Miller leaned forward in the chair and put his arms on the table. Finally, he replied, "I agree with your statement. Syria and ISIS are an international problem. But don't forget, ISIS was born out of the US invasion of Iraq in 2003."

Remmich was silent while he pulled a cigarette out of the box and lit up. He looked troubled.

"Paul, why do you get so emotionally worked up about these matters? I can't figure it out."

Remmich took a long drag, blowing the smoke out of his nostrils. With both hands, he fiddled with the wrapped striker on the empty match pack. Once again, the act entertained Miller; it was a dexterous performance. *Weird!* Miller thought silently.

"Thinking about the past and present global circumstances, I believe no one gives a damn. My military time was so-so. But my future is going to be aligned with progress."

They were both silent; Remmich fidgeted with the wrapping. He stubbed out the cigarette and dropped it into the ashtray. Drinking his last sip, he said, "Let's return to work, Eric."

Collins saw them return. He entered their workplace and focused on Remmich. "Stuttgart has contacted me. I want to discuss a few items with you about the resignation."

"I'll be there in fifteen minutes."

Nearby soldiers looked concerned. Miller turned away and didn't say anything. He shuffled through additional individual security clearance forms. He put them down and began to review another paper.

The colonel's office was across the hall. He knocked lightly on the open door. "Come in, Captain. Please, take a seat."

"Thank you, sir. You have something for me?"

"This meeting is for two reasons. First, I received a verbal go-ahead to talk to you. I want you to be aware the debriefing will be done at Patch Barracks. What we're doing now is just a preview. Second, you have the right to change your mind." He hesitated for a few seconds and looked into the captain's eyes. "Shall I continue?"

"Please do, sir."

It took twenty minutes to review ten items. Remmich had to agree to them before the military would set up a resignation conference. "You carry a greater risk to the United States than, say, First Sergeant Randolph down the hall. You know a lot. Your involvement with military intelligence matters educated you beyond your training at Fort Huachuca. In other words, we just can't kick you out and ignore your status. You have been a tremendous asset to us, and until Stuttgart notifies you of a face-to-face discussion, I hope you'll change your mind."

Remmich smiled. "I understand. However, my decision is final."

"Do you have any idea when V Corps will notify me?"

"I don't. Like you, I'm just a part of a larger framework. When I find out you'll be the first to know. Until then, you are expected to work as usual." Remmich had to initial each line item. The colonel initialed each item also. "A copy of this will be placed in your personnel file. That's all, Captain."

Remmich returned to his workplace and sat down. His buddy chose not to ask what went on because he was aggravated. He had another document in his hand, which he continued to read.

Remmich interrupted him. "What are you looking at?"

"This is about an advanced encryption course at Patch Barracks."

"Oh, they're offering the course again. You think you will enroll?"

"I'd like to, but we'll have to see how much I can handle after you leave."

They used the rest of the day to review the security clearance applications.

At 4:00, everyone but Paul Remmich decided to call it a day. He stayed behind and played around on the computer. Tomorrow he was going to meet the dentist.

17

The Comfortable Chair

Faisal Mustafa's office was on the second floor of the PX shopping mall at Leighton Barracks. There were nine dentists there who specialized in various procedures. Five were US Army dentists, and four were foreigners. The Americans identified with Mustafa, even though he came from the Middle East. He liked to discuss international politics, not being partial. And American football was a favorite sport of his.

Remmich walked into a crowded reception room. He walked up to the receptionist and identified himself. She looked at her list and spoke in heavily accented English, "Ja, gut morning, Captain. Ve've been expecting you. I'll let him know you are here. Please, sit down."

A current edition of *Time* was on one of the tables. He had only turned a couple pages before he was interrupted. It was a voice with an accent that was not German.

The man extended his hand. "I am Dr. Faisal Mustafa. It's good to meet you in person." They shook hands, and the dentist added, "Please, follow me."

The assistant directed Remmich to sit in the armchair. He relaxed as she lowered the retractable right arm. "Is this good?"

He rested his arm and said, "Yes. Thank you."

She left the room. There wasn't much to do except be patient and look at the pictures on the wall, one a colorful scene of Marienberg Castle when the vineyards were fully leafed.

Dr. Mustafa entered the room with a chart. Another assistant followed him carrying two sets of long plastic mouthpieces containing electronic sensors. She told him to open wide and bite down on the plastic. She checked its placement. "Open again, Captain." She readjusted the mouthpiece. "Okay, now bite down slowly." She changed the position of his head, and added, "Don't move." The assistant maneuvered an x-ray machine and took two images, one on either side of his jaw.

Mustafa stood between him and the computer screen to examine the results. There were no signs of cavities. He did not want to show the jaw images to the patient. Instead, he left the room with all of Remmich's information. He returned minutes later and inserted another flash drive into the computer. It showed a different image with a cavity.

"As you see, Captain, this is a very deep cavity on your right side. We can either remove the tooth or do a root canal by drilling into it to remove the cavity. That would involve deadening the nerves and filling the space. Which do you prefer?" *He didn't mention filling a tooth cavity did not always include nerve deadening.*

Remmich seemed stunned. "Strange," he said. "I've never felt any pain. What are the reasons for this?"

Mustafa was prepared for this question. "It is in the beginning stages, Captain, but your decay is close to the root nerve. Usually, a good gum structure and root will deter pain until the tooth is further decayed. To what extent I can't say as everyone is different. But I want to prevent further decay in your tooth."

Remmich didn't say anything while he looked at the images. He couldn't argue. "Well, I don't want to have my molar pulled, and so a root canal it is, I guess."

"I think it's the better choice. However, it is a lengthy procedure, and we will have to make another appointment. Today, let's finish up this preliminary visit with a thorough gum exam and teeth cleaning. Be sure to check with my receptionist and set up another appointment next week. Do not drink any alcoholic beverages the night before you come, and don't eat breakfast. Both are precautions to prepare for the surgery." Mustafa left to assist the other dental surgeons with their patients.

Remmich made an appointment for the next Wednesday at 0800 hours.

He returned to Hindenburg Kaserne at 11:30 and wondered if Miller wanted to go to lunch in town at Klaus's uncle's restaurant. After asking, his friend jumped up and was on his feet so fast everyone in the office laughed. He got his cap, stepped up to the door, and said, "I'm ready, Captain. Lead the way!"

The restaurant was somewhat crowded. The proprietor's wife, Gisela, greeted Paul and met Eric. They shook hands, and she guided them to a table. "Bier?" she asked in broken English.

Remmich looked at his buddy, who started shaking his head no.

"*Bitte, nur zwei* Colas, Gisela. *Danke.*"

"That sounded like a couple Cokes, right?" said Miller.

"You're catching on fast, my good man." They adjusted themselves better, and Remmich wanted to know, "Have you ever had a root canal?"

"Hell no! I think I'd get my tooth pulled, instead." He squirmed around, shook his upper torso, and made low-volume grunts.

Remmich laughed. "Are you doing a dance or something?"

"Why'd you have to ask? Damn! Just the thought gives me the willies."

Remmich filled him in on his dental visit while they ate. They finished lunch and returned to the office at 1300 hours.

***

Later in the afternoon, Mustafa spoke with Iyad Aboona in Istanbul. He was to build the computer chip. The dentist said, "I'm faxing the dimensions of the molar."

Aboona called Dr. Mustafa back after dinnertime. He explained a three-millimeter electronic computer chip might be too small for the tooth. He advised a four-millimeter size because it provided a stronger vibration. Mustafa hesitated before he answered. “Why don’t you craft both sizes? And be present for the postsurgical testing.” He gave the date and time.

Aboona telephoned the Istanbul international airport and was put on hold. While waiting, he studied the dimensions of the molar. He believed the tooth could fit the bigger chip. The ticket agent’s voice interrupted his concentration. After securing a seat, he telephoned the dentist’s office and gave the assistant his flight information.

***

Remmich checked in with the receptionist. He didn’t even have time to open a magazine after sitting. “Captain Remmich, will you follow me, please?” asked a cute assistant dressed in a white lab coat. They walked the corridor into a different exam room. The seating was just as comfortable, but there were no pictures on the wall and no music. She lowered the armrest. Next to the wall was a stand covered with a white cloth.

“Good morning, Captain Remmich,” said Dr. Mustafa as he hurried through the door. The dental assistant removed the white cloth, revealing surgical items and a syringe. Mustafa directed the patient. “Right now, I want you to take this sedative pill to relax before being hypnotized.”

Mustafa instructed his assistant to give Remmich a cup of water and a red pill. They left the room for twenty minutes. When they returned, they checked to see whether the medicine had taken effect. Remmich’s eyelids were drooping, and he looked almost asleep. Standing in front of him, Mustafa commanded, “Look at me, Paul.” Their eyes met, and Remmich heard the six words given to him the night he first became hypnotized: "It…is…a…cloudy…day …outside." Mustafa repeated the words slowly without losing eye contact, "It…is…a…cloudy…day…outside." He repeated the sentence one more time. "Say it, Paul."

"It…is…a…cloudy…day…outside."

"Again, Paul."

Remmich did. At Mustafa's instruction, he repeated it two more times, only slower. This time, Remmich went into a more profound, subliminal condition. The assistant dimmed the lights and walked out. Mustafa told him, "You are becoming very relaxed, Paul. You are feeling calm. You will not feel any pain in your mouth or teeth."

So that he could bring him out of the deeper trance, Mustafa said, "When I speak the words 'The...sun...is...shining...outside,' you will resume awareness of your surroundings. Do you understand?"

Remmich answered calmly, "Yes."

The assistant lowered the back of the chair all the way. She pressed a floor switch to raise it. She also reduced the room lighting, uncovered the projector, and moved the stand closer to the other side. She turned it on and adjusted the lens. The ceiling became a mesmerizing sight of stars moving through outer space.

"Watch the moving galaxy of stars, Paul. I want you to look at the stars." Remmich's eyes fixed on the scene above him, and Mustafa said, "Open your mouth, Paul." The assistant put in a brace to prevent Remmich from closing his mouth.

Turning on a small light attached to the seating assembly, the assistant focused it below Remmich's eye level. Mustafa then stuck the syringe's needle first into the outer gum and then on the inner side of the molar. The patient didn't move. He watched the display on the oval ceiling. While his attention was fixed, Mustafa and the assistant left the room.

Iyad Aboona walked into the surgical room and laid out a set of tools. He plugged the control box into a wall receptor. Its purpose was to send electronic transmission waves to the satellite and from there to the implanted microchip. The chip would vibrate in the tooth. With the destroyed nerve, the gum and mandible bone could feel the vibration.

Mustafa and his surgical assistant walked back into the room. She put the disc containing the X-rays into the computer, and the screen displayed the tooth. Mustafa began to drill out the crown section and inner pulp. The assistant sprayed Remmich's mouth with water, using a vacuum attachment to suck out the liquid and debris. The doctor now had a better view of the hollow space. For the next fifteen minutes, he used a thin stainless-steel rod to emulsify the inner root. As he worked, the assistant kept Paul's mouth clean by spraying it with water and suctioning out any debris. They took an image and displayed it on the computer screen so they could see the root sections at the jawbone. Mustafa measured the drilled-out area of the bottom molar. It wasn't broad or deep enough, so they removed more of the inner tooth.

The dentist, using pointed tweezers to clutch the computer chip, dropped the three-by-three-millimeter chip into the tooth opening. *Too small.* He removed it and did the same with the four-by-three-millimeter microchip. It went in deep enough so it could be surrounded by filling paste. The doctor removed the chip, smiling. "Iyad, this one fits better. We won't need the smaller chip."

"Thanks be to Allah," whispered Aboona in Arabic.

"Yes. The vibration will be much more evident to Paul."

The surgical assistant interrupted them. "Dr. Mustafa, we are prepared. I am starting to mix the ceramic filling paste."

He thanked her and turned to Aboona. "This microchip is going to be placed within a cement-like mixture called a flexible ceramic inlay. It's durable enough to withstand the tremendous chewing forces humans produce, and it's tough enough to protect the computer chip in place from being crushed." He primed the molar's drilled-out space to create an adhesive bond.

The assistant finished mixing the liquid and powder and said, "We are ready, Doctor."

Mustafa scooped a small amount of the filling onto a wood probe and smeared it around the bottom of the opening to fill in the root canal sections and the inner drilled section. He took the other end of the probe and pressed filling into the drilled-out space. Using another tool, he pushed the chip into the ceramic filling. More paste went around the chip before the surface was leveled. The assistant took out the brace and wiped Remmich's lips with a lip balm. Mustafa told Remmich to close his mouth and bite down. He counted to five and told him to open his mouth again. He shined the light on the filling and saw the indentation from the upper molar in the new filling surface.

He raised the back of the chair just enough for Remmich to be comfortable and to keep him looking at the leisurely revolving galaxy. Dr. Mustafa walked out with Aboona. "Let's wait about fifteen minutes while the ceramic hardens; then we'll do the necessary probes to assure the inlay is adhering."

He motioned to Aboona to follow him, and they walked outdoors onto the metal, fenced-in deck. "There seems to be a lot to see in this city. Do you enjoy living here, Dr. Mustafa?"

He told him there was much to see, including the historical Christian religious buildings, museums, and the castle. He stated that many of the more beautiful buildings were Gothic.

After fifteen minutes, they walked back into the surgical room. Their mole was still looking at the ceiling.

An assistant turned the projector off and switched the perimeter ceiling lights on but kept them low enough to prevent squinting.

Mustafa moved Remmich to an upright position. He looked into his eyes and said, "The...sun...is...shining...outside." He repeated slower, "The...sun...is...shining...outside." He was patient because Remmich was going to resume a lighter hypnotized state of mind. He looked into the patient's eyes and recited, "The…sun…is…shining…outside." Remmich blinked a couple times and swallowed. Finally, he focused on the dentist's eyes.

Although his patient was a little lightheaded, Mustafa introduced Remmich to Aboona. They shook hands, and Mustafa walked out.

Aboona told him to relax. He turned on the control transmitter and set the electronic contact at 1,000 volts. He pressed the button. The transmission beamed to the satellite in outer space, which relayed the message back to the microchip insert. A few seconds later, Remmich's head jerked.

Aboona lowered the transmitter to 750 volts. Almost immediately, Remmich's head jerked again. He blinked several times and swallowed. The voltage was still too intense.

After two more tries, Aboona set the transmitter at the lowest voltage to reach the satellite. Seconds later he asked, "Did your tooth vibrate this time, Paul?"

Remmich blinked and said he felt the vibration in his jaw, but it didn't hurt.

Aboona set the level higher at 550 volts, just to see the reaction. Remmich's face didn't move, but he claimed the "vibration" feeling became stronger.

"Wait here. I'm getting Dr. Mustafa."

They returned, and the dentist told Paul, "Look into my eyes." He waited a few seconds. "You are going to learn new communication procedures." Pointing to his cheek, he said, "First, when you feel the vibration in your tooth, you are to stay calm. If you are around people when it happens, just excuse yourself. The vibration is a signal for you to telephone this number. Read it out loud." Paul looked at Mustafa's phone showing Alzuhari's cell number and read it off. "Please repeat the number to me, Paul."

Remmich repeated the number.

"Excellent, Paul."

He explained the second procedure, which was Remmich could only use his cell phone to return a call to Adnaw Alzuhari in Amsterdam or to Mustafa in Würzburg. He was told not to use a military phone when he felt the buzz.

"Paul, do you know what my telephone number is?"

"Yes, I remember it."

"Tell me, Paul."

"Your telephone number is zero, two, two, eight, two, eight, seven, nine, two, zero, zero."

"Repeat it again, Paul," instructed Mustafa. He did. "Good. Now repeat Adnaw's number."

Dr. Mustafa looked at his schedule book and Aboona. "We need to work together tomorrow to check on today's surgery. We will have Paul practice making phone calls using his cell phone."

Mustafa and Aboona spent a few minutes deciding on a password for Remmich to use when returning the calls. The decision was his initials, P-S-R.

Remmich left after he received the dentist's appointment card that gave the date and time for his return the next day at 0800 hours.

Dr. Mustafa telephoned the Istanbul office. He described the implant success. He handed Aboona the phone and explained the outcome of his tests. Yildiz, pleased, congratulated them.

The dentist walked away while Aboona telephoned Alzuhari and Yako. He explained Remmich making telephone calls to the dentist's office over the next few days for training. "Adnaw, you are to make a call to him on Saturday morning. Paul's computer chip will receive vibrations from the satellite. I gave him your telephone number, and he has memorized it. Also, calibrate the electronic boxes you and Tara have to a voltage of 550."

***

Thursday's dental visit was stimulating for Remmich, quite literally. Each time he received a soft vibration in his tooth, he made a personal call from his cell phone to Dr. Mustafa's phone.

Before he left the dentist's office at 11:30 to return to Hindenburg Kaserne, Mustafa instructed Remmich to bring his schedule, both personal and work, during June.

June 30 was the day of his resignation.

***

It was Friday, the last practice day. Mustafa knew Yildiz wanted to get the show on the road. He instructed Aboona to get Remmich's personal and work schedule, which he faxed to Alzuhari. The vibration had created a Pavlovian routine for Remmich.

18

Resignation

On Saturday morning the apartment smelled like coffee and a toasting English muffin. Remmich was in a good mood sitting at the two-chair dinette table looking at the *Stars and* Stripes newspaper. The front-page headlines weren't very interesting today. The toaster popped up the muffin halves. He preferred seedless raspberry jam on them. He poured coffee while chewing his first bite. When his cell phone buzzed and rang at the same time, he finished pouring before he answered it.

"You up yet?" asked Miller in a teasing way.

Paul swallowed his muffin bite and said, "This is like any other day of the week. I always get up early. When did you get back from the encryption seminar at the command center?" He took another bite and listened.

"Yesterday afternoon, a little after 2:00, but I didn't want to come into the office. I went to my pad, relaxed, and called my folks in Ann Arbor." He heard chewing and sipping. "You eating?"

"Yes. Breakfast."

"Thought so. Anyway, the encryption deciphering course was demanding. Our two-inch binders included three sections. The instructors lectured for two hours each day, and then we deciphered data the remaining time."

He finished off the first half of the muffin then said, "It's demanding, that's for sure. Well, you have a challenge ahead of you. As you know the volume of work has increased. My desk has been full of paperwork since you've been gone. Master Sergeant

McClain has been a big help. I'm not sure if he told you, but he can assist you with the work. He's attended the seminars."

"He told me you've asked for an assistant officer. I guess it's me. But you're leaving, and it's going to stay the same. I'll just have to keep my fingers crossed and hope to get someone."

"Yes. So, what else did you do after talking with your folks? I know sitting around on your ass is not your cup of tea."

Laughing, Miller said, "I had a feeling you'd ask that question. I looked at new cars."

"It's about time you replaced that old Saab! Oh, and before we hang up, we're still getting together today to visit Rothenberg, right? It's a forty-minute drive."

"Okay. I can deal with a short trip. What's it like there?"

Remmich told him how it had been a medieval city with a stone wall around the older area. It outlasted the Thirty Years War in the first half of the 1600s. He mentioned it wasn't as picturesque as Würzburg, but there were other historical sights. "How's 11:00 sound?"

Soon after they hung up, he got a vibration in his molar. It was 0800 hours. In his hypnotic state, he dialed the number.

The line connected. "This is Agent PSR."

"Good morning, Paul. This is Adnaw Alzuhari. Do you remember me?"

"Yes."

"You responded as instructed. Do you have a pen or pencil?"

"Yes."

"Copy my email address." Alzuhari slowly read it to him. "Send me an email when we hang up. I will contact you tomorrow. This conversation is over."

Remmich got online and did as instructed. When finished, he closed the email. Moments later he blinked his eyes while coming out of the trance; it took a minute. He finished eating breakfast and went for a shave and shower. While getting dressed he thought about the Stuttgart debriefing. He'd never attended one before.

Today was an adventurous, touring day. Tomorrow, he'd take it easy to be fit for Monday. Thinking about work brought up another thought. It was McClain's time for promotion. Colonel Collins needed a recommendation letter outlining the master sergeant's performance. His next upgrade was to the rank of a first sergeant. He made a mental note to work on it.

He stubbed out the cigarette and decided to go to the base laundromat to get his wash done and pick up his dry cleaning. Officers had to pay to have this done but enlisted men didn't. He gathered the laundry and left.

While the clothes were being washed and dried, he walked through the PX. He passed the time playing with new laptop computers and digital-memory-card cameras. From time-to-time other officers stopped to talk with him, saying they hoped he'd do well as a civilian. Noticing the time, he bought a carton of cigarettes and went to get his clothes.

A German company owned the laundry shop, leasing the area. Their service was exceptional; two hours for washing, drying, and folding. Remmich piled the paper-wrapped items into his duffel bag and paid for the dry-cleaned uniforms.

It was 1100 hours when he drove to the PX parking lot. The Saab pulled up alongside his BMW.

Miller asked, "Hey, can you give me ten minutes? I need to buy something in the PX."

He returned and dropped a brown paper bag on the back seat and locked the car. "Since you're more familiar with the area, you don't mind driving, do you?"

"Of course not, but we're taking the countryside roads."

Miller expressed his satisfaction with avoiding driving on the Autobahn; it was the weekend. The side roads took longer, but most of the time it was picturesque. He opened his own pack of Camel Filters and offered one to Remmich. They lit up and talked.

A melancholy feeling came upon Miller. Instead of harping on his buddy's intentions, he said, "Big day coming up on Monday. Getting yourself ready?"

He exhaled and kept quiet. Thoughts of being a civilian, traveling, and making wine purchases floated through his mind. On the other hand, the secret part-time job had more positive aspects outweighing its negative ones. *He didn't know the vibrating molar guaranteed him additional responsibility.*

Miller wondered if his friend's new employment would last. He took a drag and blew out the smoke.

When they got to Rothenberg, Miller found the wall to be the most exciting feature.

***

Remmich arrived at the Patch Barracks security headquarters at 0815 on Monday. He wore his class As. The front desk sergeant told him to go to the conference room. No one was there, so he got a coffee in the mini-snack bar.

On the way back, he heard, "Good morning, Captain Remmich," from a master sergeant exiting the conference room. "Oh, good, you got some." He served as one of the administrative assistants to General Sutherland. Remmich knew him.

He returned the greeting and anticipated the sergeant asking about the resignation. However, the NCO was a polished soldier and cautioned not to talk about the situation.

The meeting began at 0900. Sutherland said, "I'm sure everyone knows each other, so I'll skip the formalities." Remmich didn't expect Major General Elliott to be there. They sat across from him. Two other officers took a seat on either side of the generals. They were witnesses. The sergeant stood by the door.

Sutherland began, "As we are aware, the purpose of this meeting is to debrief Captain Paul Remmich. It includes removing all high-military intelligence privileges. A sworn statement will be signed forbidding dissemination of any classified information."

Elliott handed him duplicate pages of the resignation agreement. It was an itemized listing of Remmich's exposure to classified documents over the years. The general told him to read off the list first.

Halfway through the list, his subconscious mind triggered him to carry out Yako's suggestion. He stopped reading and asked, "General Sutherland, what would you say if I offered my experience to V Corps as a civilian? For example, as a part-time worker to help Captain Miller. You have spoken about assigning another officer to the security intelligence team. But no officer has offered to transfer to our unit and only Eric Miller has been assigned. It is a complicated and demanding job. We were lucky to get him. The increasing encryption decoding work will limit one person being able to finish on time. Attending meetings here and at NATO will prevent timely follow-up correspondence with other units. You know I have been overwhelmed with the administrative work in the past year." He repositioned himself, leaned on the table, and said, "Finding another experienced officer to work with my replacement is going to be difficult."

The room was quiet. The generals stared at each other. All eyes darted back and forth from them to Remmich. Sutherland told him to finish reading the resignation agreement, and everyone waited until he placed the two pages on the table.

"Do you understand the content of the order?"

"Yes, sir, I do."

Sutherland's alpha personality was intolerant of uncompleted projects. He had the authority to hire a part-time person to do the security intelligence work. The individual selected had to have supervised in this area; be an officer or a civilian in military intelligence. In this case, he knew keeping the civilian to-be would be suitable.

"Let's take a break," said Sutherland. "Report back here after lunch." Everyone walked out, including Remmich. He walked to the snack bar.

The generals entered Sutherland's office. They sat down and talked. It wasn't a difficult decision to keep him on board. They knew the captain was right. There were two high-ranking officers stationed at Patch Barracks for the same reason; with the volume of responsibility, there was too much work for just one of them to undertake. Sutherland contacted his secretary and told her to get the paperwork to hire civilians.

***

They returned to the conference room at 1300 hours and sat in the same seats. The two officer witnesses did not attend.

"We regard your performance in the years you've worked here as exceptional," said Elliott. "Your suggestion to work as a civilian has been accepted. So, we have come up with this proposition. General Sutherland and I want you to continue contact here at headquarters and at the 32nd. We want you to work as a government employee. There are no strings attached. There are benefits if you continue an active role in the army as a civilian."

"So, you're saying I can resign today and be hired as a part-time civilian employee for the United States Army in Germany?"

Elliott started to answer, but Sutherland interrupted. Once again, Elliott felt the sting of his superior's brashness. He flashbacked to when they were equal rank as two-star major generals. The contention between them wasn't widely known at the time. During the tours of active duty, he was a devoted soldier. Elliott's ambitions were high and he anticipated being recognized for his service. A promotion to three stars would have given him superiority over his rival. He expected Sutherland would relocate after that since he'd already spent six years at V Corps in Stuttgart. The reverse outcome sickened Elliott, so he relocated instead.

He served three years at Fort Belvoir INSCOM. Being out of reach from Sutherland didn't reduce his distaste for the man or the insult of being passed over. During the tour of duty, he attended many meetings at NSA and the Pentagon. Every now and then a meeting permitted friendly diplomats at Washington, DC embassies to take part. Some included high-ranking military as well. Months after, word of the real reason he relocated got around. When the information filtered into the wrong hands, an Iraqi spy at the embassy found out about the promotion matter. Since the US was friendly with them on specific terms, Elliott became the target. Iraq needed scouts; any person willing to make extra money. He became a valued employee, a high-ranked soldier with an itch to get even. Thirty-six months later Elliott found himself up for another move. He wanted to go back to Germany, now with new plans.

He came out of his stupor to hear Sutherland saying, "You will have to be debriefed and sign different resignation papers."

Remmich handed over the two-page agreement. Without hesitation, Elliott handed him the civilian employment pages. They let him read them.

"This seems to be in order," said Remmich.

"This new position permits you to resign at any time. If you change your mind and want to come back, you can reenter the military at your present rank within a one hundred eighty-day period." Again, his alpha personality tendencies geared up. "Does this sound like something you can agree to today?" He sat straight and stared at Remmich over a pair of reading glasses.

They waited for his answer. Clearing his throat and leaning on the table, he faced them expectantly. He asked, "How much payment are you talking about if I agree to this role?"

Elliott answered, “Three thousand dollars monthly, minus taxes and plus expenses. This is the best I can offer, Captain. You can pick up your checks here every month at our meetings.”

He sat up straight, and his British accent seemed more noticeable as he said, “I might as well agree. One monthly meeting and encryption work won’t interfere with my new career.”

The master sergeant told him to sign both sets of papers.

The procedure over, Sutherland commented, “I think we can agree an important decision has been made today.” He focused on the recruit and quietly said, “Thank you, and we will carry out your formal discharge on June 30. Congratulations to the future Mr. Remmich.” The meeting adjourned.

Remmich wanted the next couple weeks to go fast.

The master sergeant approached him. “Sir, you need new photo IDs and an up-to-date set of fingerprints.”

***

Elliott returned to his office and told the secretary he was going across to the PX. He didn’t tell her when he would return.

Instead, he drove off base and parked at the central park in town. He used his own cell phone and made a long-distance call to Istanbul. He outlined Remmich’s new duties with V Corps.

19

New Beginning

Paul Remmich couldn't get into work mode, even though he was still legally an officer. The official resignation was days away. Occasionally, boredom clouded his responsibility. Currently his distraction triggered a nicotine urge. A familiar voice interrupted him before he could respond to it. McClain needed his signature on a document before returning it to V Corps command.

The captain didn't mean to be irritable, but the subconscious control of his mind altered his normal tolerance level. He couldn't hasten the end result just yet. He grabbed the form from the sergeant's hand, reviewed it, and signed it. McClain's presence again reminded him to sign the promotion recommendation and get it to Collins.

Miller walked into the room. Remmich's doldrums diminished and his face brightened. "Well, it's about time. Where have you been?" They hadn't seen each other for a couple days because Remmich took some time off after the resignation meeting.

Hanging his cap on the wall hook, Miller said, "I thought I told you that Collins, First Sergeant Randolph, and I had a conference call with General Elliott regarding the command takeover of this office." All eyes were on him.

"I must have forgotten," uttered Remmich.

"The meeting lasted a long time because, as you are aware, Collins and Elliott like to share war stories." He placed the notepad on the desk, sat down, and reviewed the meeting's notes with the others. He told them the subject most discussed was their office's security responsibility. All were reminded…computers turned off at 4:00 p.m., safes locked after every use, and all doors locked.

When he finished, his stomach growled audibly. He looked at his watch. "I haven't even had any coffee yet."

Remmich grinned while signing the last couple of INSCOM release papers, including McClain's promotion recommendation. Before talking, he put that in the desk drawer. "Yes, let's go to the snack bar."

On the way, Miller talked about Remmich leaving for good. "So, you're going to be in the same role." His eyebrows rose as he added, "And I suppose I'll have to treat you as if you're one of those Washington, DC bureaucrats."

Remmich grinned and remarked he liked the thought.

The captains walked into the snack bar. The tray line moved at a reasonable speed; everyone selected a ready-made item. They got to the end of the line and paid for their coffee and Miller's food. Sitting at a table near other officers, Miller asked, "You give any thought about driving to Amsterdam this weekend?"

"Yes and no. Why?"

"Because Candice is flying into Schiphol Airport on Friday and I want to see her. I wondered if you wanted to go with me."

"Oh, so you're driving?"

"I am. Besides, I don't trust your meandering mind of late. We may wind up in the Calais, France tunnel."

Remmich laughed with the nearby officers, and said with his typical British manner, "Actually, my mind is doing rather well. Thank you." His antics amused the others.

"You having second thoughts?"

"How many times do you have to ask, Eric? No." He changed the subject. "But I do want to go to Amsterdam. Do you mind if I fill your car with my personals? It will take at least two and maybe three trips to get my things to the hotel. I really don't want to spend the money for a trailer."

"No, I don't mind. Want a cigarette?"

"I'll be damned," he said with a grin, "I'm being invited to get one out of your pack again! It's a bloody miracle!"

As he handed over the smokes, Miller pointed out that he wanted to make frequent visits to see Candice and him in Amsterdam.

"Yes, continuing to get together is important." Sipping coffee, he added. "I think you should tell Randolph we want a couple of three-day passes. He's testy when his office gets flooded with work at the end of the week."

On Friday morning Miller parked in front of his buddy's apartment building at 7:30. It took the two of them twenty minutes to get the car packed up. Four hours later they arrived at the Schiller Hotel. After unloading, they went their separate ways and spent the weekend apart. Miller roomed with Candice at the airport. While they walked around Amsterdam, the Iraqi thug followed them. *He was waiting for just the right time and place.* Remmich stayed at the hotel, and Lilly was able to get free time. They discussed the wedding and spent time walking around one of the Rembrandtplein canal sectors. Miller met him at the hotel early Sunday afternoon for the drive back.

***

As he drove away, a silver BMW made a quick U-turn to follow the Saab. They got onto the Autobahn and headed southbound. Miller put the transmission into fourth gear and raced up to 120 Ks. There were two cars ahead of the BMW, which slowed him down. Two hours later they passed Cologne. A traffic sign directed them to the Badzimmern public restrooms. The thug followed the Saab to the parking lot. He, too, had to go to the bathroom. He slipped behind them into a stall to keep out of sight, then waited until they exited.

Hours later the man parked next to a curb. He watched the Saab drive up to the Leighton Barracks MP gate and stop. Miller drove his buddy to his car. They said goodbye and both vehicles drove further away on base. The man reasoned that the base must be where the officer lived. He quickly formed a plan to track his target more closely. The next day he applied for a job at Leighton Barracks. He was hired as a van driver, delivering troops' duffle bags (worn fatigues, underwear, and socks) to the wash station. His presence on base gave him ample opportunity to learn where his prey lived. Unfortunately, the thug had to change rental cars, from the BMW to a VW Beetle. He knew people would wonder how a blue-collar worker could afford an expensive automobile.

***

On Monday, June 30, at 1000 hours, a company of fifty-eight soldiers dressed in starched fatigues, field caps, and spit-shined combat boots stood in military formation to present a formal act of discharge. All the officers wore class As. Elliott stood off to the side; it was Colonel Collins's responsibility to have command.

Captain Remmich stood to attention. First Sergeant Randolph faced the men and raised his voice in his own military style: "All personnel, present arms." Randolph did a ninety-degree left-face foot turn. He looked at Captain Remmich's solemn profile, as did Colonel Collins on the right side. Both men saluted him. Remmich returned his salute as he redirected his feet and looked at the platoon formation of NCOs, Captain Miller, and lower-ranked officers. When he released his salute, Randolph and Collins released theirs. The first sergeant raised his voice and commanded them to "order arms," and they stopped saluting. Then he yelled, "All soldiers, stand at ease." The group kept their right legs standing straight and moved their left legs out. At the same time, they placed their hands behind them over their spines and crossed, fingers straight.

Remmich led the way, and Randolph followed. They walked in front of each non-commissioned and commissioned officer. Each stood at attention to shake Remmich's hand in silence, but with a smile. Collins waited at the front, talking to Elliott.

Captain Remmich ended his procession. The platoon remained at attention as he returned to the front and confronted his superior in a low tone, telling him not to forget to send McClain's promotion recommendation. Collins agreed and handed him an envelope containing the resignation documents and the civilian work contract. The new civilian walked away and drove out of Hindenburg Kaserne. It was 1100 hours.

He drove to his apartment at Leighton Barracks for the last time. After loading the BMW, he left the apartment keys on the kitchen counter. The PX was the next stop. He bought a sandwich and a soft drink at the fast-food bar, mulling over the mornings' events. Soldiers sat at tables eating and talking. He chose an empty table near them and ate while reading *USA Today*. Before leaving, he bought a carton of cigarettes. Many soldiers didn't know he'd resigned. His insides were conflicted as he exchanged salutes with them anyway.

When Remmich got back into the car, his subconscious directed an instruction. The MP saluted as he drove out, but he didn't return one. At a small shopping center parking lot, he dialed Mustafa and said, "This is Agent PSR. I am leaving for Amsterdam now. Goodbye." His programmed brain allowed him to return to his usual hypnotized frame of mind. The trip took more than four hours. He arrived at the Hotel Schiller around 5:20.

***

Elliott drove out of Würzburg onto the Autobahn. On the way to Stuttgart, he stopped at a rest spot and telephoned Major Yildiz in Istanbul. He wasn't there, so he left a message.

Later in the day, Yildiz listened to the recording. Afterward, he had Luma Samir arrange for a conference call with Alzuhari and Yako. It took a few minutes for the operator to contact both. When they got online, the operator notified the Tariq'Allah office in Istanbul.

"Good evening, Adnaw and Tara." They returned the greeting. "Our secret agent in Stuttgart told me Paul Remmich has resigned. We need to keep in touch with him. I want both of you to have contact with him on a regular basis. Adnaw, you will make full use of the transmitter box to reach him and let him get used to his vibrating molar. I want him to return calls to your phone as we planned.

"First, we want him to get settled. He needs to know our methods of contact and our demeanor. We want the hypnotism to become superior. When the time is right, I want him to get the classified document.

"I am coming to Amsterdam on Friday. We will have a talk with Mr. Remmich about his new duties."

Yildiz chuckled and declared, "Mr. Remmich is going to get the most important scientific discovery of the twenty-first century. Our scientists will use it to provide a new form of energy for Third World countries and Iraq. We will establish diplomatic relations with these countries. Then we can let the world fight it out while we maintain real national growth along with peaceful and profitable global relations."

Yako interrupted. "Major, I know you already discussed with Adnaw, but I want to be sure I understand what the scientific discovery entails. The method you are referring to is the way plants make food using sunlight, water, and carbon dioxide, and give back oxygen. I understand the photosynthesis process, but how does the new procedure convert the energy stored in the plant chloroplasts into electrical power?"

"The details are in the secret documents we will get," said Yildiz. He chuckled and added, "We will still sell our crude oil. The world's largest nations will prevent the use of anything else. Oil corporations in these countries have enough clout to influence elections with their money. It's a fact and not a theory anymore." He became serious. "If there's something the Middle East has preserved, it's the art of manifesting complex arguments." He continued after they laughed. "Petroleum refining methods and internal combustion motors pollute the atmosphere. Our new method will not, nor will we have to deal with nuclear energy mistakes and nuclear residue contamination. Who knows? One of these days, we may drive a vehicle powered by solar energy."

"I will make it a point to get in touch with Remmich tomorrow," said Alzuhari.

***

On Wednesday morning at 8:00, Remmich's tooth vibrated while he sat in the Café Schiller. He mindlessly stopped reading *The New York Times* and left the restaurant to go to his room. His subconscious controlled his actions, and instead of dialing the dentist's office, he automatically used the prefix for Alzuhari's phone and dialed 020-623-1239.

After three rings, he heard, "Hello. Alzuhari." He already saw the caller's name.

"This is Agent PSR."

"Good morning, Paul. Did you get everything moved out of Germany?"

"Yes. It's all here at the Schiller Hotel."

"Oh, you're living there too?"

"For now. I have a single room. After my wedding in September, we will have a condominium here."

"That's wonderful, Paul. From now on you are to call me, not Dr. Mustafa."

Remmich robotically responded, "Yes, I will call you from now on."

"Second, there is a meeting on Friday you must attend. I will call you again tomorrow. Goodbye, Paul."

In the minutes it took to return to the Café Schiller, Remmich's subconscious mind returned to its weaker hypnotized level of control. He sat in the same seat and got a coffee. The *London Times* had been left on a bench and he picked it up. The headline read that AIDS epidemics in African countries were growing. Another section described children's hunger, which seemed exasperating and sad to him.

The day seemed to go fast. The new resident finished straightening his personal items, such as clothing and toiletries, in his room. Things he wouldn't use frequently went into a hotel storage space. Later, he strolled around but stayed in the Rembrandtplein region. Remmich got back to the hotel by midafternoon. Lilly was still working. He went to the bar for a beer and to read more of the same newspaper.

A while later a gentle hand touched his shoulder, and he saw his bride-to-be. The bartender motioned with an empty glass, and she nodded. He brought her a half beer, and the three of them talked for a few minutes. When her pager vibrated, she complained in her native tongue.

"What's wrong?"

"I have to return to the main desk."

"Do you have to work this evening?"

"I hope not. Wednesday nights are usually not busy. I have to go."

A little while later he finished his beer, but Lilly hadn't returned, so he decided to look for her. She stood at the registration desk handing over a room card while directing a couple to the elevators. He caught her attention as the two people walked away. "I was coming to find out if you wanted to go out to dinner. I believe I heard your buzzer just go off again, and I'm afraid it might be this way all evening."

"It can be annoying."

He looked at his watch. "If we leave in a few minutes, we can catch an evening canal tour serving dinner. You can even throw your pager into the canal if you wish." She gave him a sassy smile.

***

He awoke on Thursday morning around 6:50, but he didn't get out of bed. Lilly lay beside him. His molar vibrated at 7:00, and he went into a deep trance. He got out of bed and made a telephone call inside the doorway to the bathroom. When the person on the other end answered, he spoke in a low tone, "This is Agent PSR."

"Good morning, Paul. You are to meet Tara and me at her flat on Friday at 9:00."

"Yes. I will be at Tara Yako's flat at 9:00 on Friday." He wrote her address on a pad, and they hung up.

Lilly's hearing was decent and she awakened from his low voice. She turned over to see him walking toward the bed. "Who were you talking to?"

Remmich mumbled the address to himself. It always took a minute or so for him to recover, and he couldn't shake off the deeper trance any faster. She leaned on her elbow and asked, "Are you feeling okay?"

He hesitated. "Oh, Eric called me about a problem in the office."

She blinked a couple times, yawned, and uttered, "Funny, I didn't hear the telephone ring." She got out of bed and looked at the clock radio on the nightstand. "Breakfast together is out of the question, my love. My mother is probably wondering where I am."

She got dressed, kissed him, and walked out. He lay back into bed and looked at the ceiling. He fell back asleep. When he woke up, it was past noon. He couldn't remember the last time he slept that late. He showered and went down to the kitchen. One of the chefs handed him a wrapped breakfast plate Lilly made for him.

The lobby was bustling with guests walking around. Many took advantage of the midday lunch specials in the restaurant. He saw Lilly, but she seemed too busy to interrupt. He didn't have anything to do and went outside for another walk. A couple of hours later he returned to his room and played on the laptop until she arrived at 4:30. She looked bushed but didn't want to stay there for dinner, so they took advantage of the opportunity to avoid her being called back to work.

***

On Friday morning, he ate a small breakfast at the kitchen's staff table. While eating, he noticed the time. His subconscious prompted him to go to Yako's flat. He finished and got into a cab. Twenty minutes later he walked off the elevator. The surroundings seemed familiar to him, and a deeper hypnotic trance began to overtake him.

He knocked. Yako opened the door wide enough for him to enter. He looked at her, and the mental trance spontaneously locked. She closed the door and guided him to the same sofa they had used previously. He sat on the right side as before and placed his right arm on the armrest. He sat motionless and quiet.

Unknown to Remmich, another gentleman was present. He walked over to their mole and said, “Paul, I am Arif Yildiz.”

“Yes. Adnaw spoke about you.”

“Good, I’m glad you remember. I want to talk about your training program. Remember when you gave Adnaw a copy of your work agenda?”

“Yes.”

“I need to know now what your schedule will be since you are not active duty any longer. Have you received a working outline yet?”

“Mr. Van Horn is supposed to get a schedule to me today. I think he wants me to visit vineyards in Germany and France and taste wines for purchasing.”

“Will you be doing a lot of traveling for him?”

“Yes.”

“Excellent.” They wanted to practice contacting him in different places. “I understand you also have to be present at meetings with the V Corps.”

“I will go to security meetings once a month.”

Yildiz looked closer at him. He reiterated Remmich’s job to find information about the new photosynthesis program. “It is categorized at the SCI level. But this will begin after your wedding. When is it?”

“I’m getting married on Saturday, September 14. Lilly and I plan to honeymoon for ten days in southern France.” His face remained somber but did not look abnormal.

The major repeated, “After your wedding you will find the classified data and alert Adnaw or Tara. Do you understand?”

“Yes. We are acting as a team to find classified information to assist Third World countries.”

They remained quiet for a few moments and watched him. Yildiz knew the answers to the next questions, but he wanted

Remmich to talk. Elliott had given him the details. "Paul, tell us about what you will do as a civilian."

"I will have a part-time job with the army as a civilian military intelligence specialist."

The major ignored his title. "Tell me more about the job itself."

Remmich mechanically repeated what he agreed to at the resignation meeting; attendance at a monthly security intelligence meeting and helping to decipher new encrypted text at the 32nd and Patch Barracks. My superior officers want me to translate the army's Echelon satellite's cryptograph coding for V Corps."

Yildiz already knew the solar energy find the United States possessed would be included in Remmich's decryption. Now he wanted him to tell it in his own way. "I see. So, you will have access to the same classified information?"

"Yes. I will have access to classified information all the time."

"Tell me more, Paul,"

His eyes blinked a couple times and he said, "I don't have access to this detailed documentation yet. I only heard there will be emails containing a section at a time."

Remmich's response pleased Yildiz. First, they'd made a mistake; Yako didn't get the guy targeted. Then the man she did hypnotize turned out to have as much access if not more. He leaned back and asked, "How long is this supposed to take?"

"What do you mean?"

"How many satellite transfers have to happen before you get all of the information?"

He maintained eye contact with Yildiz. "I don't know."

"What will the transfers contain?" questioned Yako.

Remmich stared at her. "I only know the plan is to help the military reduce their oil usage."

The major smiled. “Yes, it will assist many of us for a long time. And whoever gets it going first will become a world leader.”

No one said anything while they watched Remmich for a few moments. “Paul, I want you to stay here. Don’t get up.”

He looked at Yildiz and repeated, “I will stay seated.”

The major motioned for his associates to follow him to the balcony. He told them, “I wanted to take a break to talk.” He looked out over the city and said, “If he is able to confiscate the photosynthesis formula, we will be able to use him for other things. Right now, I wanted to leave him alone. Let’s see how he reacts when we go back in.”

They returned to the living room and saw their mole staring at the floor. Yildiz sat next to him. “Paul.” He waited for eye contact. “Remember to call Adnaw about your civilian work in Amsterdam and your army schedules.” Having this information would avoid having them contact Remmich when he was at either military location. The work schedules were going to inform them of his daily whereabouts.

Remmich blinked a couple times while maintaining eye contact with the major. He said, “Yes, I will call Adnaw as soon as I get them.”

***

At 10:30 Nikulin saw Remmich walk out of the building. He sat on a park bench in the grassy median strip instead of inside his flat. The median separated his one-way street from the one going the opposite direction, where Alzuhari and Yako lived. He felt lucky to find his flat. Its location provided an excellent surveillance spot for their comings and goings. Seeing Remmich leave alerted him to turn off the radio receiver and compact recorder. He waved to a taxi and told the driver to follow Remmich’s cab. The Russian assumed Remmich was going back to be his hotel.

Nikulin entered the lobby instead of waiting outside. He joined other guests in the seating area. It was too early to telephone the ambassador. *Why not relax?* He read *The New York Times* and ordered coffee twice.

The cacophony in the lobby increased as guests headed to lunch at the main restaurant. It distracted him. He looked around to locate the source of the noises and noticed the grandfather clock. “It’s time,” he said to himself. Walking to the side street, he pushed the autodial button.

The secretary transferred him to Linkov. “So, Yury, it has been over a week since we have spoken. What do you have for me?”

Linkov listened to his exploits for the missed days, focusing on one in particular. Yury boasted, “They are going to get what they think is the most important scientific discovery of the twenty-first century. Unbeknownst to the Iraqis, I will get it for us too!” They laughed.

“Yury, your humor is understandable, but let’s not become too self-confident. We don’t have the document yet. From what you are telling me, I am pleased these Tariq’Allah spies are working very hard to acquire the top-secret photosynthesis information. Well done! Now, we must wait for the classified information to arrive.”

20

The Search Begins

Schiller Hotel was busy early Friday afternoon. The grand foyer was noisy. Bellhops assisted guests with luggage. People departing and new arrivals crowded the front lobby and the registration desk area. Many got off or onto the elevators. Concierges helped guests who needed to catch a cab to the airport or train station.

There was congestion outside of the entrance. Cabs parked along the curb, motors running. The wind dispersed the smell of carbon monoxide. Private cars arrived and parked to unload passengers and luggage in areas saved for the taxis. The chaos enhanced the hotel's character.

Lilly could hear the lobby clamor all the way from the main restaurant. She'd been working there since the lunch schedule ended a few hours ago. It was a hideaway to avoid interruptions. Scheduling work times for the employees was a never-ending job. There was another page to finish changing the dates and times on the Excel outline, but for the moment, she daydreamed.

The bobbing kitchen doors brought her attention back. Her father squirmed around the tables and made his way to her corner. "Lilly, I am trying to find Paul." He handed her several printed pages. "These are his revised travel assignments for this month. Have him look it over. If there are any questions, or if it interferes with the army responsibilities, tell him to come to the office. I'll be there if he needs me." He looked at his watch. "The restaurant opens in a little while. Hope you finish!" he said with a grin.

"Thank you, Papa."

Van Horn's comment made her wonder about Paul. She awoke before him that morning and thought he'd contact her after getting out of bed. She read through the work plan and raised her eyebrows in surprise. Her father had scheduled Remmich to drive to several vineyards in the Bordeaux area. It gave her an idea, so she penciled an asterisk at the top of that page.

The restaurant's lighting became brighter, and the noise increased. Kitchen workers rolled stainless steel food islands to the buffet section where guests served themselves. Her stomach grumbled. The kitchen's pungent aromas made her hungry; she'd only eaten breakfast. Before closing the laptop, she sent schedules to the wireless printer. She walked to the office to pick up the copies, placing one in his mailbox. She found a handwritten note in her mailbox saying he was going out after breakfast. She told the front desk staff to have him contact her when he returned. The next stop was getting something to eat.

Major Yildiz left the Schiller Hotel and walked outside with his suitcase. The concierge hailed a cab for him. He was on his way to Yako's apartment.

Remmich received an unexpected vibration in his tooth. He became spellbound and took the back elevator to his floor. He entered his room and dialed Alzuhari. He listened to, "Come to Tara's apartment in one hour. Bring the work schedules for July and August." The subliminal hold over his subconscious decreased after the message ended and his perception returned to its post-hypnotic level. He needed Mr. Van Horn's schedules.

Entering the lobby, one of the front desk managers told him Lilly was looking for him. He looked into his mailbox first and found her note stuck to the schedule. Instead of looking for her, he dodged people while walking to the lobby seating area. Reading about the Bordeaux trip, he saw it included some stops along the way. He made changes on page two, adding the August 16 security meeting. He finished and walked into the office, but Van Horn was not there. A secretary offered to retype what he'd done. Because the Excel outline was on the computer, it took her a few minutes to make changes. He told her to print out three copies of the schedules; one copy was for Van Horn, one for him, which he placed in his box, and he carried the extra copy. Next, he answered Lilly's note and put it in her box. He texted Alzuhari.

The concierge hailed a cab for him. Twenty minutes later he entered Yako's building. When Remmich stepped out of the elevator, the hypnotic trance controlled him. He knocked on the door, and she walked him to the couch.

***

Nikulin watched Remmich walk into the building. The recorder clicked, indicating the start of discussion in her apartment. He increased the volume and heard English spoken. He pushed his chair to where he had positioned a Nikon camera to take shots of Yako's building. He had two photographs showing Alzuhari talking to Yildiz on the balcony. Two other photos showed the mole walking into Yako's building.

***

He didn't notice the major sitting off to the side of the room.

Alzuhari said, "We need to talk about your schedules."

Remmich reached in his black leather case and pulled out a two-page spreadsheet. He gave it to Alzuhari.

He randomly looked at the pages and said, "We also want to discuss getting the photosynthesis document to help Third World countries." He focused on Remmich and said, "We will need your help."

Alzuhari had one other subject to discuss. Although they knew the answers, Yildiz had told him to address a question regarding security. "Paul, to help us understand, tell us what the SCI letters mean."

"SCI stands for Sensitive Compartmented Information, the highest level of classification in the United States military intelligence operations."

Alzuhari told him to explain what it does. He wanted to see how much their mole knew.

Remmich described it as a system comprising intelligence sources, such as one that would function in an operational environment for military locations, hostile and friendly forces, and analytical processes. He explained there were limitations to access of SCIs. There were restrictions in disclosing the activity and conversation about its functions.

Alzuhari stroked his chin and said, "So, the photosynthesis discovery for energy would be related to an operational environment source."

"Yes."

"This isn't like the usual weapons-related classified information."

"Precisely."

"If it is under the SCI label, are you authorized to handle this high range of a classification?"

"Oh, yes. But it must be done in an approved workplace, like the security intelligence offices. It's like needing the combination to release a locked door. Since this is not weapons-related, other specialists and I are authorized to decrypt its contents."

"Good, because we expect to get the construction drawings for the building and the mechanical engineering for the machinery. Is this something you will have access to?"

"Yes."

"We want you to get it for us."

"I understand," said Remmich.

Yako wanted to know, "Can you visit the security offices more than once a month?"

"I don't know."

"What if you don't finish the decoding in one day? Will you have to stay overnight or return another day?"

"There are officers' quarters where I can stay overnight."

They wanted to find out if the SCI information could be emailed.

His brow furrowed in thought, Remmich explained there was a method. He would copy the decoded encrypted file and transfer it to his computer at the 32nd via email. There were no restrictions, as long as it went to another acceptable military base. If anyone tried to send detailed information to an outside source, it would alert CID.

"What do you mean by CID?" probed Alzuhari.

"The Criminal Investigative Division," said Remmich. "They do electronic surveillance of classified documents being sent out of an army headquarters. They can find where it comes from and the point of reception. The trained agents also listen to many military telephone conversations, and they can look at emails to make sure soldiers are not giving out classified information."

"Thank you, but you said CID will find out if anyone sends classified material," said Alzuhari. "Do you mean what you decode and email to another post can be seen by them?"

Remmich described how their system was networked to the computers in the security offices and other offices. "My computer system displays the same information. They may not understand the encrypted jargon, but they can read the decoded wording. They know if it's transferred."

"And there is a CID office at Patch Barracks in Stuttgart?" asked Yako.

"CID offices are at every US Army post."

She wanted to better understand how the decoding system worked.

He explained it was a two-column page; encrypted words were on the left side, and the right side had the words translated into understandable English.

"I have an idea," said Alzuhari. "You told us you can forward the information as it comes to you at Patch Barracks and email it to the 32nd?" Remmich answered. "Good. Then you can copy it onto a flash drive at the 32nd. Can you then take it to your computer and send the information to me?"

"Yes."

"How often is this information going to come into Stuttgart?" she asked.

"I don't know."

"Okay. Then let's agree on transferring the information to Würzburg," exclaimed Alzuhari.

Remmich needed a reason to work at the 32nd, and Alzuhari had an idea. "You are not leaving yet Paul." He discussed details of the lie Remmich was to tell.

Moments later he told Remmich, "You are not to remember any of this conversation, except when Tara, myself, or Major Yildiz talk to you. Do you understand?"

"Yes."

They said their goodbyes and Remmich left.

Major Yildiz appeared from behind the wall. "Excellent. Let's proceed as planned."

He got his suitcase and took a taxi to the airport to return to Istanbul.

***

Remmich walked into the hotel's foyer and asked the lobby host to page Lilly and ask her to call his room. He headed to the elevator and pressed the wall button. Before it arrived, a front desk clerk accosted him. He handed him a phone message and the travel spreadsheets with Lilly's notes that she'd left in the mailbox. The note told him Eric Miller was coming to Amsterdam next weekend and wanted to get together.

He heard the room's telephone ringing as he whisked the card key through the door lock. He rushed over and answered it. An annoyed voice said, "My father and I looked for you earlier. I called your cell phone, no answer. Where did you go?"

He tried to remember the reason he went out but said instead, "Oh, I got bored and walked around for a few hours."

Lilly spoke in a less aggravated way. "Well, you won't be bored after you look at your travel schedule."

"You're referring to my work schedule for the vineyards in France?"

"Yes. I got the agenda and saw the changes you made. Have you read the corrected pages?"

"I have them in my hands but haven't read through it." He studied it for a moment and said, "I can see someone made handwritten additions."

"Did you like the additions I made to include me?"

"I can tell you're smiling. What if I say no?" answered Remmich playfully.

She hesitated long enough to give him reason to believe she was pouting. "Okay, I'm kidding," he said. "Of course, I want you to go along. It will be fun."

He changed the subject. "Let's go out for dinner." She agreed.

He took the elevator downstairs and got bottled beers for the room's fridge. Returning, he rushed to answer the ringing phone.

"Hey! It's about time you showed up. I've been trying to call you," said Miller.

"Eric! How the devil are you?"

"I'm meeting Candice next Friday night. Are the four of us going to get together on Saturday?"

"By all means!" replied Paul.

Before the talk ended, Miller asked, "Are you going to the G-2 meeting in Stuttgart?"

"Yes, I am."

The call ended, and he realized no calls from Lilly or Eric had come to his cell phone because the battery had died.

***

The month went fast. The week of August 14 arrived, and Remmich's first security meeting as a civilian was about to happen. He wondered: Could he get away with it? Was V Corps' CID going to notice? He remembered how his personal telephone call to Lilly in the security office got him in trouble. He could not be entirely rational because his hypnotized mind believed he was doing this for a worthy cause.

On Wednesday morning the attendees assembled in the corridor for coffee. General Elliott waited for Remmich to arrive. He asked him to step into the conference room for a few minutes before the meeting.

"Paul, I want you to know I am pleased you decided to stay on as a civilian worker." He held out his hand. "I believe we're going to help advance global diplomatic tactics. I hope you can be the basis to get us going."

"Thank you, sir."

Sutherland and his entourage entered the room. Before sitting, the general approached Remmich and told him the first SCI email had arrived and he could leave to work on it after the announcement.

Everyone gathered around their selected seats waiting for the order to begin, then pulled out their chairs and sat down.

Sunderland first announced that Paul Remmich, who stood by the door, was now a civilian working for USAREUR. The general explained he had the same duties and responsibilities as when he was on active duty.

That pronouncement over, Remmich left and walked to the security office. He opened the SCI document and deciphered the encrypted wording for the rest of the morning.

He joined Eric Miller and others on their way to the officers' club for lunch. An hour later he returned to the security intelligence office. He continued to decipher for several hours. Finishing, he saved the information and emailed it to his computer at the 32nd. The transmit process took less than five seconds compared to the hours of translation. He wondered if he'd get questioned about it at the 32nd. He bid farewell to the others and left Stuttgart, arriving in Würzburg at dinnertime. He decided to get a hotel room off base. After checking in, he left a voice message to Lilly saying he wasn't coming back until tomorrow.

***

On Thursday morning, the 32nd administrative sector seemed to be almost empty. Remmich noticed only one man sat in the office. The officers and NCOs attended a meeting upstairs. Representatives from the US Army judge advocate office addressed security breaches, believing the cleaning crew spying had occurred in many security offices.

Specialist Cannon greeted him. He'd been working on a security clearance questionnaire form. Remmich explained he'd sent an incomplete encryption document to the 32nd from Stuttgart. The soldier listened as Remmich told him they had intermittent power blackouts and the work needed to be finished. The lower-ranked soldier understood the recurring problem at posts in Germany, so he didn't have reason to question. He turned back to the computer and resumed his work.

It took time to copy-and-paste six pages of engineering drawings that were not encrypted. Remmich finally closed the document and shut down the computer. He looked at the soldier to make sure he wasn't being watched and put the flash drive into his pocket. They exchanged goodbyes.

His stomach told him the snack bar was his next stop. He had skipped breakfast, so he bought a half cold cut sub and a soda and ate quickly. The security meeting ended as he drove out of the Hindenburg Kaserne. The lower-ranked soldier didn't mention Remmich's visit. He didn't think he had to since the army cleared the civilian to work in the office.

21

August Formula

Remmich had been on the Autobahn to Amsterdam for five hours due to a multi-vehicle accident. He entered Holland by mid-afternoon and drove into the hotel's parking area at 4:00. An attendant greeted him.

Entering from the rear door, he took an elevator upstairs and went into his room. Sitting down, he turned on the computer. It took a few moments to send the flash drive's file to Alzuhari. When it finished, his hypnotic control lowered to the normal guiding state. He went downstairs.

The Brasserie-Schiller bar-restaurant had hotel guests who sat at tables and the bar. Remmich grabbed the pack of cigarettes from his shirt pocket and chose a swivel seat at the bar.

The height of the ceilings made the room look enormous, but it was only half the size of the main dining room. Old brass lanterns hung from the rafters. They had been converted to electrical lighting. A few wall fixtures were ship wheels from old sailing vessels, carved spokes and handles confirming their bygone days. Attached to each was a lantern with a torpedo-shaped lightbulb inside. It provided soft lighting and a romantic atmosphere.

Remmich observed people sitting at the bar and nodded to a gentleman a couple of stools away from him. He started a conversation with the man as Felders placed the beer on a coaster in front of him. They talked for a while about the hotel's history. Apparently, the guy was a fabric salesman from Scotland, and he always roomed at the Schiller. Their talk ended when he felt a touch on his shoulder. He turned as she sat in the adjoining swivel seat.

Smiling, Lilly told him, "I missed you."

He looked lovingly into her green eyes, squeezed her hand softly and said, "I'm glad to be back."

"My father had to travel for you during the past few days."

Remmich started to talk but stopped as Felders put a half-liter on a coaster for her. Foam trickled down the outside of the glass. As he wiped it away, he said, "Rough trip?"

"Yes. Traffic was stopped for over an hour on the Autobahn outside of Düsseldorf due to a multi-vehicle accident."

Remmich swallowed a large sip and quietly belched. "Oh, I needed this hours ago. So, my dear, what have you been up to?"

She pulled the printed copy of his travel schedule from her dress pocket. "I'm so glad to be going with you to Bordeaux."

Remmich's eyebrows arched when he smiled. He scanned the agenda. She sipped her beer while looking at her engagement ring, swiveling it on her finger. Her eyes switched from it to him, and she said, "I am sure you recognize the changes I made. I must be sure your lover accompanies you. I don't want your appetite at the French shoreline tempted beyond your desire for me."

Overhearing her comment, the man on the nearby stool chuckled. Somewhat embarrassed, Remmich cleared his throat and said, "Ah, yes, well, do we have plans for this evening?"

"No. But let's do something away from here."

***

His visits to Belgium the following week used up a lot of time. He had so many appointments it was hectic for him. Once again, he filed electronic data giving vineyard names, locations, and quantities to be shipped to the Schiller. A vital aspect of each wine estate visit was buying in person.

He returned on Friday arriving earlier than expected. Lilly's excitement persuaded Paul to leave Sunday instead of Monday for the Bordeaux trip. They packed Saturday afternoon and went out to dinner. The following morning the trip south led them past sights of centuries-old architecture and kept them entertained. Seven hours later they arrived in the city of Cognac.

Remmich had a list from Van Horn of where to visit and stay. Their first stop was the Hôtel Girole, a medium-sized hotel. Its lobby had off-white marble panels on the lower walls with friezes surrounded by ivy perimeters carved into the marble surfaces. The upper walls and ceiling were plaster, and both the color and hairline cracks added character. A few century-old, framed watercolor paintings protected by glass hung on a wall. A couple of them showed workers putting grape cuttings into wooded buckets. Another canvas featured carriers taking the buckets to early twentieth-century trucks. There was also a charcoal sketch of the city's Gothic cathedral. The foyer boasted a spiral wooden stairway and a four-person elevator. Its dark tongue-and-groove floor led them into the check-in counter and the seating section. The room echoed a little as they wandered around looking at its paintings and decorated walls.

A desk clerk broke their attention when he said, *"Bonjour, madame et monsieur. Puis-je vous aider?"* Remmich had never mastered French and realized that he'd need to ask people if they spoke English. Fortunately, Lilly was fluent, and replied, *"Oui, monsieur. Une chambre pour deux, s'il vous plaît."*

The counter clerk finished the paperwork and wanted to know how she wanted to pay. "*Payerez-vous en espèces, ou carte de credit?*" She reached into her purse for a credit card. After signing the paperwork, the assistant gave her a keycard. Before they left, he handed them a picturesque brochure of the city and a listing of tours and places to eat. They rode the elevator up to the third floor. To their surprise, the room was a mini suite. There were two windows, which let them look over parts of the old and new town. Lilly placed her suitcase on the only rack. Paul lifted his luggage onto a sofa. They freshened up and walked out of the building. A few streets from the hotel the aroma of baking bread caused her to say, "I am thankful for my Dutch bakeries, but I like the smell of warm French bread." One establishment placed the finished loaves into bins in the shop's window and sold them while they were still warm. The bakery had an adjoining butcher shop. She suggested they buy a wedge of cheese, slices of hard salami, and a loaf of the warm bread. To complete the feast, they bought red wine. The store clerk uncorked it and gave them two plastic cups. On the way to a bench under an oak tree in the park, Remmich went to get a Swiss army knife from his car's glove compartment. She broke off pieces of bread. Paul returned and snatched one mischievously. She tried to smack his hand but missed, and they both laughed. She filled the cups halfway with wine, while he cut slices of cheese. They toasted and ate before walking around and looking at sights from the brochure.

Their first visit on Monday morning was to a vineyard in one of the six Cognac brandy districts. This vineyard was a grade below the best, and less expensive. But finding it was a problem. It was off the main road, and they weren't sure if they were driving in the right direction. At a red light, Lilly told Paul to stop at the corner. There was a policeman close by, and she got his attention, *"Excusez-moi, monsieur. Pourriez-vous m'aider, s'il vous plaît? Où est le Chateau de Cognac?"*

He pointed in the direction where the road curved and directed them to go straight ahead until they noticed the signs to the entrance.

Remmich mingled among the other Cognac buyers. Most of them just sniffed the Cognacs. He thought tasting was just as important. Lilly wanted to sample some after he remarked that the bouquet was mild and sipping it didn't irritate his throat after swallowing. The vintner heard them speaking and introduced himself in English.

"Are you familiar with our province, monsieur?" Remmich explained Lilly's father had been there, but it was his and Lilly's first time. They wanted to buy Cognac but weren't sure which ones to buy.

The vintner advised, "You simply buy the ones you enjoy the most. It's what I tell all of our customers." Satisfied, Remmich placed an order for the two they had tasted. They arranged for delivery.

They drove south to Bordeaux in less than two hours. Again, a scenic trip. Paul's agenda included visiting several prominent vineyards in the Pauillac, Pomerol, and Saint Julian regions. His work consumed the rest of the week. On the weekend they strolled the beach and saw more of everything.

It was an enjoyable drive back to Amsterdam, and they arrived late Tuesday morning. After unpacking, Lilly walked to the front desk instead of taking the elevator to her room. Paul returned to his room and turned on the computer before getting a beer out of the mini fridge. There was a message from V Corps. He needed to attend a security intelligence conference on Wednesday that might continue into Thursday. Suddenly, the subconscious conditioning compelled him to contact Alzuhari. He emailed him and wrote a notation in his datebook.

Lilly did not take the news too well. Her father wondered why he got such short notice.

Midafternoon, Remmich headed to Stuttgart.

***

Sutherland opened the conference on Wednesday at 0800. It was a meeting with mostly officers; Remmich was present so he would stay informed. The first topic of discussion included facts of another cleaner getting caught trying to make copies of a classified report. His hopes of repeating spy talks were to ingrain the problem into the minds of his officers. It had to stop. Glancing at them, he said, "The crook remains in jail here on base until he's handed over to German authorities. They will deport him. That's a strike against us because we can't prosecute. He's a resident of Stuttgart, so to speak. They control the law."

The general continued and included a problem at the Berlin MI headquarters. Like other posts, the building had a nighttime charge-of-quarters. He inspected offices on a regular basis. Walking into the admin office, he was stunned to find a cleaning crew reading and copying papers. They were just as surprised to see him. The sergeant grabbed the pages and saw the word "Secret" stamped in red. It contained information about the positive and negative uses of raw sewage from animals and how chemical companies produced crop fertilizer. He drew his pistol and called the military police, who arrested them.

"Whether you realize it or not, there are dangerous uses of fertilizers. For example, they can be mixed with certain chemicals to make explosives."

While he sipped coffee, there was a burst of raised hands from the audience. "I'll answer one question and no more." He recognized a colonel stationed in North Africa. "Joe, I'm glad you made it. What's on your mind?"

Standing up, he said, "With what you've said, General, I'm surprised there aren't restrictions to buying the stuff. Like gun controls, for example." Everyone listened, but they knew enforcement was erratic.

"Yes, I don't believe there are restrictions. At least, not in retail stores. As I said before, these people wanted the organic formula breakdown to make explosives. It's a cheap way to kill."

The group watched his expression become more serious. "Before General Elliott takes over, I need to point out one other thing. Our attitude with military intelligence glitches is still too lax. The problem is often not discovered until it's too late. The spies exchange classified documents for money. I have requested a meeting with the defense secretary at the Pentagon regarding this problem. We need more help." He stopped talking and exchanged places with the lower-ranked general.

Elliott talked of another type of espionage: cyber intelligence. He told them, "Spies are stealing top-secret information. Although it hasn't happened here yet, other army posts have arrested soldiers working in or around a security intelligence office. The spies receive the paperwork, analyze it, and use the information against opponents of the international terrorists, like ISIS and al-Qaeda. It is being used against our military, our government, and hurting businesses." He spoke for another thirty minutes. A glance at the wall clock time stopped him, and he told everyone to take a fifteen-minute break.

Paul heard someone call to him while he fixed his coffee. "You don't have to return after the break." He watched Sutherland fixing himself a cup of coffee. The general said, "I want you to go to the office. We have additional SCI data being sent in fifteen minutes."

"I'm curious, General. What's being discussed that I won't hear?"

"Not much," as he stirred the coffee. "It will be a continuation of this morning's talk, but the attendees will participate, hopefully offering ideas. Almost all of the people in this building will attend."

Remmich entered the office. He thought it was vacant until Specialist Cannon appeared from the supply storage room. They exchanged greetings. Remmich asked where the rest of the men were, and the soldier told him they were in the conferences upstairs. He explained the first sergeant was holding a meeting with the NCOs at the same time as the general's meeting.

He logged in. The encrypted message appeared. Its letters and symbols made up the script. He began to decrypt. It interested him so much he didn't notice the time. Hours later a rumble came from the corridor. It distracted him, and he looked in the direction of the noise. It was lunchtime and men were heading out. He was hungry too, so he minimized the screen and left.

Along the way, he mingled with officer friends attending the meeting. All of them entered the mess hall, paid for their food, and sat in the officers' table area. The discussions centered on terrorist threats to American embassies located in the Middle East. Some of their talk focused on political Islamic fundamentalist groups in Africa. After a few minutes Remmich noticed the time and gulped the rest of his iced tea. It was close to 1:00.

Office soldiers sat at their desks and paid little attention to Remmich when he entered the room. He resumed deciphering. He got to "Section Two," which outlined a tubular structure that housed chloroplast matter for the new energy production. Other pages displayed the actual drawings of the housing. He decided to take a smoke break and minimized the screen; as usual, he saved the decrypted information before leaving to go anywhere.

He started to leave, and the building's electricity power stopped. It happened whenever Stuttgart's power source became overloaded. The growing population demanded more power for homes, commercial buildings, and street lighting. Five years before, the US military controlled its own electrical from oil-generated furnaces. Because the German system had fewer carbon emissions, they forced the army to close their plant and follow ordinances. The US government didn't want to spend millions of dollars tearing down the old boilers and building an approved power plant. The only option was to buy the electricity, but that came with service interruptions. Remmich returned to the G-2 office and figured the power would return soon. In the meantime, the workers complained they were not going to finish the security clearance papers for soldiers. Time was not on their side today.

At 4:00 Remmich decided to leave because he couldn't do any work. He opened the datebook and noticed the dental appointment the following morning. "Dear God, I almost forgot!" he murmured. He made a note about the office losing power and told the sergeant in charge he needed to go to Würzburg to finish his work. It would forestall any criticism of him entering another workplace for the same information. The soldiers exchanged goodbyes with him, while he concealed the flash drive in its case in his hand. Outside, he put it into his pocket.

The sergeant in charge telephoned the 32nd to tell them that Remmich was coming.

He drove to Würzburg. This time, he registered at the Leighton Barracks hotel. He telephoned Klaus to rendezvous for dinner at his uncle's restaurant. He started to call Eric Miller to join them but changed his mind. He didn't want to discuss the reason he was in town.

22

Confrontation

He made a right-hand turn into the Hindenburg Kaserne base and stopped at the gate. The MP saluted and waved him forward. Remmich wondered why he greeted him that way, and then figured it out. The blue officer's stickers were still on the front and rear bumpers. He returned the salute anyway and drove on. It was 7:30 a.m.

The 32nd parking lot had its usual gathering of soldiers with coffee and smokes before the eight o'clock company fall-in. A few moved out of the way to let the BMW park. Remmich walked to both bumpers to peel off his officer's rank insignias. He walked into the building, and his footsteps on the terrazzo steps echoed in the stairwell. He went inside and dropped the emblems into a trash can.

He got to the door and was about to grab the handle when it quickly opened. The rapid action startled him. The first sergeant was just as surprised. "Excuse me, Mr. Remmich." They greeted each other while the mole went past him into the room.

"How are things going?" asked Remmich.

Randolph expected the civilian because of the message from Stuttgart. It was customary for army posts to notify other units when someone scheduled a visit.

Randolph noticed Remmich held a plastic case box like those used to protect USBs. *Did it contain classified information?* He stared at it for a few seconds. The mole's left hand held the container firmly. He told the NCO, "Well, I've work to do. See you later." The first sergeant left, insulted, and Remmich closed the door.

He greeted the crew while he walked to the desk. They pushed their chairs backward and stood to attention. He smiled and told them, "At ease, men. At ease." He ordered, "Take your seats."

He felt their stares and knew he had to say something, "I'm impressed you still treat me with military respect, but I'm a civilian now. You don't have to stand up. And the first sergeant addressed me by name, not rank. To be clear, my rank as a civilian is equal to that of a captain but it isn't necessary to salute and stand to attention when I come in. Thank you anyway."

McClain wanted to know, "Sir, why are you here instead of Patch Barracks?"

"I have to finish decoding yesterday's Pentagon SCI. The electricity stopped working after lunch in a few buildings. My building was one of them. Although I waited there until four o'clock, the electricity didn't come back on. I decided to drive here to finish. I needed to come this way for a dental appointment anyway."

The screen came on, and he clicked into the program. Satisfied, he paged down to the part where he had stopped. The more he decoded the letters and numbers the more understandable it was. He never dreamed such an accomplishment was possible.

Two diagrams showed cylinder-shaped buildings. Remmich copied them onto the decrypted page.

A short while later their sliding chair noises distracted him as the men got up, grabbed their caps, and paraded out of the security office. Remmich glanced up at the clock and realized how fast time had gone by. He saved the copied scientific discovery and minimized the monitor. He decided to get some coffee too.

In the corridor, he saw Eric Miller talking with the first sergeant. Walking toward them he listened to Miller say, "I'll look into it." Randolph eased back into the administration doorway out of sight. Miller's face was set in a frown. As they approached each other, he said coldly, "Mr. Remmich."

Sensing his buddy's mood, he countered it with, "I'm glad to see you again, Eric. I missed you at the meeting the other day. Been getting along okay?"

Miller's jaw tightened before he spoke, which heightened Remmich's interest in why he was acting so uncongenial. Finally, returned the greeting and Remmich asked, "Want to get a coffee?"

"No. Thanks anyway." After a few seconds of silence, he looked at Remmich pointedly and asked, "I was told you are carrying around a USB. Is there classified information on it?"

He lied automatically, "No. Not yet. However, I do plan to copy the Pentagon's SCI material and return it to Stuttgart."

Miller pushed for more explanation. "Why are you copying it? Aren't you emailing the decrypted sections? Maybe you'd better give it to me when you're finished. I can have someone take it down to our main headquarters."

"I think not, Eric," he said firmly. "This assignment is my duty to perform for the US Army. My job is outside your command, my friend. You know my security clearance level remains the same. Copying the SCI is a safety measure, in case there is an electrical glitch. So, I believe we've talked enough about this subject. Agree?"

Remmich's remarks made Miller's ears burn. He was thankful there wasn't anyone around to witness his embarrassment, or so he thought. Colonel Collins was on vacation, which was why the chief NCO acted rough and ready. Out of the corner of his eye, he saw the movement of someone at the door frame. It was evident Randolph had, in fact, been there listening.

Miller relented, knowing he would get no further. "I can't make a coffee break because I have to attend a meeting at the 133rd Signal Corps across the street. How about lunch instead?"

"Well, sure. Noontime is fine." Miller nodded and smiled. Remmich relaxed too, ending with, "As long as we finish a little before one o'clock. I must leave by two o'clock. I have a two-thirty dental appointment at Leighton Barracks."

"Are you still getting medical coverage? I didn't realize your privileges continued after resigning."

"I am covered as a professional US government employee."

He returned to the office and resumed decoding. Once again, the contents amazed him; obtaining energy from photosynthesis and converting it into electrical power was something new. He continued to concentrate and decipher.

Screeching chairs distracted him again. It was lunchtime.

Remmich followed a group of soldiers into the snack bar. Sophie Litz waved her hand to get his attention and called melodically, "Hello, Captain Remmich. Yoo-hoo! Captain Remmich."

He walked over to the stand. The German woman blurted out, "It's gut to see you again, Captain. I was surprised to find out you retired." Her countenance changed to a more serious mode. "I hope you vill still visit us. We missed you."

He gently squeezed her hand and answered, "Thank you." Her smile conveyed a kind spirit. "I will visit as often as I can." Miller joined him. Sophie greeted him too. He smiled back at her before he and Remmich got in line.

There were many soldiers getting food ahead of them. It took five minutes to slide their trays to the food they wanted, get a drink, and pay. Miller's eyes widened because Remmich's plate included a large order of fries, a quarter-pound burger with cheese, lettuce, tomatoes, and mayo, and a large Diet Coke. Miller insisted on paying before they walked to their favorite table. He chuckled, "With all of the food on your tray, it looks like you haven't eaten American for a while."

Showing great restraint by not stuffing his face immediately, he replied, "Eric, I can't get the good old American greasy cooking at other places. No Dutch or German restaurant cooks fries like this. And to get a beef quarter-pounder outside of the army's restaurants, you practically have to slaughter the bull yourself. Europeans eat mostly veal, pork, and lamb. There are fast food restaurants all over Germany, but their burgers are thin and tasteless."

"So I have found out," said Miller.

They finished. Remmich leaned against the back of the chair and gently rubbed his stomach. "Damn, that was delicious!"

Miller laughed. "It sure was. Now I have to fast for several days before getting more fried food."

"Do you fry food at the apartment?"

"Rarely. I bought a toaster oven and a small propane grill at the Leighton PX soon after you moved. I broil or barbecue because it's a healthier way to cook. How about you? Do you eat a lot of fried stuff?"

"Actually, no. The Dutch cook by baking and boiling. There is some frying, but Lilly is health conscious, and I'm lucky she cares. Perhaps I need to barbecue, too. Besides, before resigning, I had my annual physical and found out my blood cholesterol is high. The doctor told me to change my usual style of eating."

"You sure as hell are not following the advice today!" exclaimed Miller.

"Listen, sinning occasionally isn't going to tip the world off its axis. Agree?" He got a grin.

Miller accepted a cigarette, and before using the lighter, his buddy lit the last match in the book. He fiddled with the empty book by bending the wrapper around the striker section, bending that in half, and then using his finger to move it back and forth.

Miller leaned on the table and spoke in a teasing way. "You enjoy destroying those things, don't you?"

He maintained silence and played with the matchbook. His concentration was somewhere else. Miller couldn't remember when this behavior became a part of Remmich's personality. *Was a subconscious force directing his friend? Can a person change so much so quickly? It was evident Paul's mind was somewhere, but where?*

Unexpectedly, without looking up, Remmich blurted out, "So what are your plans?"

Miller kept watching the bending shenanigans and answered, "I enrolled in the continuing courses for coding and decoding encrypted satellite email."

"Do you think this second-level course is going to be as challenging as the introductory class we took?"

"Probably. I'm sure there will be similarities." He did not continue, because he wanted to talk about something else. While he sipped the soft drink, he wondered how to ask his question without seeming intrusive.

Before he could ask, Remmich added his thought. "I believe continuing a course in the same subject is a good omen for our records." He stopped bending the matchbook.

Quietly, Miller said, "Are you still carrying the flash drive?"

Remmich looked down at the table, temples pulsing, and contemplated how to answer. He raised his head, staring with aggravation. He repeated, "Eric, it's no one's concern whether or not I carry classified files with me. I'm permitted to do such things. If Collins were here, he'd tell both you and Randolph to mind your own business." He added, "Why did you ask me again?"

Miller couldn't miss the irritation in his friend's voice and answered, "No reason, but I agree with you that Randolph's manner is bossy."

"Definitely. He can be a pest, but you have to appreciate that you outrank a first sergeant," advised Remmich. "Anyway, let's change the subject."

Miller agreed because dragging out a controversial issue would only incite an argument. "What are your plans for the month?"

Remmich began to answer, and suddenly, a vibration in his molar took command of his thoughts. His expression became somber and his eyes seem to glaze. Miller observed the transformation curiously. "I have to be excused." Miller watched as he lifted the cell phone to his ear when he stood up. He walked toward the entrance and disappeared. "Weird," Miller thought to himself.

"Yes, Adnaw, I have the information. What? Just a minute. A truck passing by is making it hard to hear. Hold on." Remmich moved inside and turned to face the wall, holding a finger in his other ear. In a low volume, he said, "I will email it to you when I return to Amsterdam."

Miller began to stand up. When he noticed his buddy walking to their table, he sat back down. While Remmich seated himself, Eric asked, "What was that all about?"

Still somewhat transfixed, he couldn't answer right away. He rubbed the bridge of his nose and improvised as best he could, "Oh, it was...Lilly's father. He wants to know when I'm returning."

"Funny. I didn't hear your phone ring. You just got up suddenly and walked away."

Unsettled, Remmich changed the subject and replied, "I must return to finish the encryption deciphering, and then leave for the dentist's appointment. Let's get a refill before going back."

They refilled their cups at the soda machine, paid, and went outside. Miller asked, "So, what are your plans for the rest of the month? I was thinking about coming to Amsterdam."

"I plan to go home today after I finish at the dentist's office. Thankfully, I won't have to take any more trips to visit vineyards in another country for a while."

Miller thought about the answer. "So, you are driving directly to Amsterdam and not to Stuttgart?"

The question reminded Remmich he had not mentioned returning the flash drive there. Calmly, he said, "I just remembered. After the dentist appointment, I have to return to Stuttgart. I guess my plans to go home will be delayed a few hours."

"I see. But, man, you are going be driving for a lot of hours. Do you want me to assign one of the men to return it for you?"

"No. No. I'll drive down after my dental appointment, and just get home later."

Miller didn't pursue it.

They entered the security office. McClain accosted Miller, telling him they had to leave. Remmich sat at his desk and watched them walk out. He finished decrypting in an hour and saved the information on the hard drive. Next, he interrupted Staff Sergeant Ramsey. "Where did those two go?"

The soldier stopped typing and answered, "They went to the 133rd Signal Corps for a meeting, sir."

Remmich nodded.

He copied all the decrypted data to take with him. Then, he emailed everything to Stuttgart before turning off the computer. He placed the flash drive into the case and put it into his jacket pocket.

Just then, the captain and the master sergeant returned. Remmich told him that he was leaving. Miller told him, "I want to walk outside with you."

Remmich opened the car door and tossed his jacket to the passenger side. Facing each other, Miller told him, "The reason I wanted to come out with you is you seem to go off on strange tangents sometimes as if you're somewhere else. You abruptly stop paying attention to our conversations. It kind of reminds me of when we visited the castle together. Remember?" Remmich started to say something, but Miller added, "When we were in the snack bar you just walked away and held your phone to your ear." He studied Paul's eyes, wondering if everything was all right. "I mean, are you under some pressure, or is someone threatening you? Are you in trouble? Why didn't you make the call from our table?"

Remmich's eyes darted around. He couldn't answer his best friend. There was a void in his head. It was embarrassing. The words "threatened" and "being in trouble" made him cautious. Instead of getting into another argument like they did at the Marienberg Castle and today, Remmich took a deep breath, put his hand on Eric's shoulder and affirmed, "Hey, I'm doing okay."

"Dammit, Paul. You sure?"

Instead of giving Miller an answer, he smiled and sat down in the driver's seat. He started the engine and opened the window and came out with, "I never got your apartment address. Lilly needs it for your wedding invitation. And by the way, are you and Candice coming?"

Miller lifted a business card out of his shirt pocket, wrote down the address, and gave it to him. "As for Candice, I'll ask her. Her flights now are scheduled to be in Amsterdam on certain weekends."

"Yes. I understand. Okay, Lilly is going to send the invitation to you. Give me a call when you visit Candice in Amsterdam."

He put the gear in reverse, backed out of the space, and drove off. This time the MP did not salute. He only saw the emblem on the window identifying Remmich as a US government civilian employee. Miller stood there wondering about his friend's psychological condition. He went into the building with his forehead creased. *What in the hell is wrong with him?*

***

Remmich took the stairs up to the second floor of the dentist's office. He entered and signed in. Five minutes later a dental assistant escorted him to a room, and he sat in a patient chair. Another assistant approached and placed an X-ray negative into his mouth. She took the picture and displayed it on the monitor. Mustafa entered the room and made a visual exam of the molar and glanced at the x-ray image. Pleased, he told his patient the filling was secure. "We set up your next appointment for you." He gave him a card with the date.

Congested traffic lessened on the Dutch highway going west. Remmich's thoughts along the way centered on the Third World countries needing him to fulfill a mission. Another was getting married. The last idea led him to wonder if Miller would telephone Stuttgart about him returning the data. He debated about which general would be contacted if Miller notified them.

The hotel was a block away. Remmich turned and drove into the back parking entrance, and an attendant took over. He rode the freight elevator up to his floor. It was close to 8 p.m. After turning on the laptop, he sent the copied science data. He waited until Alzuhari responded that he'd received the email. His regular post-hypnotic suggestion condition returned. He decided to contact headquarters in the morning. No one was there now, except the CQ and the cleaners. He turned off the laptop and walked down the stairway to the Brasserie-Schiller bar-restaurant. While blowing smoke out of his nose, he motioned with his hand to the bartender. He ordered a sandwich and a beer. Patiently, he waited to be with the woman he loved.

23

Operation Find

Captain Miller received a follow-up email from one he'd sent a few days before. It asked if he intended to be present at the CIC meeting. He printed the page and conferred with the colonel.

"From what I know, it means USAREUR is going to talk about the counterintelligence group here in Germany. They need to find qualified personnel," said Collins. "Paul Remmich is cleared to decipher the encrypted code. But, if you agree to talk to them, they will offer you a broader position." He looked at his watch and uttered, "Hell, it's time for a coffee break, Captain. Care to join me?"

Rank didn't have any privileges in the long breakfast line at the snack bar. Miller looked at the printout again, ignoring the moving line. Collins nudged him to move forward. He took a couple of sideway steps, still reading. "Why me?" he asked the colonel.

"Like I said, it simply means they may ask you to become part of the covert operations team. They pursue offensive espionage, including spies and secret groups. The counterintelligence group, or CIC, believes active-duty spies are here in Germany. Unfortunately, like other branches in the army, they are being forced to downsize by thirty percent. Early retirement for older people, both military and civilian, is a reality. The army will replenish but with a smaller number. They want younger people." He paid for both food orders.

"Care for a smoking section, Captain?" asked Collins.

"I'll leave it up to you, sir."

"I smoke a pipe, so you pick the table."

He followed Miller to the same place he and Remmich used.

"Thank you for the coffee and doughnut."

"Don't mention it, but don't expect it all the time."

After Collins finished his doughnut, he stuffed tobacco into the pipe and lit it. The white smoke had a cherry-vanilla aroma. He puffed one more time and told Miller the CIC favored personnel who work in his area of expertise.

"I'm not sure I understand, Colonel."

"I don't want to go too far into this subject because I don't know everything about the details. Let's wait for the meeting."

Miller's naiveté with the CIC group made him ask, "Is it similar to the monthly meetings, sir?"

"No. This is different," said Collins, while he read a short article in the *Stars and Stripes* newspaper someone had left on the table.

"Is Paul Remmich going to attend?"

He stopped reading while holding the paper. Looking at the captain, he said, "No. This is for active-duty personnel only. It isn't a regular meeting."

He took the last sip of coffee and suggested they return to the office.

Collins wanted to share a thought. "Do you realize, Captain, the newspaper article I just read states there are covert dealings between the various Shi'ite and Sunni people? Many secretly work with ISIS."

They reached the front of the building and stopped. Collins smacked his pipe against the palm of his hand to empty it onto the grass. "It's going to take a good kick in the ass to stop the espionage of hired foreigners." Out of the blue, he added, "I wonder if Russia has the same situation? Just talking among us is not going to change the problem."

The colonel found a note on his desk to call General Elliott. He dialed and was put on hold. He noticed Miller passing by the room and motioned for him to come in and sit down. While they waited, he put on the speakerphone.

The general clicked on and identified himself.

"Good morning, Jerry," said Collins. "I got a note saying the date changed for the upcoming meeting. It's now on September 3rd."

"Yes. Good morning, Joe. Sutherland changed the date to give the troops in Northern Africa and the Mideast more time to get here. After the meeting, people interested can talk with CIC at length."

The colonel explained he and Captain Miller were going to arrive Tuesday afternoon, and asked, "Care to have dinner with us, Jerry?"

Elliott hesitated, then answered, "I'd love to, Joe, but you are familiar with how things are before a meeting. I'll tell you what; if I'm free I'll be glad to join you and Captain Miller. Why don't you call me the afternoon you arrive? I'll know better then."

"Will do, Jerry. Take care." Collins hung up.

"I take it we're going to leave early afternoon on the second, sir?"

"Yes," he replied, while changing the date in his daily organizer.

***

Paul Remmich was bent over under the car hood, fiddling around to see if the engine oil was clean and full. When he unscrewed the transmission cap to check the liquid level, he felt a vibration in his molar. His conscious mental state shifted, and he left without tightening the lid and closing the hood.

He went to his room and woodenly pressed the phone's autodial. He recognized the familiar voice and identified himself. "This is Agent PSR."

Alzuhari greeted him. He told the mole the information sent was not enough. It didn't seem to have an ending. There should be additional data to copy. "Look for it and send me the rest of the report."

Remmich told him it will have to be after the next security meeting at Patch Barracks.

The order embedded in Remmich's subconscious took precedence over his job in Amsterdam, even his marriage if need be.

"Before we end this talk, your schedule shows you are getting married later this month. When I get the remaining material, you will be left alone to arrange for the wedding. I see you and Lilly are going to the French Riviera for a honeymoon?"

His mole thought for a moment, then answered, "Yes." The line went dead.

He returned to the parking lot to find a hotel attendant standing next to his car. The employee said, "You left the transmission cap laying aside and forgot to close the hood." Remmich thanked him.

***

Miller and Collins drove separately to Stuttgart. The main entrance to Patch Barracks Kaserne was full. Miller followed behind the colonel. Another MP on the right waved them to the adjacent gate. The MP's hand computer verified their car tags with a distinctive "buzz."

The V Corps first floor swarmed with officers and NCOs.

One of the sergeants at the reception desk led them to Elliott's office. He got to the reception desk and told the sergeant secretary the general expected them. He led them to the office. Elliott was with his assistant, speaking on the phone. He ended the call and introduced Major Thomas Shott to Collins and Miller. The general explained, “Gentlemen, it’s good to see you, but I’ve got a lot to do organizing tomorrow’s meeting. I won’t be able to have dinner with you.” They spoke for a few more minutes. Elliott didn’t want to get too friendly with the colonel, other than exchanging war stories. The guy usually asked too many questions.

***

On Wednesday morning, Collins led Miller to the large conference room. They entered and chose a place to sit. Others talked with them about the meeting. Major Shott entered and brought everyone to attention. Sutherland and his attaché walked in behind him. Shott ordered, “At ease.”

The generals stood at the middle seats at the front table. When they sat down, everyone took their seats. Two other high-ranking officers representing CIC sat on either side of them. They introduced themselves. Thirty other people attended the meeting. Lower ranked officers and NCOs sat in folding chairs along the walls.

“Good morning, fellow officers and NCOs,” said Elliott. “General Sutherland and I want to welcome you to ‘Operation Find.’” He looked down at his notes with pursed lips, clenching his jaw. Looking up he added, “I’ll make this short and sweet. We are aware of some of the spy activities of the foreign cleaning crews. We are now aware internal espionage is a reality as well. We believed active-duty moles are stealing classified documents.” The room was silent.

“Now, to confuse matters even more. Some of the Middle East cleaners have let themselves get caught as part of a scheme. We pay too much attention to prosecuting them and ignore the continuing espionage. We've managed to put some of them behind bars. They know our JAG lawyers must follow Geneva Convention rules. A German lawyer represents the spies. Why? Because they have to register as migrants with the German immigration offices, they are protected until found guilty. Fortunately, they get expelled from this country. The Germans are not stupid. They are cautious because the same thing has happened to their government."

Elliott stopped talking, stood up, and leaned on his hands on the table. With another stern look, he pointed out, "We must be more vigilant. Leaving classified material lying around for easy access is a crime punishable by court-martial and prison."

He let the CIC officers talk for a few minutes. It included what Collins and Miller talked about; early retirement and recruiting new blood for CIC. The conversation continued for another hour. They told people, for those interested, more discussion would follow. The officer sitting next to Elliott ended their portion of the meeting telling them a soldier needed six years of completed service to become eligible.

Sutherland glanced at his notes while he sipped coffee. A sergeant dimmed the lighting and focused on the overhead projector. While this took place, the general acknowledged, "For your information, we found that espionage activities are varied. One, in particular, involves small and large rocket constructions, not just Middle East troops' field maneuvers. I'm referring to ISIS."

He hesitated for a moment. He got a nod and said, "Master Sergeant Jenkins, please begin."

A spreadsheet listed the number of immigrants working for the armed forces in Germany. It included what they did, their native countries, and which ones returned to their native countries when their visas expired. There was a column showing which ones were spies. The last column showed the amount of money used to employ them.

Sutherland explained, "The information that is most important to one person here today may not be known by another one. You are going to receive a directory of today's attendees. We expect you to communicate with each other using email and phones. Being aware is just as important as sharing ideas. What if a spy gains access to bio-weaponry? Like an ampoule containing an infectious disease. Alert readiness is what we were taught. Let's use it. We need to stop the moles from providing the enemy with information. Lack of attention to detail will damage the technical procedures of the United States military and our industrial technology."

He had one last thing to say. "This afternoon we will discuss the primary sources and get answers. I urge all of you to talk to each other at lunch. For example, what security problems exist at your posts or embassies? Spy activity can prepare the way for terrorist suicide bombings and chemical attacks. It can't be stopped without knowing ahead of time. We need a group effort."

Sutherland stopped and looked at the clock. It wasn't noon yet, but he wanted everyone to return on time for the second part. Letting the group go early to beat other GIs to the snack bar would ensure they could do it.

The group got in line holding trays and utensils. Miller and Collins were among the first to get their food. During lunch, soldiers shared their experiences. Miller just listened. He wanted to talk in the meeting about something different, although it somewhat paralleled the subject matter. They returned to the conference room at 1:30.

The generals and CIC officers sat back in their chairs to let the soldiers ask questions and allow others to answer and share ideas. Occasionally, the conversation drifted off into tangents. Soldiers complained they had too much to do in their units; limited time would prevent them from getting involved. *These weren't the soldiers CIC wanted.* Others liked the idea of getting a directory. *Communicating, even if only due to speculation, was better than ignoring a potential problem.*

Two hours later, the discussion ended. Elliott asked if there were any questions. He saw a lot of hands raised. He selected a man vigorously waving his hand. "Yes, Captain Miller?"

He stood and said, "Excuse me, sir. I have an off-the-wall question about my job." He cleared his throat. "Since Captain Paul Remmich's resignation, he has been appointed to the same military security level as when he was on active duty. However, he is a civilian now, decrypting for the army. Are we going to operate by a combination of military staff and civilians?" He hesitated for a few seconds and then added, "That's the first of my questions, sir."

"I guess that means you want me to answer it first?" He got a yes. "Captain Miller, Mr. Remmich's duties include decrypting classified communication. Only a limited number of INSCOM officials in Washington and here at USAREUR V Corps share his vast knowledge. In other words, Captain, he's very valuable to us."

"So, he's the only civilian in V Corps who can do the encryption reading and interpretation?"

Elliott got agitated. "Yes. I told you what he can legally do. For now, he is the only one at V Corps, besides you."

"Yes, sir, I'm part of the team too." He wanted to assure himself the civilian was going to be kept on board. "Are we letting Mr. Remmich remain employed and accountable?"

Now Elliott looked irritated. "For the moment, Captain Miller, I do not worry about his access to classifieds. Yet, I understand the point you're making, and I agree we need more V Corps military people to do this work at other posts." He hesitated for a moment, then added, "I recall, Captain, I believe you're an officer considered for training for the CIC also. Am I correct?"

"Yes, sir, I am going to look into it."

"What's your second question, Captain?"

"Sir, just after the last security meeting over a week ago, Mr. Remmich drove to the 32nd. He brought a flash drive with him. It had encrypted security information he got from Stuttgart."

People in the room began to mumble. Elliott ordered, "At ease, everyone. Captain, Mr. Remmich used his better judgment. He couldn't do any more work at this command post. We experienced electrical failures here in several buildings." He decided to emphasize the problem to get Miller to stop talking. "Everything, including lighting, elevators, computers, and communication, went dead in three buildings. As I understand it, Mr. Remmich waited until 4:00 and only then decided to go to your unit in Würzburg to finish it. Yes, he transferred the decrypted information onto a flash drive. We do things like that here at V Corps because there have been glitches before. You will begin to do this at your office, Captain Miller. So, to make a long story short, if we would have lost the information, he'd have something saved."

An officer interrupted when the general stopped. He verified what Elliott had said. Talk among some of the others stationed there confirmed they had experienced the same problem.

Meanwhile, Elliott had a chance to think and add confusion. The clincher statement was, "Finally, Captain, Mr. Remmich is one among other civilians working in security intelligence. Do you suspect him to be a spy?" Miller shook his head. Elliott smiled and added, "We're positive this man has no affiliation with any espionage group."

"I agree, sir."

Elliott waited for other officers or NCOs to comment. They didn't, because the general's disposition was evident. With raised eyebrows, he asked, "Are you finished?"

"Yes, sir."

He sat down, still troubled by Remmich carrying around the flash drive. Elliott's dismissal made him forget to ask if it was returned to V Corps.

Sutherland ended with, "One final thing for those of us stationed in Germany. The next V Corps meeting is the eighteenth at 0800 hours. For those of you interested in talking to CIC, you can wait here."

Elliott turned to his attaché and nodded. Major Shott announced, "This 'Operation Find' meeting is adjourned." The generals stood up and walked out. Everyone stood in attention.

Miller stayed there with two other officers. Unbeknownst to them, the two CIC officials they were talking with were conducting an interview. The general discussion evolved into questioning by the higher-ranking officers. They evaluated opinions and possible solutions from the lower-grade officers. It ended an hour later. Miller wondered if doing this work would remove him from his present job.

24

Luck

Remmich's early morning drive to Stuttgart was as crazy as usual on the Autobahn. He left early to beat traffic, maintaining a speed of one hundred miles per hour. *The BMW loved it!*

He slowed down and stopped behind several cars at the Patch Barracks west gate, four and a half hours after leaving Amsterdam. After the MP scanned and verified his entry credentials, the corporal waved Remmich on base. The Patton Drive parking lot was not full. He parked and strolled into the headquarters building in a good mood. *He had a plan.* After he signed in at the front desk, the sergeant directed him to go to the conference room. Sutherland wanted him to be present at the meeting.

The place was packed. Remmich exchanged greetings with a few people and sat against the wall. Minutes later everyone heard, "We're going to begin." All those in the room stood to attention. The upper brass entered the conference room. General Elliott told all of them to take their seats.

Sutherland welcomed everyone. They returned the greeting. As he spoke, his demeanor changed. "There was another killing at UNIMI in Stockholm. It was one of our men. Captain Frank Jenkins. Some of you may have seen him at the conference a couple of weeks ago."

Remmich watched Miller walk into the room. They exchanged glances. He sat down with the other officers. The only thing on Remmich's mind was what went on in that meeting he wasn't invited to attend.

The general explained the captain had been shot twice at close range with a snub-nose Beretta 9mm. The Stockholm forensics report believed the murder was probably committed by someone he knew. The general offered his opinion; spies are seeking potential moles. He based the idea on Miller's experience before his transfer from UNIMI. He said the unknown suspects were skilled in their maneuvers. They carefully selected the person they needed for their plan.

The general saw a waving hand. "Okay, I'll answer one question for now." He pointed to an officer, who stood up.

"Sir, from what you just stated, do you think the killing resulted from him refusing to do what they wanted? I'm assuming it's connected to espionage."

"Yes," he affirmed in an angry tone. The young officer didn't expect such an abrupt answer and sat down slowly.

Sutherland leaned onto the table and folded his hands. "There is no rational reason for this murder. UNIMI dealt with the local authorities. They told the police the instructor made a roll call every morning. One day our man wasn't there. They found him dead in his studio apartment." He flattened his hands on the conference table. "The detectives believe another killing by the same people occurred before this tragedy. Lieutenant Bernie Bliss, a British soldier, got a bullet in his head. The forensics match in both killings." Leaning back against the chair with his arms outstretched and hands flat on the table, he added, "Our own Captain Miller had an altercation with Iraqis when he attended UNIMI. There may be a connection." He didn't go into detail.

The conversation was so interesting, nobody noticed the time except the general's attaché. He announced a fifteen-minute break.

As bodies scattered out to the corridor, Remmich approached his friend and they said good morning to each other. "Eric, I didn't see you before we got started."

"I wasn't here. Collins called me and wanted to review tomorrow's next encryption seminar with me."

"Ah, yes, I remember talking about it with you. So, tomorrow is the second day." Miller answered yes while they got coffee. Remmich suggested, "Let's go out for a smoke." They walked out onto the sidewalk with others. Standing near the butt can, he asked, "So, what's going to take place in this encryption course?" He lit his buddy's cigarette first.

With caution, Miller responded. "It's a carryover from the binary vocabulary code in our introduction a few years ago. These are three-day classes, and that's it." He stopped short, sipped, and took a puff.

Remmich decided to bait him. "I'm confident you'll do just fine."

He wanted to avoid talking about it anymore. "Look, it's not worrying me. Everything's computerized, anyway."

The mole didn't waste any time. "So, tell me about the 'Operations Find' meeting."

Miller felt cornered and took a coffee sip to stall his response. "It wasn't anything new. Most of us are aware of the espionage tactics by Middle East workers. Sutherland and Elliott discussed civilian retirees and getting new army recruits." He stopped talking to omit his involvement with CIC. He took another sip and puffed on the cigarette. The explanation satisfied Remmich.

A soldier interrupted everyone from the entrance door, telling them the conference was about to resume.

"I suppose I'll see you later, my friend."

"Aren't you going upstairs?"

"No. General Sutherland told me to only sit in for the first session. He wants me to continue to decode the Pentagon encryption document. I'm working on the part I couldn't finish yesterday."

He entered the office and hung his jacket on the back of the chair. After sitting down, he turned on the computer. While it booted up, he said, "I wonder if another power glitch will occur today."

"We hope not," replied a private. Other NCOs expressed their concerns.

He moved the mouse to click into the system, and the cursor froze. *You've got to be kidding me,* he thought. Frustrated, he shut down the machine. While waiting for it to boot up again, he wanted to know when the electricity came back on. A couple voices answered together, saying after dinner. His computer finally came on, but the screen froze.

"Oh, no, not again!" he blurted out.

"What's wrong, sir?"

"Now this damn thing keeps locking up."

An E-4 soldier understood his frustration and said, "I guess you're going to have to talk to someone in CID."

Remmich pursed his lips because he knew the way things worked. He placed his hands flat on the desk and said, "Okay. I guess that's what I have to do."

He went downstairs and walked along a dimly lit, dungeon-like corridor. Halfway down the hallway, he opened a door labeled "CID—USAREUR."

An attractive PFC soldier sat behind a computer. She turned to look at him and asked, "Can I help you?"

Remmich introduced himself and explained the problem.

"Do you have any identification?"

He scanned the large area. There were other offices, and cubicles lined the wall in the central office. There was no one sitting in them. He removed the lanyard around his neck. The private walked over to the counter. He handed his ID to her, and she also asked for his valid driver's license. He got it out of his wallet and gave it to her.

The private returned to her desk to look for his name and photo on the computer. Satisfied, she returned to the counter. Before she said anything, he told her the reason for the visit. He also questioned why there wasn't anyone else there. The soldier gave the details. "All of the staff is attending the meeting upstairs. The junior repair specialist is with them, but he's not the man you need. He understands a little bit. He's new. You're going to have to come back when the senior technician is here. Sorry." She returned the ID and his license.

Remmich thought for a moment. Hoping his British accent and polite manner had put her at ease, he smiled disarmingly. "Private Sellers, I'm capable of correcting glitches myself. Time is crucial, Ms. Sellers, and the higher brass wants the encryption decoding done soon. Mind if I try?" He didn't go into detail.

Sellers hesitated before saying, "I suppose."

He knew she was hesitant about letting him in the room by himself. "It's okay." He reassured, "You probably don't know my civilian status is equal to my past active-duty rank. I'll make sure you don't get into any trouble. I promise."

"What rank are you equal to?"

"Captain."

She relented, and he followed her to the adjoining electrical circuit room. It had cabinets containing surveillance and telephone wiring for the base. He glanced through several cabinet windows and studied the connection labels. The third cabinet had a tag identifying his office and the wiring connection locations.

She stood beside him with a master key and opened the wood-framed glass door. "My duty station chief explained to me sometimes the wire shoes disconnect because vibration loosens the screws. He told me when the electric current flow returned from the blackout, it had a stronger jolt."

He thanked her with another smile, and she left.

Years before when he first arrived at Patch Barracks, Remmich had been given a tour of the building, including the CID office. He spent time being taught about the connections. Since he was mechanically inclined, learning the connections' technical data wasn't confusing. A staff sergeant, who was the stand-in technician, showed the circuit switching system to him. He explained how the different color-coded wires were connected to computers and communication systems. All the machines worked from colored cables. Each attached to a particular processor for the transfer of classified material. If something went wrong with a network, the wire connections got examined first.

The first snag he saw was a loose end wire shoe. *What luck!* But he didn't have any tools, so he decided to get the PFC. She found a tool packet in a desk drawer. He returned to the circuit board and used a Phillips screwdriver to tighten the screw onto the horseshoe fitting. For good measure, he pulled out a business card and sketched a diagram of the wiring layout on the back.

Now he needed to find out if the upstairs security encryption machine was operational. Making a call to the office would be faster, but it was more advantageous to maintain a smokescreen. He walked back to his office and sat down at the desk. The computer turned on, but he lied in an aggravated way. "Ah, god, it still isn't working." He put it in sleep mode. No one said anything to him or paid attention. They kept working because they just thought he complained too much.

He reentered the CID office and saw PFC Sellers still by herself. She didn't notice him. She wore headphones and was concentrating on copying a recorded telephone conversation. He walked up and lightly touched her arm. He pointed to the circuit boardroom. She nodded to indicate it was okay to go back.

He unscrewed two wires and switched a green cable with a black wire. He went upstairs and was able to log onto the Internet. Next, he typed in his email address. Seconds later the file appeared on the screen. That was all he needed to do. Now he could send the secret files directly without CID's knowledge.

Remmich walked back downstairs to the CID office. It was fifteen minutes before lunch. There was a problem; he'd lost track of time and the office crew had returned to their workplace. Straight-faced Staff Sergeant Jones accosted him, and Remmich had to go through the whole verification process again. He handed his ID card and license to the NCO, who conferred with the private. The guy listened to her explain what was going on. A few minutes later he returned to the civilian and gave him the IDs. They entered the circuit boardroom. Concentrating on the wires, Remmich told the sergeant, "I have to tighten a few of the mounting screws." He looked at the guy and pointed, "These colored wires must be tightened securely in place." He moved his forefinger across the area to show the NCO, but Jones looked confused. "Do much work with these things, Sergeant?"

Jones looked embarrassed as he straightened and answered, "No, not me. Although I've had electrical training for this work, I'm new to this job. My senior NCO does not want me to do anything that might cause a problem. Besides, I've never fixed anything inside these terminal boxes before. Our senior NCO in the other office does this kind of work. He's teaching me. But he's on a NATO field maneuver." Remmich asked what he did. "Right now, I listen to telephone chatter, identify people who are making personal calls with military phones, and monitor classified security information discussed over the phone." This guy seemed to be the right person to follow up with. *Remmich remembered getting his ass chewed out for the illegal telephone call.*

A delivery worker entered the CID office and set three large boxes with pizzas on the counter. A delicious aroma filled the area. There was a lot of chatter about being hungry. The delivery man took the money and left. Jones quickly said, "excuse me" to Remmich and bolted for the hot pizza. Now the mole was home free. For the time being, he left the two switched wires in place. Sometime in the future, he planned to pretend the system was stuck again; he'd return them to their proper place. The pizza aroma stimulated his hunger, and he decided to do the rest of the work after lunch. He couldn't wait to email the decrypted information.

Remmich got into a crowded cafeteria line. General Elliott noticed him and walked in front of several soldiers to talk to him. Wisely, no one complained.

"Oh, General, I didn't realize you were here. How was the last part of the conference?"

"It concluded with being aware espionage is a twenty-four-hour reality. Infiltration of espionage agents into V Corps must stop, not decrease."

"Yes. I agree."

"By the way, did you finish with the decrypting?"

"No, not yet." Then he lied and told the general the computer stopped responding, and a technician had to reboot it more than once. He ended the explanation by saying everything was operating again.

In a frustrated tone, Elliott asked, "You mean to tell me it took until now to get the damn job done?"

"Yes, sir, it did." Remmich didn't pursue the matter, and so he asked an off-the-wall question. "Planned your leave time yet, General?"

The lunch line moved forward, and Remmich caught a glimpse of his buddy waiting to pay. He looked back at Elliott, who said, "My wife and I enjoy vacationing in Spain. We're going to San Sebastian, a city on the Atlantic."

"How did you find this vacation?"

In a better mood, the general said the trip he and his wife had purchased was an army discount package. He elaborated about the costs for round-trip air travel, hotel costs, and other features.

"That's a hell of a deal, sir."

He saw Miller paying the cashier. Remmich and the general stood behind three people in line. After the two paid, they separated and walked to separate tables.

Miller started to read *The New York Times*, Frankfurt edition. Hearing a food tray placed on the table interrupted his reading. He looked up and saw who it was. "I thought you left to go home."

"The decoding is taking a little longer than expected."

They both took bites of their sandwiches. "How come?"

Remmich deftly repeated the lie he gave to the general, hoping his friend accepted the answer.

He took his last bite, swallowed, and said, "I wanted you to know I rented a tux for your wedding. Plus, I'll be staying at Candice's place from now on. If you remember, she recently signed a lease for a one-bedroom apartment on the south side of Amsterdam."

"Sounds serious."

Miller smiled. "Yeah, it's getting better. She is an interesting person and a sweet woman. We like a lot of the same things."

While he talked, Remmich half listened. He wondered how much of a burden his buddy could become visiting Amsterdam. He finished speaking, and Remmich suggested, "Have you talked about getting her to visit you in Wurzburg? I mean, you know there's much to see. You have an apartment there."

"We've talked about it."

"I guess with her in the air so much you guys must have costly telephone bills."

"Not really. She has an unlimited call package with the cell phone company."

"Of course, but what's the cost of your bill?" asked Remmich.

"Well," he began, his eyes lighting up in amusement, "it's high."

Grinning also, Remmich said, "I'm afraid to ask how much your last payment was."

Miller chuckled to cover his embarrassment and to avoid answering the question. "We've kicked around alternating our visits between Würzburg and Amsterdam. Do you remember her friend, Alice Johnson, at the Blues Alley jazz restaurant? She's the Delta Airlines general manager at the Schiphol Airport." Remmich said he did. "Anyway, she offered to let Candice borrow her car occasionally. But Delta can also arrange a rental for her."

Remmich talked about how he and Lilly had alternated getting together. A few times she visited him, but he drove to see her more times in Amsterdam during the courtship. He lit a cigarette and exhaled dual plumes of smoke out of his nose. "You didn't forget meeting me on Friday afternoon for the rehearsal, did you?"

"No, of course not."

"Since I've never done this before, I hope it doesn't drag on too long. The faster the better, so we can go out and party."

Miller burst into a laugh and said, "Sounds like you're ready. Yeah, we can go out. You don't mind if Candice goes with us, do you?"

"Of course not. Hell, you and Candice will keep me pure."

"We'll watch your butt." He smiled in an ornery way, and Remmich chuckled.

Calming down, he said, "Lilly's parents aren't having a dinner party after the rehearsal. They're traditional. After 6:00 p.m., they believe it's bad luck to see my bride and vice versa."

"That is old-fashioned. Superstition, I guess, from old beliefs. At least, we know they're not true."

"Whatever," said Remmich. He began again, a thoughtful look on his face. "Oh, so you don't drive around in circles, Eric, do you have the name and address of the church?"

"Yes, but Candice and I are taking a cab. When you and I are finished with the rehearsal, we're going out by taxi again. It's safer to let someone else take me where I want to go in case I get tipsy."

After lunch, they went back to the headquarters building. Miller attended the afternoon session, and Remmich went to the office to finish the work. He secretly opened the Internet and his email station. Within seconds, it had copied and transferred the decoded photosynthesis information to his home desktop. He used the army's email to send the same to the central G-2 office. He turned off the computer and bid farewell. The few soldiers did the same.

No one mentioned the flash drive.

25

Ring Exchanges

Remmich returned to Amsterdam and drove the BMW into the hotel's driveway. An attendant wasn't there, which led him to think the place must be busy. He got out and noticed the time on his watch. *Long day,* he thought to himself. Finally, a driver arrived and drove the car to the parking lot.

He wanted Lilly to eat dinner with him to talk about Friday's wedding rehearsal. He stood with his back to the opening elevator door and saw her at the end of the corridor working as the restaurant's hostess. He turned and pressed the button to his floor. As soon as he walked into his room, the telephone rang.

"Hello,"

"I saw you get on the elevator. Care to join me in the kitchen dining area for something to eat in a half-hour? I'll be off then."

"Good. I'll be there."

Remmich sat at the desk, and his subliminal training took over. He turned on the computer and waited while it booted up. He logged in and opened his electronic mail. *Bingo!* The data was there, and he double-clicked to open the file. He scrolled to the end of the last page. He pressed the control and home keys and returned to the beginning. Going to his email contacts list, he clicked on the code name for Adnaw Alzuhari. A minute later a return message appeared on the computer screen confirming the information arrived. The stronger mind control reduced, and he reverted to his normal subconscious state. It was time for dinner. He wanted to discuss the weekend's plans.

***

Eric Miller sat among other soldiers attending the three-day encryption coding and decoding course taught by the CIC. At the front of the room, two officers introduced themselves: Colonel Jim Kirby and Lieutenant Colonel Mike Hoppes. "For purposes of making this seminar less stressful," said Hoppes, "I want all of you to understand there are no dumb questions. Encryption of top-secret and SAP, or Special Access Program, security information is not easy stuff to learn. This course is like your introductory classes earlier in your careers. You will be dealing with binary codes. Your computer system has been programmed to translate into English." Using a remote, he lowered the wall screen and pressed a button to turn on the ceiling projector. "This is the binary code alphabet. As you see, there are uppercase and lowercase letters with numbers to the right of them. You will notice that the figures consist of only zeros and ones.

"In a way, this alphabet is similar to the old Morse code system that replaced letters of the alphabet. Then and now, it used an arrangement of dots, dashes, and spaces to form words. You will learn how to associate the binary code letters and numbers with letters to form words and sentences."

Miller was as confused as the others. He'd learned security intelligence encryption translation before, but nothing like this.

Colonel Kirby got up to talk. "Each of you has the training handbook. Also, these booklets are for your use when you return to your duty stations. Only you, your office, and your executive officer are allowed access."

Unlike the introduction class, they took a break for ten minutes every hour. At noon, a bus drove all of them to the officers' mess. When they returned, Hoppes took over again.

The following two days were challenging. The classmates felt like they were pushing an Abrams Main Battle Tank up a hill by hand. Sometimes the material was confusing; sometimes it was fascinating. Fortunately, there was no time for daydreaming; teaching and interaction kept them busy.

Finally, the third seminar day ended. Miller drove out of the base back to Würzburg on the Autobahn north.

***

Nikulin hailed a cab and told the driver to wait. He'd watched Alzuhari and Yako meet on the sidewalk and get into a taxi. The Russian spoke in his accented English, "Follow that black cab." He believed he was lucky because they always traveled together. During the ride, he telephoned Linkov. The ambassador was having lunch in his condominium.

"Hello?"

"Good afternoon, Ambassador. I am following the two Iraqis. They are going out again." He finished by saying, "I will catalog where they visit, and the time spent in each area." They hung up just as the cab arrived at the Blues Alley jazz bar-restaurant.

***

The next morning the blinking light on the dark computer screen signaled that messages were waiting. Alzuhari tapped the space bar to wake the screen. Among various emails, one was Remmich's. It reminded him of the wedding and ten-day honeymoon.

Alzuhari was pleased Remmich wouldn't have to save documents to a flash drive anymore.

***

Paul and Lilly finished reviewing the guest list for the wedding and reception during dinner. She alerted the head chef of the tentative final number. The main ballroom could seat more than fifty people. There was enough open floor space for a small orchestra and dance area.

The next day Paul took a taxi to the tuxedo shop and put on the tux, but no adjustments were needed. While walking back to the hotel, his cell phone buzzed. It was Miller.

"Listen, I called to let you know I am in town. Candice's plane arrived an hour ago, so I guess she'll be here soon. I'll call you back when she arrives, and we'll set a time to meet." Before he hung up, he added, "Hey, your time being single is getting short! Care to buy a one-way flight ticket to the Bahamas before tomorrow morning?"

Remmich's eyes sparkled as he laughed and answered, "No. I'm had."

The quiet afternoon time gave him time to rest in bed, with intermittent periods of sleep. When he woke up, his stomach rumbled and he decided to eat something before going out. A half-hour later he took a cab to St. Bavo's Church. The wedding rehearsal finished at 7:30. Afterward, a driver took Lilly and her sister and two bridesmaids back to the hotel. Candice, Eric, and Paul rode in a taxi to the Blues Alley bar-restaurant.

A maître d' showed them to a table. Sitting, Miller looked at his friend and told him the tab was on him. A waiter approached, and he asked what they wanted to order. Candice wanted Chardonnay. The men ordered Amstel on tap.

Remmich saw Tara Yako on the other side of the horseshoe bar. *Strange!* She seemed somehow familiar, but he couldn't imagine how he might know her. He looked around the room hoping to trigger some recollection. Then he looked at her again, searching his memory to no avail.

Alzuhari returned after he used the men's room, and he noticed something was bothering Tara. He sat in the chair and asked, "What's wrong?"

"Do you see who I see?"

"Where?"

"Almost straight ahead where people are sitting in the table section. Two black people, and a white man."

"It's Paul Remmich."

"Yes, and his black friend is with him. The woman must be his girlfriend."

Alzuhari leaned closer and tried to calm her. "Paul Remmich does not know you or me. Please remember, Tara, the hypnotic trance controls him. He only knows us when he is told to meet us at your flat or on the phone after he gets a signal."

"But what about the black man? Eric is his name."

"I don't think he will recognize you."

"I hope." Frantically, she added, "But you're sure Remmich doesn't recognize us?"

"No. As I pointed out before, our mole's conscious mind is in a dormant mode, and the subconscious mind controls the behavior and obedience to us. Don't forget, he's hypnotized. He was told *not* to remember us in public. Remember?"

The waiter returned to Remmich's and Miller's table. While he placed their drinks, Candice asked, "You're not having second thoughts, are you, Paul?"

With a lopsided grin he said, "Actually, I'm looking forward to marrying Lilly. I'm hoping our marriage will reduce some of her workload. The Schiller Hotel needs an additional assistant or two to ensure local regulations are followed."

Candice told him, "I hope they hire another worker for her sake."

Miller asked, "What are the health regulations in this country compared to other European countries?"

Remmich stated, "They are very health conscious. They demand safeguards to prevent bacterial outbreaks from restaurant dumpsters containing decaying food." He faced Candice and added, "The health department makes monthly examinations of all establishments, including those in the canal quarter red-light district. Eric and I visited the area the first time he came to Amsterdam."

She changed her attention to her beau and asked in a perturbed tone, "You did what?"

Remmich laughed, and Miller stifled a smile.

She had him in a corner.

He lowered his voice to sound serious and explained, "You have to understand. Paul was giving me a tour of the city, which included the hot-spot areas. The important thing is that we wound up here." She stared at him with disbelief, and he added, "That was the night we met."

Candice looked skeptical. "You mean you were just touring and not participating in the street goods?"

"Yes. That's what I was trying to say. Honest. Ask Paul."

She scoffed, "Ask Paul? Right! I'm going to ask the one who set you up in the first place. I mean, how else would you have become aware of one of the world's most renowned cities of prostitution?" She sipped her Chardonnay and added, "Hmm?"

"He's telling you the truth, Candice," interjected Remmich. "I was only trying to provide local cultural education to my friend." She covered her mouth quickly, almost spitting out the wine. Shaking with amusement, she swallowed and wiped her lips with a napkin.

Guests clapped as the bandleader and piano player approached the microphone stand while his cohorts set up. "We're going to continue our evening with more of the renowned United States jazz composers. We're starting with a Cole Porter song,

'You Do Something to Me.' But first, I want to introduce my German friend, Beatrice Schmidt, who is going to sing it."

The music began. Candice suggested, smiling, "Want to dance?"

Miller held her close as they danced slowly to the music. His eyes wandered along the circular design of the bar. Then his eyes focused on a woman, and his jaw tensed. *It was her!* Miller tried to force himself to be rational. It wasn't so much that she had disappeared for a few hours with his friend weeks before. His issue was that since then, Paul Remmich seemed a different person. Did she have something to do with that change? The music ended, and before the next song, they returned to the table.

The waiter came by. Miller ordered another round.

"Where did Paul go?" asked Candice.

He didn't answer. Miller had been looking in the direction of the bar at someone. Candice repeated the question.

His attention returned to her, and he said, "I guess he had to go to the men's room."

Miller took a sip of beer, and for a moment he gazed at the table. She interrupted him and asked, "Is something troubling you?"

His thoughts centered on the activities of the first night he met Candice. He leaned his arms onto the table, exhaled, and looked up at her. "Oh, it's just that I've been thinking about Paul's resignation and how disappointing it is to me."

"I can understand that." She moved her hand to his arm. "I lost friends after my resignation in the air force. I still correspond with a few, and you still have Paul as a friend. Look, he's made you his best man, and he's with us tonight. Just because he chose a different career doesn't mean you're going to lose his friendship."

"You're right, thanks."

She smiled and added, "And I never dreamed I would meet someone in the military. And a person I enjoy being with." He smiled. "Maybe it'll develop into something more."

"Maybe it will." He got tingles in the back of his neck.

The bandleader announced, "I have a request to sing an old-time favorite, 'Unforgettable,' by the great American singer Nat King Cole."

They danced leisurely; their arms draped around each other. Candice's head rested against Eric's chest. A slight turn on the dance floor showed Paul Remmich smoking a cigarette inside the front entrance. He was looking toward the bar. Miller tried to figure out what or who his buddy was staring at. His eyes scanned the bar. He saw that woman again and realized Paul had his attention on her. "Jesus!" he mumbled.

Candice lifted her head and asked, "What's bothering you, Eric?"

He shook his head and stopped staring in the direction of the entrance. He wondered, *What's he going to do?*

Remmich saw two open seats near the woman. He dropped his cigarette into the ashtray at an empty table in passing and sat in the swivel chair next to Yako. Hoping she'd turn and look at him, Remmich ordered another Amstel. He put a five-euro bill on the bar and shifted to get her attention while she talked to Alzuhari in Arabic.

The singer started to begin another song.

Miller saw his buddy sitting to the left of the woman. It was apparent Remmich wanted to confront her. While he sipped, she turned toward the man on her other side and tilted her head left to alert him to the person sitting there. They got up and walked onto the dance floor. *Why is she avoiding him?* Miller wondered. When the woman and her male companion started to dance, they held their bodies too far apart for them to be lovers. *They're hiding something for sure,* he thought.

"Is he still looking?" Tara asked, dancing with her back to Remmich.

"Yes, and his friend is dancing near us."

"What?" she uttered. "We need to leave."

***

Paul Remmich was in a good mood on Saturday morning when he woke up. He did his morning rituals and went downstairs to get breakfast. He wondered if marriage changed a man.

Before he knew it, it was time to get ready. He returned to his room and got dressed. He knew he looked good; the tuxedo fit him well. When he got outside, a concierge pointed out the black limousine waiting for him. The head chef and his wife accompanied Paul.

Eric and Candice were already at St. Bavo's Protestant Church. Candice was excited because she had never attended a wedding in a foreign country. A church assistant directed Miller to follow him into the sacristy. The minister was putting on his vestments. Candice listened to the magnificent organ, a 1520 vintage. With hundreds of organ pipes, the sound was incredible as the organ master played Bach interludes. He began with Cantata Number 147, or "Jesu, Joy of Man's Desiring." After a few minutes, the organ master changed to another Bach masterpiece, "Sheep May Safely Graze." A few minutes before 11:00, the music stopped and the church became quiet.

Remmich and Miller walked to the center of the altar and took their places on the side.

The music resumed in full force with a quartet playing. To honor Paul Remmich's American nationality, and in keeping with traditional US Christian weddings, they played "Here Comes the Bride." The procession slowly approached the altar, the bridesmaids first. Franz Van Horn accompanied his daughter.

When they reached their destination, he put Lilly's right hand into Remmich's left.

Paul and Lilly exchanged vows while a violinist played "Ave Maria." The minister gave his blessing. Paul kissed his bride, and then they turned around and walked down the aisle. The quartet played parts of Mendelssohn's "A Midsummer Night's Dream." The new Mr. and Mrs. Paul Remmich smiled as they passed their guests, while tiny rivulets of happy tears rolled down Lilly's cheeks.

***

The Remmichs' flight landed in Marseille on Sunday morning. They rented a car and drove to the Le Mas de Chastelas Hotel in Saint-Tropez, a coastal town on the French Riviera situated between Nice and Marseille. For ten days, they relaxed. The Mediterranean Sea was a beautiful sight from their second-floor condominium villa, and they enjoyed the clean sea scents and fresh breezes.

They often sat on the front balcony overlooking the water while sipping wine. A few nights, they walked in the town. Later they would watch ship lights in the distance and gaze at the flickering stars. They took day trips to the neighboring cities. Paul entertained Lilly with stories he'd learned in history classes. Two of his favorites were the escapades of the Phoenicians' sea adventurers and the Romans' conquest of Europe. Lilly was fascinated. The setting was perfect for the newlyweds to become even better acquainted and they didn't want to leave.

26

Another Tactic

High winds forced the pilots to bring the jet to a lower altitude. It bounced as it landed, swaying back and forth. The engines reversed, and the brakes engaged. The aircraft taxied along its designated route. A ground controller guided it to the jetway, and the plane stopped. A flight attendant opened the fuselage door for deplaning.

Lilly excitedly started to walk faster, but Remmich slowed his pace as he passed a newsstand and noticed the front page of a Frankfurt-English edition of *The New York Times*. The headline declared Iraq was withdrawing from Middle East associations—the United Arab Emirates and the oil cartel. Another section mentioned Iraq's possible withdrawal from the United Nations. She walked back and nudged him to come along.

A Schiller aide met the Remmichs at the baggage area. They accompanied him to the van outside. He loaded their luggage, drove off, and radioed the hotel. Thirty minutes later they stopped in front of the entrance.

Her mother and sister stood outside, anxious and smiling. The newly married couple exchanged hugs and kisses with them. The bellhop took their luggage up to their new residence.

The lobby was busy with its usual number of guests arriving, departing, and milling around. Remmich excused himself and stopped at a newspaper stand and got a copy of *The New York Times*. He folded it in half and placed it under his arm. After returning to the group, his mother-in-law moved in between them and looped her arms around theirs. They went into the elevator.

Karelle Van Horn unlocked the condominium's front door. She handed each a key and a keycard—one for a deadbolt and one for the regular lock. She made it clear why there were two. "I don't trust the plastic keycard by itself to prevent break-ins, and so I had a deadbolt system put on."

They walked in, but Remmich was more interested in a newspaper article. He slowed down and let the women go ahead. Karelle noticed him pause, so she interrupted and said, "Paul, please come and see your new office."

He continued to read and didn't respond. She rolled her eyes in consternation. Turning away and joining her daughters, she grumbled loudly. That distracted him enough to follow her request. It was a bedroom converted into a work office. There was a new desk with his laptop, an empty bookshelf, and a reclining chair. He sat in front of the computer and turned it on.

Remmich heard Franz enter the condo talking to a waiter. His father-in-law saw him concentrating and left him alone. There were over two dozen emails. It took a few minutes to erase most of them, except two. One was Alzuhari's, and the other was from V Corps. Suddenly, he felt a vibration in his molar. He blinked a couple of times, succumbing to the trance. He robotically pressed the cordless telephone buttons for the number he had memorized.

The line rang. "Hello?"

"This is Agent PSR."

"Welcome back, Paul. How are you?"

He recognized the voice. "A little exhausted, but otherwise I'm doing fine."

"Tell me your work plans for October."

"I do not have it yet. I'll call you back."

He disregarded Remmich's hypnotized state and asked, "By the way, did you get the wedding gift from Tara and me? It is cylinder-shaped, wrapped in brown paper. Open it and tell me if you like it."

He struggled to think and added, "I don't know because I just got back home."

"Okay. Get the schedule to me as soon as possible. Also, our commander needs six recent photographs of you. They must be front facial. It doesn't matter if they're color or not."

"I will have the photographer send six singles to me."

"Come to Tara's flat Tuesday morning at 10:00."

"Goodbye."

They hung up. As the hypnotic trance subsided, Remmich became aware of the voices in the other room. The women were having a good time opening wedding gifts. Suddenly, they heard a "pop" sound. A waiter was ready to pour champagne. The server handed him a glass as he came into the room.

When all their glasses were filled, Anna made a toast. Everyone smiled, saluted by raising their glasses, and sipped. Another waiter served hors d'oeuvres.

The parents placed their glasses on a serving tray and went into the living room. A cylinder-like package was on the hardwood floor. Paul heard Franz ask, "Karelle, what's in this long package?"

Paul and Lilly walked over to watch as Anna and her mother ripped off the covering. They unrolled it to reveal a beautiful Persian rug with a multicolored floral design surrounding a more prominent, lighter-red center. Everyone commented on its beauty. Remmich knelt on his right knee next to the rug and read the cloth tag sewn to the underside. "This writing is in English. It is a Persian rug from the province of Sarouk in Iran. It is approximately four meters by two and a half meters." He figured out the size in US measurements to be about eight feet wide by thirteen feet long.

After final congratulations, Lilly's parents and Anna walked out of the condominium to let the newlyweds be by themselves.

Lilly told him she needed to rest for a bit. She lay down on the sofa so he went into his office, but left the door open a little. Remmich called the central office and told them to send October's work agenda. While he waited, he used the minutes to look at some of the honeymoon pictures in his camera. When the schedule arrived, he studied it and emailed to Alzuhari along with thanks for the rug.

Alzuhari sent it to Yildiz in Istanbul. He telephoned Alzuhari and said, "I see he has two free days on Monday and Tuesday next week, but his work schedule for the rest of the week is busy. My office booked a morning flight for Iyad Aboona to come to Amsterdam this coming Monday. I am sending him because he is our electronics engineer. You and Tara are to be present when Iyad instructs him. My contact also said the PX stores carry the tools he will need. Iyad will explain. He will instruct Paul Remmich how to install transmitter devices at V Corps Headquarters. Did you receive the listening devices and radio receiver?"

"Yes, Major, I have them," said Alzuhari.

"I cannot give you his name, but a high-ranking US military intelligence officer notified me about a construction project. The headquarters at Patch Barracks is presently under renovation. The officer said the corridors are being used as workplaces. Construction will finish in a few weeks."

***

Remmich read the other email message. It was a follow-up notification from Colonel Collins. "Upcoming meeting scheduled for Wednesday, 15 October is canceled. Building renovations in progress and will last into next month. You are to come to headquarters after you return to Amsterdam. More encryption work is needed. Call to confirm message received. You will have to stay for several days. Finally, the November meeting date has not been selected."

Paul erased the Wednesday meeting in his datebook. He used a sticky note to remind himself to ask about the November meeting date. He sat back and resumed reading the newspaper.

The UN's lack of international awareness about Middle East crises caused alarm to the United States government. The ongoing argument about ISIS's relations with Iraqi and Syrian officials made the US Department of State question whether there is a scheme between them and Putin's Russia.

The article ended with a quote from Secretary Mitchell: "It isn't a problem of one enemy anymore but a glut of issues outside our reach. Russia may be supplying the Bashar al-Assad regime with military artillery and guided missiles."

Remmich forgot about his fatigue and mumbled to himself, "This is absurd. Iraq doesn't want to ruin their hope to expand in international relations. Using less prosperous countries with trade potential is smart business." He put the paper down and, smiling, said in a low tone, "Surely, the government is irritated because they can't legally interfere." He read other information and found it appalling, especially a story about North Korea having ICBM capability.

He returned to the living room and saw Lilly still asleep. Without waking her, he wrote a note and left it on the rug near the couch. He went to the Brasserie-Schiller bar to get a beer and smoke a cigarette.

***

Iyad Aboona's jet landed Monday, and he took a taxi to the Hotel Schiller. He identified himself in English at the reception desk. A clerk took a moment to verify the reservation. The attendant handed Aboona a room card and advised him which elevator to take. He called Alzuhari after he got into the hotel room to tell him he'd arrived. They arranged to meet the next day to discuss the plans for Remmich and the next steps. They also decided to have dinner together at 6 p.m.

***

On Tuesday morning the Iraqi took a cab to Alzuhari's flat at 8:00 and they walked to Yako's building carrying a satchel and a box. When they got there, Aboona removed two architectural drawings from a shoulder bag and put them on the table. While he unfolded one, Yako placed a flat, rectangular device with an attached wire on the unfolded drawing. It was a receiver-transmitter.

They leaned over to familiarize themselves with the graphics. Aboona pointed to the wall sections in the two second-floor conference rooms for the placements. Showing the device to them, he said, "Paul Remmich will hide one behind a chair rail in each of these. Right now, German carpenters are remodeling, and the finished walls are being painted." He explained that some of the personnel had to work in the hallways while their offices were being remodeled. The first-floor rooms and the second-floor conference rooms were closed off.

Looking at the drawings again and pointing he said, "These pencil markings show where he is to hide the devices." He reached into the carrying case and placed another page on the table. It had five sketches showing how to do the work. Next, he pulled out a piece of chair molding and a section of wallboard. "I am going to show you how the work will be done. This is one of two pieces of the wallboard. I have another one for Paul Remmich. I am using these two items to demonstrate how this thin black part will fit into a scraped surface of wallboard." He described how to remove the wallboard's plaster between the markings. When the scraping finished, the hidden part fit snugly between the wall and the chair molding.

Aboona said, "Adnaw, Major Yildiz wants you to get a part-time job at the Blues Alley restaurant. You are going to assist Tara, and possibly Paul, in the future to get another spy."

***

Remmich drove to Yako's building and rode the elevator up to her floor. The routine level of his subconscious mind no longer controlled his actions. He knocked on the door.

Yako opened the door and said, "Good morning, Paul. Come in." She knew Remmich didn't remember the engineer from the dentist's office, so she introduced him to Aboona. She told him to pay attention to the engineer.

They stood at the dining table, while their mole looked at the drawings. Remmich took a receiver-transmitter and examined it without saying anything.

Aboona said, "You will install these two receiver-transmitters behind the chair rails in the two conference rooms. You are going to leave today."

Aboona showed Remmich the page outlining the things to do. He detailed each work procedure. Remmich was told to scrape the other section of wallboard. Next, he would place the receiver-transmitter into the gap and hold the molding section against it.

Next, he demonstrated how to pull out the piece of wood from the wall before scraping the wallboard. Then he continued to the next step of placing the device in between wood and wall before hammering the wood back against the wall. He reviewed the last two work items. They included gluing the antenna wire to the outside along the bottom of the chair rail. Aboona explained why glue needed to be finger-tooled to the underside of the chair rail to secure the wire. The final demo showed how to use a small tube of drywall paste to fill the surface holes where there was a countersunk nail.

"One last thing," said Aboona. "You are to take both drawings with you. I am sure someone will question you as to why you are there. Do not show the person this smaller drawing. Explain that you need to inspect the rooms for security reasons, like soundproof wall work. Do you understand?"

"Yes."

Aboona placed a lithium coin cell battery into each receiver-transmitter. He gave him a list of hardware tools to buy from any PX." He asked Remmich if he understood what he needed to do.

In a somber mode, they heard, "I will install the receiver-transmitter in each conference room on the days I am scheduled to do encryption work."

The trio realized he could be discreet. He had all the right information. The plan was a go.

Alzuhari said, "If you see a possible problem, stay away." He handed Remmich a wad of euro bills to pay for expenses and the list of tools. The meeting ended at 11:00 and Remmich left.

Aboona said, "Next week Major Yildiz will be visiting on the weekend. He will notify you. For your information, there is going to be another project for Paul Remmich."

***

Remmich informed his wife about the army work, and said he'd be there for a few days. He did not give her an exact number. She told her father, who was beside himself with frustration. There was nothing he could do; he couldn't fire his son-in-law.

***

Paul was on the road by 1:00, arriving in Stuttgart at 5:30 p.m. *Once again, he drove at record speed.* He exchanged euros into US dollars at the American Express bank at Patch Barracks. The PX supplied the tools. Minutes later he entered the headquarters building and stopped at the front desk.

The CQ didn't know him. He verified the mole's ID from the list of people working in the security intelligence department. He noted Remmich's work schedule was supposed to start the following day. The sergeant wondered why he was there in the early evening. But the soldier overlooked it and asked to see what was in the bag. He found tools and no weapon. Remmich partially unrolled the drawing and explained he had to look at the construction work. The CQ stated he could roam anywhere he wanted.

Clear plastic sheeting hung from the upper walls and sealed off the working areas to prevent dust from settling in the corridor and other rooms. Remmich walked into the first room to bug. He scanned the partially completed construction work, including the wood railing. There were workers in there getting ready to leave, and he asked in German if anyone spoke English. They all did, so Remmich acted as if he was an official military inspector. The foreman answered the question of why they worked so late. He explained it was because materials were late being delivered on Monday. Remmich told the painter not to paint along the chair molding areas until he finished inspecting. He lied and said he wanted to show the army the excellent job they were doing on the walls. They believed him.

He waited until they left before examining the locations he was to work on.

***

On Wednesday morning he reported to the security office; it was not being renovated. The computer he used had the encrypted document. The routine was the same, except he wasn't required to copy anything else and email it anywhere. He labored all day conscientiously, except for a coffee break and lunch. Being occupied helped the time to go faster. At 4:00 he turned off the computer and followed the others into the corridor.

Remmich went to his car and waited, smoking a cigarette. He needed to make sure everyone left the building. The higher brass were the last to leave. He watched their cars go off the base before he got the tool bag and blueprint from the trunk.

There was another CQ on duty. He'd never met Remmich as he'd always had night duty. Asking for identification, the sergeant took the lanyard and his ID. It showed name, photograph, and employment position. The mole explained he was there to inspect the finished renovation work. The British accent didn't trouble the guard, but he asked to look into the sack to check the contents. Just tools, no weapon. Next, he unrolled a portion of the blueprint. It seemed legitimate. Since Remmich had a legitimate ID and equipment, the sergeant didn't question further.

Upstairs the painters and carpenters had finished work and packed up. As they walked out under the hanging plastic sheets, Remmich entered 203. The painters had done as he asked and left the wood molding alone. He worked in there for two hours, removing the chair rail, scraping the wallboard and finishing. No one interrupted or questioned him, despite his hammering.

***

There were vehicles lined up at the gates on Thursday morning. When it was his turn, the MP verified the sticker and waved him to go. Remmich parked at the General Patton lot again. He could see the German workers through the open windows in 203. But he was surprised to see men wearing formal Class A military attire also. It was common for everyone but officers to wear fatigues and combat boots. He figured they were USAREUR from Heidelberg, the control center for soldiers in Germany and other countries. It made him wonder if there were full-time inspectors. *It would put a glitch in his orders.*

Remmich went into the security office. Not all the soldiers were there yet. He exchanged greetings with those present. When the others arrived, he was not disturbed. They knew the coded documents were a challenge. The rest of the day was routine. He left at the same time as the others. Once again, he sat in the car until the brass drove off base, including the ones in class As. A few minutes later, the German workers left. Feeling anxious, he got the equipment and blueprint out of the trunk. The CQ on duty the day before recognized him. The same inspection procedure took another five minutes, but Remmich expected it.

He started work in room 205, undisturbed, and finished in less than two hours. Satisfied, he had one more thing to do.

***

Friday morning there were long lines out to the street. It took fifteen minutes for the MP to pass the BMW through the gate. Remmich found a spot in the same lot and saw the workers through the windows. He also saw other people roaming conference room 203. He didn't think it unusual until he saw Sutherland talking to people. He stayed in the car, watching. When he couldn't see anybody except the workers, he got out and went inside.

There was additional work to be decrypted. Remmich worked diligently until the workday ended. Some of the inspectors were there. They examined other renovation sections on the first floor. The contractor superintendent accompanied them.

Remmich waited for an hour in his car. The inspection continued so he had no opportunity to go back inside. He left, knowing he'd be back Saturday morning. To his advantage, the day's decryption work wasn't finished either.

27

The Tests

On Saturday at noontime Remmich finished the rest of the decrypting. He walked out of the building and sat in his BMW. Personnel walked out of the headquarters building. When he believed it empty, he opened the back door and lifted out the tool bag and blueprint. The CQ on duty remembered him, and Remmich said, "I guess everyone is gone?"

The sergeant chuckled and answered, "Hell, the diehards didn't even stay here today. This place is a mess. But, yeah, there isn't anyone else here, just you and me." He searched the carrier sack. Satisfied there wasn't a weapon, he permitted the spy to enter.

On the second floor, he listened for voices or footsteps on the wooden floorboards. Nothing.

Entering conference room 203, he texted Alzuhari. This was the signal that sound tests could begin. He dropped some wood pieces on the floor. A reply text confirmed the sounds were loud and clear. He repeated the same procedures in meeting room 205, and the reply was the same.

Remmich left and went to his vehicle. This time he put his supplies in the trunk. Before driving off, he looked at the post's entrances. Because of the sticker on his windshield, it was likely he wouldn't be questioned. He couldn't afford to have the trunk opened by an obsessive MP. He chose the busier exit. As he neared the gate, three vehicles beat him in line. Then several cars got in line behind him.

He smiled to himself when he saw there was only one MP. He knew there should be more; one for entering vehicles and another for the those exiting. This MP appeared to be double-timing to achieve the tasks of two; he crisscrossed the entrance to the exit repeatedly. Remmich tension level dropped and he took a deep breath of relief. He wasn't likely to be searched.

***

Nikulin, who had been in Stuttgart for as many days as Remmich, followed him. Stuttgart traffic was heavy, which made it easy to track the American. And with the stop-and-go city traffic, he had the opportunity to call Ambassador Linkov. After listening to multiple rings, he remembered the embassy was closed on Saturdays. He left a message explaining the state of affairs.

***

Remmich drove back to Amsterdam, a satisfied spy. He met Lilly in their condo. She wore a bathrobe and said she was going to take a bubble bath. He asked, "Did you make reservations for dinner?" She answered yes and went away to bathe. He got a glass of wine before going to the office. A minute later Alzuhari received a message telling him all was well.

The mole didn't know it, but Baghdad had an additional task for him.

***

Miller returned to his apartment building mid-morning while talking to Candice on the phone. He was about to insert the key into the lock when he stopped talking. The front entry was not completely closed. His heart started to race, anticipating a trap. Without explanation, he told her, "Let me call you back." He slowly walked in, placing the grocery sack on the kitchen table. A squeaky noise revealed an intruder's possible location. That particular bedroom door hinge needed oiling. *Maybe it's only that the window is open and blowing the door?* Sneaking quietly on the corridor carpet to the doorway, he could see that it was not open. His memory flashed back to the invasion and killing in Stockholm. He needed to be careful; a repeat of that incident could get him a penalty harsher than a mere transfer. Silently, he walked back to the sofa and pulled out his Beretta 9mm pistol from under a cushion. With outstretched arms, he tiptoed to the room. His right forefinger stayed against the trigger.

As Miller walked through the doorway, a person jumped out from behind. The thug pushed Miller's gun up while forcing him against the chest of drawers. The gun fired into the ceiling, and plaster dust spattered down on them. Miller violently shoved the man's pistol hand backward onto the chest of drawers. The weapon bounced out of his hand, landing on the floor behind the partially opened door. The invader quickly karate-chopped the Beretta out of Eric's hand and onto the carpet. They both lunged for it, but his opponent was quicker. He forcefully rammed Eric's shoulder into the nightstand. When the intruder bent over to grab his semiautomatic, Miller quickly side-kicked the attacker's legs, toppling the brute over.

It was now a matter of kill or be killed. The attacker swiftly turned with the firearm in his hand. Miller had a few seconds to push the muzzle away. He felt the heat of the bullet pass his ear. Before another shot could be fired, Miller grabbed the inside of the assailant's left forearm. Holding it up, he broadsided the left hand. The pistol popped out and landed by the bed. They both dove for it. This time Miller snatched it first and turned toward his assailant, shooting into the attacker's right armpit. The guy flinched but managed to get his left hand around Miller's throat and began to squeeze. He couldn't breathe but was able to turn enough to shoot into the side of the man's abdomen, hoping not to penetrate any organs. The guy fell backward onto the floor, motionless but breathing.

Miller pushed himself away, still pointing his firearm. His face was flushed from the exertion and anger. He briefly considered emptying the magazine of bullets into the animal. *He would watch every bullet impact the body.* As his breathing slowed, his good judgement returned and he called the MP station instead. As he waited for an answer, he recognized the man as the second of his Stockholm intruders.

Two MPs arrived at the apartment followed by a pair of medics. They bandaged the intruder's wounds and inserted an IV, before getting him to the hospital. The military police asked Eric what happened. For ten minutes he described his ordeal. When he finished, they told him he still needed a complete debriefing and settled on 3 p.m.

During the time between the incident and the debriefing, the CID investigators discovered their criminal had a double identity. His documents showed he worked as a van driver at Leighton Barracks, but the man's true identity was revealed when the thug was interrogated. He didn't plead for mercy; he declared diplomatic immunity. His passport showed he was an Iraqi serving at the Stockholm embassy.

***

Once the debriefing and paperwork finished he returned to his apartment. An Army truck was parked behind his car with two men inside. The soldiers got out of the truck and greeted him while saluting. He returned the salute.

"Sir," said the taller one, "we texted you a couple of times but you didn't answer." Miller felt around in his pockets and realized he didn't have his cell phone. Watching him search, both soldiers noticed his wrinkled clothes but said nothing. They knew why he was unusually disheveled.

"Captain Miller," said the other NCO, "we got a message from the CID office about the break-in and were sent to fix your door. We checked it out a little while ago to assess the damage, but we didn't go in. It looks like it's only the lock and we have a replacement kit. We can fix it right now if that's okay with you."

"Yes, of course."

They left to get tools and equipment and met him inside. He left them alone while looking for his cellphone, finding it on the side table next to the sofa. There were several texts. Two from the repairmen and one from Remmich: "Call me when you can."

Exhausted, he walked outside and sat down on a circular bench surrounding a large tree. Before he called Remmich, he wanted to talk to Candice. He explained what happened and told her the intruder was the man from the Stockholm incident who got away. "And you know the rest of the story." Before hanging up they planned a visit for the following weekend.

"I don't want to get together with the Remmichs because I think we need a weekend by ourselves." Candice was happy to hear that but was curious as Eric seemed to be leaving something out.

"Too much has happened in the past weeks. Paul is secretive about what he does in his spare time and he asks too many questions. It's like he wants to know everything that's going on with the S-2 division all the time we're alone."

"Strange," she commented. "Do you think he just wants to keep up to date?"

"I thought of that also, and I'm not sure. I guess I have to take it a day at a time."

They ended the call confirming the weekend rendezvous.

He didn't want to tell Remmich about his future plans with MI and about the trip to Amsterdam to see Candice, so he composed his response before pushing Paul's autodial button. After three rings he heard, "Hello, Eric. Thanks for calling back."

Miller's assumption was correct. *Remmich wanted to get together the following weekend.* Eric said that wouldn't work and they concluded the following weeks were not possible either. Remmich's excuse was business travel for three to four weeks. Miller breathed a sigh of relief that he didn't get pressed for details about what he had planned. His possible new position was still his secret. The call ended cheerfully with them promising to see each other when they could. Both hung up and wondered why the other man has seemed so agreeable.

END

The Tariq'Allah is not finished. They want to add another mole to their secret ranks of brainwashed spies. Find out what happens to Remmich and Miller in book two of the series, *Counter Identity*. Will everyone survive?

Dear Reader,
I hope you enjoyed this book. I would appreciate it if you would leave a review for it on one of the many book sites, such as Amazon, Goodreads, etc.. Honest reviews are valuable, constructive ones help me write better, and positive reviews help other potential readers find my books.
Thank you in advance.
Karl
karlbraungart.author@gmail.com
www.karlbraungart.com

Printed in Great Britain
by Amazon

39415775R00145